CITY PROBLEMS

CITY PROBLEMS

AN ED RUNYON MYSTERY

STEVE GOBLE

OCEANVIEW PUBLISHING
SARASOTA, FLORIDA

ISBN 978-1-60809-443-1

Published in the United States of America by Oceanview Publishing

Sarasota, Florida

www.oceanviewpub.com

10 9 8 7 6 5 4 3 2 1

PRINTED IN THE UNITED STATES OF AMERICA

For Gere, who always believed

ACKNOWLEDGMENTS

I want to thank numerous people who helped me along the way.

My agent, Evan Marshall, is always a good sounding board. He initially took me on to represent my historical mysteries featuring the pirate Spider John. He sold those and then found a home for Ed Runyon. It has been a good ride, and I've learned a lot about this crazy publishing business from him.

Bob and Pat Gussin and the whole team at Oceanview Publishing wowed me from the start with their enthusiasm and professionalism. I look forward to continued work with them.

Other writers inspire me, of course, and have helped in many ways. Go read some Andrew Welsh-Huggins, Kristen Lepionka, Tracy Clark, and Mark Pryor. I predict you'll start gobbling up their books.

My friend Tom Williams reads my books before I send them off to Evan, and he offers many insights and suggestions. I can't thank him enough for that support.

More than anyone else, though, I need to thank my wife, Gere, and my kid, Rowan. Gere (pronounced "Jerry") helps me unravel plot problems, gives me time and space to write, and does stellar proofreading—all while being the best life partner anyone could possibly have. She amazes me every day. And Rowan thinks it is pretty damned cool that Dad has books available in libraries and bookstores, although you won't catch the kid saying that out loud. It's OK. Dad knows.

CITY
PROBLEMS

CHAPTER ONE

Early Sunday, Time Unknown

PAIN. DEEP, SHARP pain, physical and spiritual, forced her up from whatever merciful blackout zone she had found. That was the first thing she noticed.

The next thing to break through the barriers of her consciousness was the whispering. Drunken, panicked whispering. Nothing concerning her or the horrible things that had happened to her, nothing about her pain. They were worried about themselves, not her. Like bad things had happened to them, but not to her. She could not make out many words, but none of the words she comprehended were about her.

It was like she didn't matter.

Then, motion. She was still in the back of the truck, rolling down some unknown road, bouncing occasionally and hitting her head on the truck bed so the pain would scream again and again. She tried to touch the hard, wet spot on her skull, but stopped when she realized her hair was clinging to the truck bed and her right arm was trapped beneath something, or someone.

One of them is sitting on my arm.

The knowledge froze her. Her right arm was a useless thing; the moment she tried to move it they would know she was awake, and they would hurt her again. She tried to swallow the scream building inside her, and felt her tongue swell with the effort. Breathing became more difficult, and she thought she might choke. Her body fought for air, her lungs suddenly working hard, and she feared they might realize she was awake. But the truck's bone-rattling motions apparently disguised her feeble efforts to breathe. She concentrated on inhaling and exhaling slowly through her nose.

Don't panic. Don't let them know you are awake. Don't let them hurt you again.

She calmed down, and tried to figure out where she was. Everything smelled of beer and whiskey and wet grass.

She risked opening her eyes, afraid of what she would see, then grew more afraid when she saw nothing.

God, it's dark out here, wherever this is. Am I blind?

No. After a moment, she could just barely make out the dark, tinted windows of the truck bed cap, which revealed a darkness slightly different from that inside the truck. The window shapes seemed to shift, as though the glass were fluid. No real light got in through those grimy windows, and she could see no faces to go with the voices that surrounded her.

The truck hit a new bump. The back of her head slammed the truck bed, and she closed her eyes against a nebula of swirling colors and a host of dagger-stab pains. As the pain slowly dulled, the colors faded slowly, but she still saw them even after she opened her eyes again. She felt it very important to open her eyes.

The mad kaleidoscopic whorls persisted, but beyond them she thought she could discern half-formed images. Boys. Sneers. Booze. Faces that shifted from human to monstrous. Smiles full of fangs, with spit and grunts and curses forcing their way through sharp, clenched teeth.

Next came more sounds, and she struggled to determine if they were real, or if they were memories. Music cut through the hum of tires on pavement. Droning rock, heavy bass. It made her head and body throb. It seemed she'd been hearing it forever, even before her universe had been reduced to pain and fear and darkness.

A flare of light blinded her. The orange flash illuminated a leering face, and a sulfuric odor emphasized the hellish, uncaring eyes. The match flare vanished with a swish, and only the bright glow of a cigarette was left. The tossed match landed on her cheek, burning her, and she yelled and kicked.

"Jesus! She isn't dead!"

"Oh, fuck, man!"

"Hush," a voice said. The weight pinning her right arm to the truck bed lifted, and a rough hand slapped her face. She did not see the blow coming, so the sudden sharpness was worse for being unexpected. The sting of it was so distinct she could feel the salt of her own tears on the smacked skin. She stifled a scream, and chewed her lip.

"Better," the voice said. Someone else snickered.

"Guys, maybe we should—"

"Shut the fuck up! Jesus!"

One side of the truck bed brightened, and she heard the whine of a big rig rolling past. For just a second, she could see the silhouettes of her tormenters. She tried to memorize their positions, envision herself kicking out into their faces, hurting them back.

Then the darkness returned and someone slapped her again. Hard. She gave up fighting, then.

"No," she said. "Please, no."

She tried to tell them she would never, ever tell anyone what had happened if they would just let her live. She got out three words before a smack in the face made her eyes water and the foul boozy taste rise in her throat again.

"Shut up, bitch!"

"No. No. No." She fought again, though she could not see. Her arms and legs were sluggish, responding slowly when she tried to kick or punch or scratch. Fingers coiled like snakes around her wrists and ankles. Her shins and elbows rapped painfully against the cold truck bed, and something sharp dug into her right shin.

She felt herself sinking again, back into oblivion.

CHAPTER TWO

Tuesday, 11:10 a.m.

I HAD OLLIE Southard's head tucked under my right armpit, with enough pressure to cut off his damned howling. That caused a vibration against my ribs that tickled, but a cop has to learn to ignore that kind of thing.

Ollie's ordinarily a gentle giant, and he wasn't bellowing at me. He was yelling at the guy who had pissed him off.

That guy was on the bar floor, bleeding from the nose Ollie had probably broken. The skinny guy, a stranger to me, dug his boot heels into the wood floor to scoot away from me and Ollie. His hand wandered toward his belt in a way that said "knife."

The music—something by Soundgarden, I think, but I did not really know—suddenly stopped. "Watch it, Ed! Stranger's got a knife."

"Yes, Tuck. I see that." Tuck owns the place, and he's a friend of mine, so I did not want him involved. "Now duck behind the bar."

I'm a fairly big guy—six feet, two hundred pounds—but Ollie had fifty pounds on me and stood a head taller. The guy scooting across the floor was dark and skinny. He looked like he should have been able to easily duck a big, slow man like Ollie, but he hadn't. Maybe he was drunk. Or high. Or both.

I already knew he was stupid.

I wouldn't have grabbed Ollie at all, but my attempts at peaceful mitigation succeeded about as well as my date nights lately. Just as I'd yelled "freeze," Ollie had snatched up a wooden chair and wielded it like a club, ready to bash the skinny guy. Cops aren't supposed to let stuff like that happen, even on their days off, so here I was trying to quiet things down. A well-timed armlock and a hard pivot got the big fellow under control. The chair he'd grabbed tumbled harmlessly aside, but one of its legs broke. I hoped Tuck wasn't going to make me pay for that.

Ollie smelled like old socks soaked in cat piss and sprayed by a skunk. The other guy smelled like a gallon of some body wash that was supposed to make supermodels swoon and strip. I suddenly wished this tussle had taken place in the open air rather than within the dim confines of a one-bar town's one bar.

The advantages I had over both of these brawlers were sobriety and training. That, and the fact I knew Ollie Southard would not go for my gun. Ollie absolutely hates guns, and writes letters to the editor every week to make sure everyone knows he hates guns. The editor actually limited Ollie to one printed letter a month years ago, which Ollie never stops bitching about, but Ollie writes them anyway. Ollie believes the NRA is an evil cult, so I knew he'd ignore my weapon.

Even so, I kept my left arm locked down tight over the holster while my right arm played boa constrictor around Ollie's throat. Sometimes, cherished opinions about the evils of guns wilt under combat conditions.

My sobriety was purely accidental. These jokers had started fighting before Tuck could finish pouring my first glass of Commodore Perry, so I had not yet had a single drop of India pale ale to drink. This made me want to throw some punches. I had planned a good day, and these guys were fucking it up. Despite the provocation, I was determined to resolve this as peacefully as I could. I am a professional. I can be reasonable.

I had intended to take a few hours off from my job as a sheriff's detective in northern Ohio farm country. We'd gotten a guilty verdict that morning on a guy who'd tossed his wife down the stairs, breaking both her legs, an arm, and her ribs. She was an addict, and her husband had claimed someone else had hurt his wife, probably a dealer tired of taking bad sex instead of money for his product.

The husband had discounted her claims that he had been the one who attacked her, saying she was probably too damned addled on heroin to have any goddamned idea who had thrown her down the stairwell, and maybe she had just fallen down the stairs all by herself because drugs made her woozy. Why would we listen to anything a drug whore said anyway, he asked on the witness stand. He called me both a liar and a motherfucking liar, after having sworn on the Bible, no less, so help him God. The prosecutor had objected to defend my honor, of course.

I took no real offense. Cops get used to being called names, even in farm country. Instead of taking umbrage, I just watched Baker Thomas, the husband. I watched him the way a raptor watches a mouse, and I could not help noticing how goddamned pleased he seemed every time someone mentioned Kate's injuries.

Heroin is a real goddamned problem around here, just like everywhere, and people were ready to believe Baker Thomas when the crime happened. This was just one more drug incident to them, they thought. Drug whore got hurt? Meh. How'd the Browns do last night?

But the guy's reaction to her fall had seemed a bit off from the start, and I had never quite believed him. Neither did the deputies working with me. He always seemed to be in on some private joke. Sometimes, you just know when a guy is guilty, whether you have the evidence or not.

He had presented us with what seemed like a solid alibi, though—witnesses who swore he was at a bar while his woman got busted up. It had taken me a month to break that alibi, but I eventually used my powers of persuasion, by which I mean I put one of those witnesses against a wall until he shit his pants, and that convinced the guy to talk. That cracked things open, and we proved Baker Thomas had stolen heroin from his wife and traded it for lies that established his alibi. Now the husband was on his way to prison.

I call that a good day.

My plan had been to take the rest of the day off, drink some beers, and get Tuck to play some Steve Earle and Willie Nelson on the good speakers, instead of his usual hair band shit. That plan was now in jeopardy because the skinny stranger had snarled something about fucking faggots at the talking heads on the TV screen just as Tuck had tipped the tap handle for my India pale ale.

The man's timing was unfortunate. Ollie, who had been sitting nearby draining a double bourbon, planned to marry a big bearded guy named Rush who looked almost like Ollie's own twin. Read into that what you will, but I don't care to examine it too closely. Anyway, Ollie didn't like the stranger's comment about gay people one damned little bit. Words were exchanged, drinks were spilled, and the next thing you know I've got a very large smelly man in motorcycle togs locked under my arm and a scrawny perfumed stranger scooting across the floor and leaving black marks from his boots.

My damned cell phone was buzzing in my pocket, too. That probably was a work call, and another reason to be cranky.

I locked my eyes on the skinny stranger, who had a pinched face, goatee, and dark arched eyebrows that made him look like a ringmaster at a circus run by Stephen King, or maybe Neil Gaiman. I hoped to keep the combatants apart long enough for them to see sense. I knew Ollie and figured he would calm down quickly. I did not know the scarecrow with the broken nose, but if he gave up, I thought I might even get out of this mess without paperwork. There was a chance of that, anyway, as long as the string bean on the floor didn't pull the knife.

He pulled the knife.

I rolled my eyes at the switchblade that suddenly appeared like a magician's paper bouquet in his right hand. "I'm a cop. Drop that."

"Fuck you," the idiot said, trying to get up.

The key to such situations is remaining calm, dispassionate.

I shoved Ollie away, calmly and dispassionately, and he crashed into the wall. I considered calmly and dispassionately kicking knife boy in the nuts, and figured I had every right to do so. That would have been unprofessional, though, and probably would have gotten my leg sliced. I drew my weapon instead.

"Mine shoots a lot farther than yours," I said. "Drop the blade."

He dropped the blade, but something in his demeanor told me he had stared down the barrel of a gun before.

"Shove that thing as far from you as you can," I ordered, and he complied.

I stepped back so I could keep both men covered, even though I was not too concerned about Ollie.

Ollie moaned, "Holy shit."

"It's going to be OK, Ollie." I looked at the skinny idiot. "I am Detective Ed Runyon, Mifflin County Sheriff's Office, and you both are under arrest." I recited the rest of the Miranda stuff. I don't think either guy was really listening.

"I can't get arrested," Ollie said. "Rush is gonna be pissed."

"You can kiss and make up later," I said. "I can't ignore a bar fight, Ollie." I really wished to hell I could ignore it, but taxpayers wouldn't like it, and neither would my boss.

The phone in my pocket kept buzzing.

Ollie inhaled deeply, hands on his knees, and blew out a loud sound, something between a "whoa" and a "whew." It could have been a blowing whale, it was so loud. He spun, lost balance, and fell back against the wall again. With that additional data, I concluded the double bourbon had been Ollie's third.

One of the traffic signs that pass for fancy decor at Tucker's Bar and Grill clattered to the floor as Ollie slid down on his ass. The sign said "Falling Rock Zone." I didn't have time to laugh at that or make a wisecrack. Neither did the huge dead buck's head hanging above.

Somewhere behind the bar, I heard Tuck say "thanks." He popped up from cover and placed his cell phone on the bar. "Help is on the way, Ed. Dispatcher said they are close by."

The stranger stayed on the floor, and snarled a bit. "Fucking cop, man. This was a setup."

"You are under arrest for attempted assault with a deadly weapon," I told the stranger. I aimed at his sweaty face. "Plus, you know, actual assault. Probably some other shit. I will figure it all out later. Do not move."

He didn't move.

"Me, too, Ed?" Ollie's question was expressed mostly in burps.

"You're under arrest, too, Ollie."

"Damn, Ed. Sorry." His face, the part that showed through all the beard, anyway, was beet red. It got redder.

A few minutes later a siren split the air somewhere nearby, and I heard tires squealing through a tight turn. Another siren sounded from the north, and I heard a cruiser brake hard outside.

"Hail, hail, the gang's all here," I said.

Tuck had a short-barreled shotgun leaning against his shoulder. "I popped your brew into the fridge, Ed."

"Thanks. Best service anywhere." My phone was still vibrating, but I ignored it and kept an eye on the man on the floor. "You can put the shotgun away, Tuck. Cavalry's coming."

"Right."

Soon after Tuck had put away his shotgun and Ollie had started breathing normally, Deputies Scott Baxter and Irwin Trumpower came through the door, guns drawn. Bax was low, Trumpower was high, and they made it look just like on TV. Trumpower was more Hill Street, while Bax was more Mayberry, but still, just like on TV.

The guns went back into their holsters pretty quickly, though. Irwin, the senior of the two, spoke. "Got it all under control, Ed?"

"Looks that way, Trump."

"Do not call me that." His forehead, which always looked crinkled with concern even when he was telling a dirty joke, folded into deeper furrows.

"Everyone calls you that," I said. "Have for years."

"Not anymore," Trumpower said. He added under his breath, "I watched the news today. Fuck that fucking guy."

"Should've heard him this morning," Baxter whispered, aiming a thumb at Trumpower. "Madder than a wet cow on a Tuesday."

"What does that even mean, Bax?" Bax was known for having a blender somewhere between his brain and his mouth, and things came out of him a little mixed up.

"Just means Irwin was upset about being called Trump, is all." Baxter looked a little wounded.

"OK," I said. "Irwin it is. Cuff these guys for me? The gentleman there on the floor first, please. A count of assault against each, and attempt with a deadly on a peace officer against Skinny. Bag the knife there, too. It's under that table." I pointed. "It belongs to Skinny. Got his nice, grimy fingerprints all over it."

Trumpower cuffed Skinny. Baxter, who swears he's older than thirty but looks like he should be playing the nice teen boy next door on an old-fashioned sitcom, cuffed Ollie and raised his eyebrows. "What started it?"

I holstered my gun, and pulled my phone from my pocket. "That one there," I said, pointing at Skinny, "exercised his free speech rights to say nasty things about gay people. Ollie exercised his free speech rights to call Skinny a stupid piece of shit, if I recall correctly. He might have called him a fucking stupid piece of shit, actually. I wasn't really taking notes. Anyway, things sort of went downhill from there. The marketplace of ideas in all its glory, the epitome of civil debate. Like Twitter, only you could actually smell it."

"Huh?" Baxter never knew what the hell I was talking about, which evened the score a little bit regarding my inability to translate his habitual mixed metaphors into English. Trumpower got a laugh out of it, though. He had a good sense of humor, even if teasing him about his last name apparently was a bad idea now.

"Never mind, Bax." I finally glanced at my phone, and it buzzed again. It was the sheriff calling. I did not answer immediately. "You guys have any idea why Daltry might be calling me? He knew I had a date with a few beers."

"No idea," Trumpower said. "He doesn't have to check in with me before he calls detectives."

Skinny was standing, but wobbly. His nose was swollen, but the blood stream had slowed to a trickle. For a peacenik, Ollie hits pretty goddamned hard. Trumpower had the man's head tilted back.

"You need an ambulance, sir?" Trumpower, as always, was a professional.

"No," Skinny said softly, through a lot of drool. "I need a lawyer. I am going to sue detective man here. For false arrest! I was defending myself!"

"Be sure to tell your lawyer you pulled a knife on me," I said. "That will impress him. The judge will love that shit, too."

"Or her," Tuck said, grinning.

"Huh?"

"You assumed the lawyer would be a *him*, Ed," Tuck said. "Not cool." He dates a lawyer.

"Or *her*," I said, nodding. "Duly noted."

Skinny got agitated. "Hey, what about my ride? My Harley, man . . ."

"We'll take care of it, sir." Baxter grinned. "Saw that when we were coming in. Real nice."

"Better not scratch it up!"

"We will be very careful."

I looked at Bax. "You thought I was in here fighting for my life and took a minute to admire a motorcycle?"

"Just noticed it, is all," Bax said. "Couldn't help it. It's sweeter than a pancake in heaven."

The road deputies hauled out the combatants after we discussed combining our eventual reports. I sat at the bar, not at all looking forward to writing my eventual report, and Tuck turned off Fox News and gave me my beer.

"Damn, Ed, for a man who professes to dislike violence, you are awfully damned good at it."

"I kind of have to be."

"You are snake-quick, my man, snake-quick. Had those bastards under control in no time." Tuck ran a handkerchief across the pearls of sweat on his forehead. "Thanks for handling that, man. I thought I was going to have to shoot someone. That would fuck up my perfect record. So, drinks are on me today."

"Thanks, bud." I took a sip, nodding in appreciation. "And I'll keep my mouth shut about the shotgun."

Then I called Sheriff Daltry.

"Ed, I like it when my people answer on the first ring or two."

"Sorry, John," I said. "I was hugging a big gay guy."

"What?"

"Just joking, sort of." I tried to sound like I didn't want to flush the phone down the toilet, but I don't think I succeeded. An actor, I ain't. "Little bit of a fracas here at Tucker's Bar and Grill, and I had my hands full of skinny dumbass and angry gay guy. They got in a fight. Road patrol came and mopped up, no one hurt bad. Skinny stranger took a hard punch in the nose, not from me, by the way. I thought it was broken, but maybe it's not. It stopped bleeding bad, anyway, and he didn't want an ambulance. Stranger pulled a knife and was professionally subdued at gunpoint."

"Any of that shit on body cams?"

For a sheriff who always worries about what might show up on a deputy's body cam, Daltry was forever saying such things out loud and forgetting he might be on speakerphone, or that calls can be recorded. "No," I said. "Road guys got here after all was quiet."

"Good. You hurt?"

"Not a scratch. I'll type it all up tonight."

"Sure, Ed. OK." John Daltry is a bit of an asshole, but he knows the job we do, so he didn't ride me any further. "Listen, we have a detective from Columbus coming here on a missing person case. Teen girl, pretty blonde, I hear, and the cops think she might have come our way. I want you to help out on this end."

I do not like the words "missing teen girl." They were not words I ever wanted to hear again.

"Why does this Columbus cop think the kid was coming here?"

"I don't know, Ed. Maybe they suspect foul play, maybe the girl knows someone around here. We'll know when we know. In the meantime, I'd like you to assist."

"Can't Bob do that?" Bob Dooman was the other detective in the Mifflin County Sheriff's Office. "I have racked up a lot of hours lately, John, and I'm already two beers in." That was a lie, but Tuck was setting down my next one, so it was only a little lie. I planned to be two beers in by the end of this phone call, anyway.

"Bob has OT issues, too, thanks to that Quincy bitch, and his kid is sick and Amy's working. And I don't like them Columbus high-and-mighty types coming into our turf anyway, so someone is damn well gonna babysit, and it's gonna be a detective, not road patrol. The job is yours."

"All right, Sheriff." I sighed, and took a sip of brew. The Quincy woman had stopped taking her depression meds and run off with her baby boy, and Bob Dooman had been busting ass for three weeks calling and driving to every town she had friends or family in. I'd been helping with that while handling most of the routine stuff—tractor thefts, barn burglaries, marijuana grow operations—in the meantime, along with breaking that wife-beating bastard's alibi and showing up in court. Bob had found the woman and the kids, all safe, and had earned a little relaxation. His sick kid trumped my desire for beer and good music, too, so it looked like I would get to babysit a Columbus detective. "He coming to the station, or am I meeting him somewhere?"

"She," Daltry said, sounding like he disapproved. "Yes, she's coming to the station. Ought to be here in an hour or so."

"Fine," I said. "I'll be there." That was twice in the span of fifteen minutes I had incorrectly assumed someone working in law enforcement was a man. I decided to work on that.

Daltry could have said thanks, but he ended the call instead. I put the phone down and hoisted the beer. Tuck squinted against the afternoon sunlight beaming into his otherwise properly dim drinking establishment.

I drank my brew, enjoying the solid hops kick. "Tuck, my man, queue up Willie for me. 'Heaven and Hell' ought to do it."

"Since you kept people from dying all over my bar, I'll do it, but you know I hate that Willie Nelson shit." Tuck kept all kinds of music on his computer here, and played whatever seemed best for whatever customers he had at the moment. Left to his own devices, he was a metalhead. He shook his head hard, and his long black hair whipped like a flag behind his head, and all the beads in it rattled together. "I hate that Willie shit."

"I like Willie, and there's no one here but you and me now, and I have to go back to work soon, so buck up," I said, winking. "Oh, can you write down your witness statement for me? I want to relax, not interview you." I took another sip, a deep one. "I'd leave out the part about you pulling a shotgun, if you know what I mean."

Tuck fired up Willie. I handed Tuck my notebook and a pen, and he started writing, tapping his bead-laden hair with the pen now and then in search of just the right words. When he isn't pouring beer or listening to metal or dating a lawyer, Tuck writes poetry.

"It doesn't have to be Elizabeth Barrett Browning," I said. "Just write it. Fast."

"A phrase well expressed has life, Ed," Tuck said, smiling. "Always strive to put just the right words down on paper when you know the world might see them later. Every written line can be a legacy."

"Well, no one but a couple of lawyers, a reporter or two, a judge, and maybe, I say maybe, my boss will read this, so create fast and skip the iambic pentameter. I'm due back at the S.O. soon."

I was not looking forward to meeting this Columbus cop. I was pretty sure my week was about to start sucking hard. This cop was bringing city problems, and I'd had my fill of those.

Not that life as a country detective was all IPA and roses, of course. It was not what I had expected when I left NYPD almost five years ago. Not at all. It was dangerous and depressing in its own way, but not every damned day, and not in a way that rips out your soul and stomps on it.

Columbus, Ohio, wasn't New York, either, but it had some of the same city problems I'd hoped to never see again, and now some detective was coming here and maybe bringing some of those problems with her. And they might become my problems.

Law enforcement in Mifflin County wasn't easy. We had drugs. We had break-ins committed by people who needed money to buy drugs. We had spousal abuse. We had drunken brawls. But we didn't have that special kind of crazy that cities grow like bumper crops, the kind that makes people kill just for the hell of it, or plunge off a high roof because, hey, it's Tuesday. The kind of crazy that breeds human animals, complete sociopaths. The kind that made me leave NYPD in a drunken tailspin, with a head full of my own special kind of crazy.

I did not want city problems. No, no, no.

I especially did not want missing teen girl city problems. I'd had my share of those, too. More than my share.

I eyed the bourbon on the high shelf just beyond Tuck's head, but signaled for another beer instead. I knew drinking more before meeting this cop was a bad idea, but that didn't stop me.

Tuck placed my third beer in front of me, and started to ask why I was agitated, but decided against that.

I told myself it was probably a simple runaway case. Maybe the girl ran off with a boyfriend. Or a girlfriend. Maybe they were in a hotel somewhere, doing things teens do, and no one was getting hurt. Those cases tended to end after a day or two, with no real tragedy. Mom or dad would call us, say the kid came home. We'd ask a few questions, write a report, and file it. This case, quite likely, would be the same.

I told myself that, but I knew there were other possibilities.

Aside from drugs and discarded murder weapons, the most common criminal export around here was bodies. They killed people in the city, then drove them out to corn and woods country to dispose of the remains. I'd seen a few of those in my five years here, and counted myself lucky I hadn't seen more. Counties closer to the big cities see that more often. None of the found body cases I'd handled here had been a teen girl.

God, I said in my head, *don't let this be a dead teen girl.*

I wondered why I had so quickly gone past the scant evidence and jumped to the most morbid possibility, and drained my brew a bit faster than I had intended.

Willie was singing on the good speakers, about how he couldn't always tell whether he was in heaven or hell.

I didn't know, either. I'd fled New York's hell for something that was not quite heaven, but it was close on good days.

And now I worried that hell had followed me here.

CHAPTER THREE

Tuesday, 12:30 p.m.

I RUSHED TO my trailer, which is only a few miles from Tuck's but is around the bend from town and secluded behind some woods, out of sight from any other human dwellings. Just the way I like it. The F-150 tossed up dust as I turned off of Big Black Dog Road and rumbled down the long dirt driveway. Pine branches scraped at the truck in a few spots, but I could not hear them because I had "Lonesome, On'ry and Mean" playing pretty loud.

I rent the trailer from a farm couple. It sits by a pond that really ought to be called a lake, but my landlords say it's a pond and I don't argue with my elders over what they call their own property. The late September sun was a bright floodlight on the oaks and maples and made the pond ripples shine like white gold. Burnt orange leaves swirled like drunken butterflies in the air. I didn't have time to enjoy it, though, because some Columbus cop was looking for a missing girl.

I showered fast, then scarfed down a ham sandwich and a Mountain Dew. I put on khaki pants and a dark blue Mifflin County Sheriff's Office pullover shirt, then donned my tennis shoes and tucked the Smith & Wesson M&P 9-millimeter into my belt holster. I stepped outside, sighed at the red-tailed hawk circling over the giant hollow sycamore across the pond, then got my ass into the truck. I replaced the Waylon Jennings disc with Doc Watson and headed to work.

My little slice of heaven is near Jodyville, where Tucker's Bar and Grill is two doors down from the only traffic light and across the street from the only general store. The Mifflin County Sheriff's Office is in Ambletown, about ten minutes away unless I use my siren and step on the gas. There was no need for that now, of course. I was going to be on time, unless a tractor got in my way.

I passed the store, then braked hard. What the hell. I owed Nancy a fry pie, and the Columbus cop could wait. I parked, ran in for two strawberry pies, and returned to the truck. A few minutes later, I stepped up to Nancy's porch, a fry pie in each hand.

"Strawberry?" She smiled. "Oh, Ed, you did not have to do that."

She smiled widely, not caring a bit if the world saw she was missing a tooth or two. She had a big straw hat on, as always, and white strands of hair sprang from beneath it at random intervals.

"Yes, I did have to do it." I sat on the porch swing next to her and handed her a fry pie. She tore into the wax paper wrapper with glee. "I pay when I lose a bet, Nance. You won, fair and square."

"You been around as long as I have," she said, "and you figure out how to win at checkers. I'll be eighty in a week, Ed."

"No way," I said. "Eighty?"

"Yep!" She smiled big. "Gonna be a party after church Sunday. You coming to church Sunday?"

"Nope."

Nancy sighed. She had asked me to go to church every week since I'd found her stolen lawn mower, almost two years ago. "One day, you are gonna say yes."

"Not likely," I replied. I consider theological matters to be too complicated and personal for discussion in committee, and I'd found most preachers get pretty irritated when you ask pesky questions. "I will try to drop by for the party, though."

I ate half of my fry pie in a couple of big bites. Nancy nibbled patiently at hers.

"I hope you will come," she said. "Lots of nice people will be there."

"There aren't many people in Jodyville I don't already know, Nance."

"Well, you need to know them better."

"OK, well, at the party, then. If I can. Cop's work ain't ever really done, you know." I finished my treat and licked my fingers.

"I know." She waved at a bicyclist speeding down the road. The guy on the bike nodded and kept pedaling hard. "I'd like to ride fast like that," Nancy said.

"Speaking of getting somewhere fast, I have to run. Enjoy that pie."

"Thank you, Ed! You be careful, sweetie."

I ran back to the truck and headed toward Ambletown. Despite the pleasant visit with Nancy, I wasn't really at ease, and I realized I had used the pie bet as an excuse to delay the inevitable. I shut the music off after a while. Doc's guitar usually settles my mind, but this time it didn't.

I saw tractors in the fields harvesting corn, but encountered none on the road, so I pulled into the sheriff's lot just a couple of minutes late.

I went through the lobby instead of the "Law Enforcement Officers Only" door, because Debbie Maynard was dispatching today and Debbie is gorgeous—long brown hair, great curves, a smile like a supernova. She's married, and she's not the kind to cheat, but I like looking at her anyway. She knows I like looking, too, and doesn't mind a bit. It makes the workdays more interesting for me, and she at least lets me think it makes the days go better for her, too.

She peered at me through the bulletproof glass and opened the little window. "Hey, Ed. How are you?"

"Good, Debbie, good." I tried to sound like I meant it, but this whole missing girl thing kept rolling around in my head. "You?"

"Fine. Wishing I could get home and back to my book. I am at the good part."

"Sex and violence?"

"Ghosts. Shirley Jackson." Her brow furrowed, and she waved a hand in front of her nose. "Strawberries and beer? You know how Sheriff feels about drinking on duty."

"And he knows how I feel about going on duty when I'm drinking. We're even."

She flashed the nova smile and buzzed me in. "Stay away from him anyway."

"I'll try."

"Farkas called. Wants a quote or two on the trial this morning."

"I got no quotes for the press. Tell him to read my report."

"Already did. Oh, there's a message on your desk. Mr. Green called again, about the tractor."

"His son-in-law didn't steal the goddamned tractor."

"Tell Mr. Green that."

I had told Mr. Green that, probably a half-dozen times, and I would tell him again, but not right away. He did not believe his son-in-law was fit for his daughter, and he probably was right about that, but being drunk and jobless and stupid didn't add up to being a farm gear thief. The poor son of a bitch didn't have enough property to hide a stolen tractor, and he didn't have enough brains to sell one without getting caught. I didn't think he had the energy to steal a donut, let alone an antique tractor.

I snuck one more peek at Debbie, who caught me doing it and smiled, then headed down the hall and entered the squad room. Only one deputy was in the room. Irwin Trumpower sat at one of a half-dozen desks, probably writing up his report on the fight at Tuck's. I asked, and he confirmed that. "I will write mine tonight," I told him. "Thanks for the assist today."

"Thank me with a beer," he said. "I forwarded you the name of the skinny guy, and his priors. Nothing major. He's a guitar man, plays devil music."

I nodded and ducked back out to the hall.

Sheriff Daltry was in his office with the door closed, so I continued on to the detectives room. There are six desks in that room, but we had only two detectives. The taxpayers recently had funded a nice shiny new building and jail for us. The office had big windows to let in a lot of afternoon light and illuminate all the empty desks. Daltry spent a lot of his time these days trying to convince farmers to pony up for a few more bodies to sit at those desks, but the county had fallen short in two straight elections. Farmers prefer paying for jails to paying for manpower, I guess. And then they wonder why it takes a deputy twenty minutes to rush from across the county whenever they call about something.

I plucked the sticky note about Mr. Green's stolen antique tractor from my computer screen and tossed it in the garbage can. I sat at my spot, by the big window with a view of a barbecue place and a hot dog joint, and started typing up my report on the incident at Tuck's.

According to Trumpower's email, the skinny guy's name was Bob Van Heusen. Age forty-two. He claimed to be a professional guitar picker out of Columbus, but he seemed to make most of his money selling pot. Picking on Ollie got him hurt, and busted, which was bad for him because he was wanted on misdemeanor charges from a couple of other jurisdictions. The dumbass should've kept his head down and his mouth shut, but dumbasses seldom remember that. Dumbasses often make my job easier. I made a phone call to Columbus to let them know we had Van Heusen under lock and key.

I had left the door open. Sheriff Daltry leaned in and said, "Hey, Ed, meet Michelle Beckworth."

He waved her in, and she maneuvered around his towering bulk. His potato nose dipped as he took a peek at her ass.

Michelle Beckworth was cute as hell. I put her at thirty-two or thirty-three, a few years younger than me. Dark brown hair, curly and almost to her shoulders, framed a good smile, brown eyes, high cheekbones, and a few freckles. She wore a white short-sleeved blouse and faded jeans, along with a pair of running shoes. She had a Columbus Police Department badge and a holstered pistol on her belt, and carried an official-looking file folder. A blue windbreaker was draped over her arm. She hung that on the back of a chair.

Daltry hadn't bothered to announce her as Detective Michelle Beckworth, but then again, he didn't think women should be cops. I had asked him once if his attitude might make female voters decide he didn't need more tax money to hire deputies. My question did not endear me to him.

I came around my desk and shook her hand. "Detective," I said. "I'm Ed Runyon."

"Hello." She had a deeper voice than I expected, and it had a smoky quality. "Call me Shelly."

She grasped my hand firmly, then let go. She didn't have colored stuff on her fingernails, and she didn't wear any rings.

The sheriff cleared his chubby throat. "Shelly here has a missing person case—girl might have come up our way. You show her around and help her out, Ed."

"Will do, Sheriff." I looked her in the eyes. "Hungry?"

"I ate on the way up here, but coffee would be great."

"I will let you get to it," Daltry said. He gave me a hard look before vanishing, and ran a hand through his gray hair the way he does when he's annoyed. I figured he had smelled the beer on my breath and planned for us to have a little talk. I figured I had better rehearse speaking in one-syllable words.

I pointed Beckworth toward the coffee station in the squad room and followed in her wake. She had a nice walk, so I was inclined to forgive her for making me go back on the clock. "It isn't fancy, so if you want better coffee, I know a place."

"No, this will be fine. I am not fussy as long as it isn't decaf. Black, please."

I poured two cups, black. "OK, so tell me about your missing girl. Runaway?"

"Maybe. The girl's name is Megan Beemer, an Upper Arlington charter school junior. We're assisting Upper Arlington PD on the case."

"Upper get to call in Columbus PD every time a girl disappears for a couple of days?"

"Her dad owns an arc welding business and contributes enough to local political campaigns to get their attention."

"Ah. Lucky for her she's not a poor kid."

"Whatever her circumstances," Shelly said sharply, "it's my job to help find her."

"True enough. OK, so runaway?"

She shrugged. "Maybe not. Girl has good grades, no record with us or Franklin County or anyone else."

"Boyfriend?"

"A very recent ex, in fact."

"Those make great suspects."

"Yeah. But he has a very strong alibi. He was gaming online with friends in three countries, shooting alien zombies or some such. The whole thing was recorded, time-stamped, everything. Our online forensics people doubt it could have been faked, but they are checking anyway, and the kid is cooperating. Seems genuinely worried about her, too, despite the breakup. The kid looks exactly like the type to spend so much time online shooting alien zombies that he bores his pretty girlfriend. His name is Matt Foreman, and there is a sheet on him in the folder."

I declined to look at the sheet. Columbus PD could worry about Matt Foreman. I was more concerned about whatever Mifflin County connection the girl had.

She took a sip of coffee, closed her eyes, smiled like God was whispering in her ear, sighed, and set the cup down. For a moment, her expression was rapturous. "This coffee is way better than advertised."

"Locally roasted beans," I said. "And we clean the coffeepot at least annually."

She laughed, then she was all business again. She handed me a photo from the folder, then picked up her coffee.

"Megan went to a party Saturday night, one of those warehouse one-night-stand things where they rent a place and get a band or two and some booze and some drugs and some strobe lights and dance their little brains out. She never made it home."

This was Tuesday. "So, a couple days missing." I looked at the picture. The pretty face in the photo—a yearbook picture shot in front of a brick wall decked with ivy—looked familiar, like maybe she was a Disney actress or something. Wholesome, fresh. Blue eyes, blonde hair, bright smile. She was sixteen or seventeen, I figured, wearing a bright floral sundress and posing with her arms wide open, like she was announcing her imminent conquering of the world.

Now she was missing.

The image reminded me too much of another girl, in another place, who was not so pretty when we finally found her. That was the night I left the big city, full of bourbon and mental pictures I could not erase. I hate thinking about that night. I had spent a great deal of time and effort learning how to not think of that night.

I shoved those thoughts aside, shoved the photo back into the folder, and reminded myself this detective had not come to Mifflin County just to drag my nightmares into the light of day.

"Did you give this info to Debbie?"

"The hottie in dispatch? Yes. She jumped right on it. She probably has it on your Facebook and all that by now."

"Good. So . . . what makes you think your girl came this way? Did she want to see corn and cows?"

"First, I just don't think this is a runaway," she said. "She didn't fight with her parents. No history of unruliness or any other issues. We talked to her friends, and her teachers. She liked her life, by all accounts. And . . . she drove herself to the party and her car was still in the parking lot."

"OK." Her words stirred up some stuff in my mind that I didn't want swirling around in there. I took a deep breath. "It does not fit the usual runaway profile. What else?"

"She texted a friend from the party, said she had met a guy. Said he was from Hicksville."

I shrugged. "Well, we have a lot of hicks and a Jodyville, but no Hicksville."

"I assumed she meant it generically," Shelly said, "although there is a Hicksville in Defiance County. We got a guy looking there, too. Anyway, we tracked down the warehouse owner, a disgusting creep named Kerr, and hit him with a shitload of charges related to the party. He said he didn't know anything about Megan, but he remembered seeing a lot of Mifflin County plates in his lot that night."

"That's a slim lead," I said. "I do not suppose this guy gave you complete vehicle descriptions and license plate numbers, by any chance."

"Lots of pickups, he said." She took another sip of coffee. "NRA stickers, Browns decals, shit like that. No license plates. And we checked the security cameras in the parking lot. Low resolution piece of shit cameras shooting in the dark from an angle too high to begin with. Couldn't read a damned plate in the lot. Couldn't make out a single face, either. Just saw the tops of the ball caps."

I sighed. Someday, I'll write a primer on where people ought to put their security cameras. The cheap ones ought to be put up the manufacturer's ass. "Well, that narrows it down to, oh, about eighty percent of the vehicles we have around here." I drained my coffee mug.

She grinned. "I noticed that driving here. My thin lead gets a bit thicker, though. And the guy did not notice a preponderance of plates from any other Ohio county."

"How much thicker?"

"We found Megan's phone, busted and wet and muddy, off the interstate near Alum Creek. You ever try to separate a teen girl from her phone?"

"No, I am not brave enough for that."

"State worker cutting weeds saw the phone and called it in to his dispatcher, and they called the sheriff and he called us because he'd heard of our case."

"Pure goddamned luck."

"Yep, but I will take it. It was an iPhone with an *Attack on Titan* phone case, just like Megan's."

"What is *Attack on Titan*?"

"An anime where they battle gross naked monsters."

"Like Godzilla?"

"I don't think so," Shelly said. "I don't really know the show. Anyway, our forensics guys have been able to confirm it is her phone."

"Any prints?"

"None useful, just partials. Phone got rained on, and it was busted up pretty bad. Not too far from the road. It was hurled from a vehicle on 71, maybe, based on the damage. Not merely dropped, in any case."

"OK." I pondered for a couple of seconds. "So Alum Creek is north of the party venue, sounds like."

"Yes." Shelly nodded.

"But not far north, so while the phone headed in this direction, it did not head far this way, right?" I poured more coffee. "There is a lot of Ohio between here and Columbus that could be accurately described as Hicksville."

"Right, but combined with all the Mifflin County plates in the parking lot . . ."

"Yep, you are right. It is a logical starting point. Anything useful on the phone? Photos, texts, anything like that?"

"Tech guys are fishing around in there to see what they can retrieve. The phone was found Monday morning—took a while for all the planets to line up and get it in our hands. Damage is extensive, but our guys are pretty good."

"And they have a backlog, no doubt." Crime labs always have a backlog—it's just a fact of life. They work their asses off, but they can't possibly keep up. Unless you have a hot lead or a solid suspect, your evidence usually has to wait for its turn under the microscope or whatever other digital watchamajig they are using these days. "At least we aren't waiting for a tox screen. So, there is hope we'll hear soon?"

"I have filed paperwork trying to get us moved up on the priority list," Shelly said. "The girl's parents have money and friends in high places, so that will probably help. And one of the lab techs likes me a lot." She winked.

"OK, so in the meantime we'll see what we can find out here. You working with Ambletown PD, too? They're the city here, county seat, but they've got hillbillies, too. Sort of Hicksville, but with more traffic lights and better Wi-Fi."

"My partner has a pal at Ambletown, a guy named Dyson, who said he would work the city for us. So I get corn country."

"I know Ray Dyson, good cop. OK, then. Finish the coffee, we'll saddle up in my truck and go find your girl."

She looked me right in the eyes. "You been drinking, Detective?"

"Until the sheriff told me you were coming, I was off duty. I'm fine."

"OK."

CHAPTER FOUR

Tuesday, 2:10 p.m.

"WE'VE GOT TWO high schools in the county, aside from Amble-town, that is. We'll start with Hollis High," I told her, swinging the pickup out onto the main east-west highway.

"OK. Why?" She was thumbing through the CD case I'd moved so she could sit down, and I think she was trying not to laugh. "You know you can just stream music from your phone these days, right?"

"I spent a lot of time collecting CDs, and this truck is older than Spotify." I gunned it a bit. "Still runs good, though. OK, so why Hollis. One, they'll be letting kids out about the time we can get there. Two, I know a friendly face there—things might go faster. Three, they had a big football win Friday night, so maybe some kids from here went down to Columbus to celebrate."

"Cool." She shook her head slowly. "This music all seems older than you."

"I like the good old stuff," I said. "Waylon, Willie, Johnny Cash, Bocephus..."

"Bowhatsit?"

"Hank Williams Jr. It's a nickname. Mostly sings about booze and his dead daddy, a country legend, by the way. Anyway, I like that stuff. I even play at the guitar a bit, and sing when no one sober is listening. My dad gave me a nice guitar when I was a kid. I just strum, never learned to really pick. Dad thought I could learn that, but I was too impatient."

"I haven't heard of most of this stuff." She put the case back into the console and started filling me in on the scant details of her case. "Aside from the ex-boyfriend, Megan Beemer had no big issues with her parents or classmates, but she had an independent streak. She supported LGBTQ rights, railed against the machine on Twitter and Instagram and Tumblr, all that. As happens to anyone with two X chromosomes who dares to speak her mind online, she'd attracted her share of anonymous assholes who thought a lot of ad hominem attacks and sexist bullshit would set her straight, but she generally handled those with humor and grace."

"Sounds like a good kid."

"Yeah."

"You looking into those online guys for a possible suspect?"

"Yeah," she said. "Looking for guys who stand out from the crowd, or who might be in the area, or whatever. None so far seems to be a strong candidate, and they almost all go by anonymous nicknames because they are cowards, but we'll try to get an IP address or something to identify one of them if we get a good suspect."

"OK," I said. "Tell me about the party."

No one had gone to the warehouse party with Megan; in fact, her friends had tried to talk her out of going at all, on the theory that it sounded too wild.

"I wish she had listened to her friends." I sighed.

"Me, too. Young people. Fearless as ever."

"Yep."

I wrestled the Ford onto the two-lane road that led toward Jodyville and Hollis High School, and we left town behind. About a half-mile later, a big-ass corn combine took up almost all of the road ahead of me. I glanced around, figured I could make it easily. "Hold on, Detective."

I steered the truck into a harvested field to my right. Thank God for four-wheel-drive. I gunned it, threw up a big cloud of dirt, and passed the farm gear. I got back onto the road, and the F-150 stopped rocking like a toy boat in a kid's tub.

"You have different road rules here," Shelly said, grinning and catching her breath.

"Yeehaw." I slapped the steering wheel. "That actually is the first time I have ever done that, but I have been dreaming of it for years. Most of the time, there are ditches along the road that make it sort of impossible. We got lucky here. But I have practiced that little maneuver in my head about fifty billion times."

She looked around at the autumn show of painted leaves. There was little to see besides woods, fields, farmhouses, and more fields, but it all added up to pastoral beauty. "Nice out here."

"Yes, it is," I said, hoping it would still be that way once this case was over.

She turned toward me. "You know you look a little bit like Heath Ledger?"

"Who?"

She laughed. "C'mon. Heath Ledger? The actor? Played the Joker? You look like him, just bigger."

I knew the guy she meant. She wasn't the first person to tell me that, of course. But the only movie I had ever seen Ledger in was that one where he painted his face with deathly white paste and bloody gruesome lipstick, and went around scaring people and killing people for no damned reason at all. The Joker was a trickster God in a universe without rules, sense, or justice. I didn't want to live in a universe like that, and maybe sometimes I still worry I do live in a universe like that. I'd used booze, pills, therapy, and meditation ever since New York in an attempt to not see the universe that way. And now, here I was looking for a missing girl while memories stalked my mind, like Grendel at Herot.

Anyway, I get tired of hearing about how I look like the fucking Joker.

"Nah, I don't look like him."

"It's not a bad thing, Ed." She grinned. "Lot of women would say it's a good thing."

I glanced at her. "Yeah?"

"Yeah."

Well, then, maybe looking like the Joker sans makeup could have advantages, after all.

I was a professional cop working with another professional cop, though, so I changed the topic. We just chit-chatted the rest of the way to Hollis High—a flat, one-story building with a library at one end and a gymnasium at the other, with hallways and classrooms and a cafeteria in between. The marching band across the parking lot was rehearsing "Billy Jean." Don't ask me why.

Kids were streaming from the doors already, lugging books and bags and wandering toward the line of vehicles where parents waited to collect their offspring. Some wandered to the right, where a string of yellow buses waited to take them home. A lot of the girls reminded me of Megan Beemer, and of a different blonde, back in the Bronx, who I didn't really want to remember.

I parked the truck and got out in a hurry, spitting on the gravel lot. I had thought about NYPD and that damned Bronx case too many times today, and the beer was wearing off.

"You OK, Ed?" Shelly shut the truck door. "You look pissed."

"Yeah, I'm fine. Let's go."

We walked toward the front door. Principal Del Reed saw me and headed my way. He waved. I waved back.

He dodged his way through the swarms of kids and hurried toward us as quickly as his short legs would allow, his black tie flapping over the shoulder of his blue shirt. He wore his usual walleye expression, the same one I always got when I came poking around Hollis. Reed was worried more about bad publicity than just about anything else, because there was always a school levy coming up and it ain't easy prying money from farmers who think you are indoctrinating kids to believe in evolution and vote for Democrats. Reed would rather lose both legs under a lawn tractor than give farmers another excuse to deny his school funds, so he was hoping we weren't here to do a drug sweep.

"Can I help you, Detective?" He had jogged about a hundred feet, and was huffing a bit. He tried to look happy to see me, and failed miserably.

"Mr. Reed, this is Detective Shelly Beckworth, from Columbus PD. Shelly, this is Principal Del Reed, in charge of all these kids here."

They nodded at each other and muttered hellos.

"Shelly is working a missing persons case, Del, and we're hoping some of your kids might be able to help us out."

"Columbus, you said?" He made it sound like a disease.

"Yeah. None of your kids are in trouble," I assured him.

"Oh, well, of course," he said, showing a genuine smile at last.

"At least, we have no particular reason to think so. We just hope some of them might have heard or seen something. Actually, I was hoping to start with Miss Scott."

"Ah," Reed said, peering down at his shoes. He looked back up, trying to hide a grin. He suddenly looked like a window peeper. "Well, you know where to find her, I am sure. Please . . . try to be discreet. Please? And thanks for not showing up in a marked cruiser. Thank God for small favors." He went on his way, saying goodbye to departing kids and waving at parents in the pickup line.

"You didn't want to start with the principal?"

"Nah. He's so worried about the district's image he won't say much of anything, even if we put a gun to his head. If a cop asks him what's on the lunch menu for tomorrow, he'd check with the school board for permission to answer before committing himself."

"Yikes."

"Yeah. Kids don't tell him much, anyway. No one really likes him. We'll get more help from one of the teachers. Linda Scott's an English teacher, and helps the arts teacher a lot, and the kids adore her because she treats them like people. If any Hollis kids went to Columbus this weekend, I think there is a pretty good chance she might know about it."

"Sounds good. Principal seemed amused when you mentioned her, though."

"No idea why."

We entered the building. The lobby opened into the cafeteria. A few students sat at tables, and on tables, gabbing away. A couple were reading, and one was writing furiously. I figured they were hanging around for some after-school club or something, or maybe just waiting for rides. I doubted they just loved school so much they didn't want to rush away at the final bell.

We turned right, headed down the hall and past the offices, then turned right again. Another left, and we were at Linda Scott's classroom. Literary quotes hung in a row across the wall. "There's many a man has more hair than wit. —William Shakespeare." "I have never let my schooling interfere with my education. —Mark Twain." "Love doesn't just sit there, like a stone; it has to be made, like bread, remade all the time, made new. —Ursula K. Le Guin."

I always scanned those quotes, looking to see if Linda had added the one I had suggested. Lo and behold, there it was. "I prefer rogues to imbeciles, because they sometimes take a rest. —Alexandre Dumas."

I spotted Linda, shelving a book. Her back was to me, but I recognized the flowered skirt, the curves, the nice legs, and the long red hair streaming down the back of her white sleeveless blouse. The three freckles that formed a triangle on her left forearm were still there.

"Knock knock," I said.

She turned and smiled big. "Ed!" Her blouse had a couple more buttons loose than was probably wise in a building full of teenage boys, but I didn't mind if she didn't. It is sometimes a good thing when September is unseasonably warm.

Linda came forward quickly and gave me a hug, then smiled at Shelly. "New girlfriend?"

"Fellow cop. Detective Shelly Beckworth, out of Columbus. Shelly, this is Linda Scott, reader, writer, artist, and cupcake expert."

They shook hands, and seemed to be sizing one another up. Maybe that was just my imagination working overtime. It does that.

"I am looking for a teen girl missing out of our jurisdiction," Shelly said. "We have reason to believe she may have encountered some Hollis students at a party in Columbus on Saturday night. Maybe she left the party with one or more of them, or maybe they saw her leave with someone else or heard her mention some plans for afterward. Anything that might help."

"We were hoping you might have heard if any Hollis kids went up that way," I added.

"I see." Linda's green eyes met mine for just a moment. We'd had a thing a while back, and it had been a pretty damned good thing up until she'd asked me what I was thinking one too many times. What I had been thinking wasn't anything I wanted to talk about. Linda liked to try to fix people and thought making them talk would do that. She probably was right, but I didn't like it much anyway and it tended to make me surly and difficult to be around.

Anyway, we had parted on good terms, and seeing her now I had to wonder if maybe I should have talked more.

"As a matter of fact," Linda said, glancing heavenward, spinning toward her desk and clasping her hands together with what seemed to me a small air of victory, "you came to the right place. There were plenty of celebrations this weekend. Big Green beat the Dusters, you know. Rivalry game, rah rah rah." She smiled at me, and leaned against her desk. I knew she did it just to stretch those long legs out in front of me. She crossed the right one over the left, slowly, smiling all the time.

"Halls were filled with hushed talk of parties, getting wasted, getting laid, getting caught, you know how it goes," Linda said. "Most of it sounded like parties around here. But I do know of at least three boys who went to Columbus."

I whipped a notebook from my pocket. Shelly did the same and asked, "Names, please?"

"Soul Scraped."

"What the fuck?" I snorted. "You got a student named *Soul Scraped*? I know Bob and John are kind of out of style these days, but . . ."

Linda laughed. "It's a band, Ed. Soul Scraped. Hollis High's very own power trio. Dark, angsty, poetic stuff, very fast and very loud."

"They were in Columbus Saturday night?"

"They had a gig there, yes," Linda said. "They were very excited about it, although they tried to act as though it was no big deal. You know, like a guy in the bigs hits a home run and casually trots around the bases like he hits one every day, that sort of thing. But they talked about it a lot, and clearly had a night they described as epic."

Shelly tapped her pen against her chin. "Do you know where they performed?"

"No idea, but I think it was a party, rather than a campus bar or something like that."

Shelly and I exchanged glances. I asked Linda for the names.

"Jimmy Norris. Sorry. He prefers Buzz these days. He is the guitar man and lead singer. It's his show, really. Johnny Burke plays bass, Gage Thomas plays drums, but I think Buzz writes it all. A lot of Poe and Lovecraft and Clark Ashton Smith riffs in the lyrics, but some Emily Dickinson and Yeats and more, too. They auditioned for our yearbook assembly, but Mr. Reed thought they were a bit . . . too . . . much."

I nodded. "Hell, I know Buzz Norris. Trailer park across from the cemetery near Jodyville. Our road guys get called out there to shut down the noise a couple of times a week."

"Are they any good?" Shelly finished writing the names.

"No," I said.

"Yes," Linda said.

"I have heard them," I said. "About as melodic as a chain saw."

The teacher laughed and flipped her red hair back over her shoulder. "You voluntarily listen to Kris Kristofferson, may I remind you. Musically, Soul Scraped may be an acquired taste. But Buzz's lyrics have some real poetry to them. He thinks things through. And they are a very enthusiastic power trio. They jump and bounce and really shred the instruments."

"Kristofferson's a poet," I muttered. "And Willie doesn't shred."

Shelly gave me a puzzled look, then returned her attention to Linda. "Do you know of any other students who went to Columbus this weekend?"

"No, sorry."

"Gage Thomas," I said. "Any relation to Baker Thomas?"

Linda's eyes flashed quick anger. "The son of a bitch who threw his wife down the stairs? No, Gage is not related to that piece of shit. He's been pretty vocal about that." Linda usually tries to save the adult language for after hours, but the Thomas case had everyone riled up.

"OK." I jotted that down.

"Thanks for catching that garbage," Linda said, calming down as quickly as she'd flared up.

Shelly pulled out Megan Beemer's photo. "Have you seen this girl around? If she came this way with a hot guitar player, she may have met him here after school or something, or maybe you've seen her around town."

Linda looked at the image, and sadness clouded her face. "No, haven't seen her. Pretty girl. I hope you find her soon. God, I really hope so."

"Thanks. We will do our best."

"See that?" Linda pointed to the Dumas quote on the wall.

"Yeah, I did," I answered. "Thanks."

We said our goodbyes and headed back to the truck. On the way we showed the photo to a few straggling students, and asked if anyone knew of any excursions to Columbus, but we had no luck.

Back behind the wheel, I radioed dispatch. "Dee Two to station."

"Station. Go ahead, Dee Two."

"Debbie, have we had any noise complaints from the Norris place today? Out near Jodyville?"

"Indeed. Got one just now, almost as soon as school let out. Loud drumming, that's it so far, but you know the rest of it will start up soon. Always does. Unit Three is set to respond, but he is way up north just now. It's gonna be a while."

"I'll take the noise call; you can wave Unit Three off."

"Gonna request some real country music, Ed?"

"Dee Two out."

"Station out."

We listened as Debbie called off the road guy. It was Trumpower, and he sounded relieved. I figured I could get a beer out of him for taking the call.

"OK, Shelly," I said as the truck engine rumbled. "Let's go be music critics."

"Who's Kristofferson?"

"Jesus Christ." My eyes widened as I pulled out of the school lot. "Really? 'Me and Bobby McGee'? 'Sunday Mornin' Comin' Down'? 'Help Me Make It Through the Night'?"

"I know the Bobby McGee one," Shelly said. "Janis Joplin sang it, right?"

"Yeah," I said. "Kris Kristofferson wrote it. He sang it, too, well, growled it really. Growls and grumbles, mostly in tune, but not always. Anyway, a damned good songwriter."

"Never heard of him."

I sighed. "Why me, Lord?" I've always been told my musical tastes are older than I am, but I felt like I was beginning to catch up.

CHAPTER FIVE

Tuesday, 2:47 p.m.

"Dude, we're fucked."

"Not so loud, dumbass. Jesus, you might as well be on speakerphone. Why don't you call the fucking TV news and tell them all about it?"

"Sorry. It's cool, though. I'm all alone. No one close enough to hear me. Which is good, because we are fucking fucked."

"Calm down. How are we fucked?"

"Cops. Came to the school. Asking about Columbus and a missing girl. Showing pictures, asking students do you know her, have you seen her around, shit like that."

"Columbus is a big town, dumbass. Lots of bitches disappear. Every fucking day."

"I said they got pictures, dude."

"Pictures of us?"

"No!"

"Then who the fuck cares? Is it her?"

"Fuck, dude, I didn't talk to the fucking cops, OK? You think I'm a moron?"

"Yes."

"Fuck you."

"Anyway . . ."

"Anyway, I hear it is a blonde they are looking for, a pretty blonde. We are fucked."

"Will you chill? Jesus! Dude, lots of people were at that party. No one is going to find her; no one is going to connect her to us. Unless, you fuckhead, you lose your shit and start sweating and gulping and shitting your britches in front of the cops, you got it? So calm the fuck down. Figure they got nothing, because if they had something, they wouldn't just be asking random fucking people random fucking questions, see?"

"Yeah, maybe. OK."

"So we will figure out our next move. Relax. We'll figure it out."

"OK. I said OK. Fuck."

"Calm down."

"OK."

"They might get to us, you know, because we were there and people know it. So they might talk to us."

"Oh, fuck. Oh, fuck. Oh, fuck."

"But that don't mean shit, OK? Other people were there, too. Remember?"

"Yeah."

"So us being there don't prove shit, right?"

"I guess."

"Right?"

"OK, fuck it. Right."

"So they come around, they ask questions, we don't know shit, sorry, dude, never seen her. Right?"

"Right. OK."

"And we stay calm. Got it? We went to the party, we saw people but not her, sorry we can't help you, blah blah blah. We don't stammer like a dumbass, we don't drip sweat all over the fucking cops, we don't start yammering like a nervous fuck, right?"

"Right."

"We don't shit ourselves."

"Right."

"Because we are dudes."

"Right."

"We are dudes."

"Right. Fuck, yeah. Right! We are dudes!"

"OK, we cool?"

"Cool."

"We dudes?"

"Dudes. Fuck, yeah."

"We rock and roll machines?"

"Fuck, yeah, dude. Fuck, yeah. Rock and roll machines."

"Keep cool. Later, dude."

"Later."

CHAPTER SIX

Tuesday, 3:19 p.m.

I HAD SKIPPED lunch, so Shelly and I stopped at the Jodyville Market for fry pies and coffee, since it was on the way. It would be my second fry pie of the day, but, well, that's happened before. They're really good.

Jenna behind the counter smiled at me as though she knew a secret. The market was the only real option for shopping nearby, unless you wanted to drive into Ambletown, so everyone in or near Jodyville popped in here regularly for smokes, ice cream, bad beer, and lunch meat. Jenna knew everyone by face, if not always by name. Some people collect stamps or coins, but Jenna collects gossip.

She looked at me the way a birder looks at a green-winged teal, then her gaze zeroed in on Shelly. "Who is your friend, Ed?"

"My friend is a cop, here to do cop stuff." I poured two cups of joe to go. "Her name is Shelly. Shelly, this is Jenna, and she's wondering if you and I are getting married anytime soon, and if we are going to invite her."

"He's not my type," Shelly answered, and selected a strawberry fry pie.

I selected a peach pie, paid up, and then we got back to work. I aimed the truck for the trailer park. We ate on the go. It's a skill all cops have to acquire.

You could hear the damned drums and bass long before you could see the trailers. Rapid-fire tempo, only one chord as far as I could tell. The closer we got, the more I could feel the rumble climbing up from the road, through my truck and up my ass. I'm sure Hank never done it this a-way.

Once we had the place in sight, I could hear someone singing. Droning, really, with no more tonal range than one of those big machines that suck autumn leaves up from the curbside. I tried to make out the alleged poetry, but the only thing I could clearly discern was a phrase that sounded like "turd blossom." It sure as hell didn't sound like Robert Frost.

Everyone in Jodyville called it a trailer park, but that was something of a poetic expression itself. The collection of six trailers had just sort of gathered off the main north-south route south of town over the years on what used to be farmland. There was no fancy name for the place, no attempt to pretty things up. One dirt road slanted off the main paved route, and all the trailers were on the north side of that. Pickups, four-wheelers, and beat-up cars were tucked in anywhere there was room. Grills stood in front of every trailer, and everything smelled like burnt meat, dead grass, and gasoline.

I found a spot for my F-150 and got out. The unseasonal warmth was slowly giving way to the tyranny of the calendar, and low gray clouds had parked themselves above all the fiery leaves. I grabbed a windbreaker from behind the truck seat. We started walking toward the god-awful din emanating from the last trailer in the row.

Shelly tried to say something, but all I could hear was a dude yelling "turd blossom." She wasn't reaching for her gun or anything, so I figured she wasn't trying to alert me to danger. I shrugged and headed behind the trailer. She followed. I think she was dancing a little. Damned if I knew why.

The rockers were thrashing and shredding or whatever the hell they call it on a platform made of two-by-fours and plywood, and painted black with a lot of white skulls on it. Some of the skulls were bleeding. So were my ears, I am sure. The platform covered most of what passed for the trailer's backyard.

Buzz Norris, the guitar player who kept shouting into the mic, was scrawny, tall, and wide-eyed. There was no audience, and he hadn't yet noticed me and Shelly, but he was playing to an invisible crowd anyway. His jeans were black, his T-shirt was black, his tennis shoes were black, his guitar was black. The poor excuse for a beard he wore was black, like his hair. I suspected both had help from a bottle. The sole spot of color on him was a yellow handkerchief or bandana, tied around his head in a way that made his hair stand up like bristles on a porcupine. A skull earring dangled from his left ear, and it, too, was black. I couldn't remember if an earring in the left ear meant he was gay or a pirate, but I didn't really care.

He went at the guitar strings like one of those TV chefs chopping meat. The rapid slashing made a blur of his hand. The other hand was locked into a bar chord that I suspect was supposed to be A. I wondered how long it would be before a string broke. I wondered if he'd even notice when it did. I hoped they would all break.

Beside him, Johnny Burke played a bass that looked like a cheap replica of McCartney's Hofner, but he wasn't playing anything that sounded like The Beatles. Blond and bewhiskered, he jumped like a pogo stick and pounded a single note on the biggest string, basically providing a low drone behind Buzz's vocal. Burke wore a *Star Wars* T-shirt and jeans, both in great danger of falling apart.

The kid on the drums, Gage Thomas, looked younger than the other two. Maybe he was a freshman. He had a pale face, short reddish hair, a cigarette dangling from his lips, and a Reds baseball jersey. A beer bottle stood precariously atop the bass drum on a set that seemed to have been cobbled together from remnants of three or four different kits. Every time he thumped the foot pedal, that beer scooted around on the drum. Judging from the stains on the brown wood, he'd already spilled a couple million beers on that drum, so this one wouldn't really do any more damage when it eventually tumbled. His right hand struck a crash cymbal in time with the bass drum, about once every three seconds, while his left tapped out sixteenth notes on the snare.

Every now and then, Gage did a short roll, silenced his crash cymbal, and everyone stopped for a second while Buzz screamed "turd blossom." Then the aural assault resumed.

I flashed my badge, but the power trio kept on playing. I walked slowly toward Buzz, glaring, and he stepped away from the mic and stopped punishing the guitar strings. "Chill, dudes," he yelled.

Mercifully, they chilled. The sudden quiet was enormous. Mark Twain once said that truth hurts, but silence kills, but Twain never heard these guys.

I put my badge away. "I'm Detective Ed Runyon, Mifflin County Sheriff's Office. This is Detective Shelly Beckworth, Columbus Police Department."

"Damn! Columbus? We have moved on up!" Buzz ran fingers through his dark hair, knocking the yellow kerchief sideways a bit. "We haven't had detectives come out to tell us to quiet down before. And now all the way from Columbus? Awesome!"

"We're not here just to quiet you down," I said. "But, yeah. Quiet down. Anyway, Detective Beckworth is working a missing persons case, and she has some questions."

"Yes," Shelly said, fishing the photo out of her folder. "You guys can rock, by the way." I think she meant it.

"Fuck yeah," Gage said.

"You know it, dude," Johnny said.

"We fucking suck," Buzz said, sucking some snot back into his nose afterward.

"Amen," I said, but low so no one could hear it.

"You had a gig in Columbus this past weekend?" Shelly made it sound like the coolest thing that ever happened.

"Party," Buzz said. "Private thing. We got paid, though."

"Paid by Eric Kerr?"

"Yeah," Buzz said. "He rented a warehouse, or bought it maybe, I don't know, and had a big party. He saw us on YouTube and asked if we wanted the gig and, you know, money for nothing, chicks for free, right? Hell yeah, we wanted the gig."

"Sure," Shelly said.

"But if that dude Kerr is into some evil shit or pot or even actual real drugs or anything, look, we just got paid to play, OK? We didn't take nothing, we didn't snort nothing, we didn't shoot nothing."

Shelly held the photo of Megan Beemer where Buzz could see it. "Yeah, sure. This girl was at that same party and she never went home after. Her parents are worried sick, and we're hoping you might have seen her and can maybe tell us something, anything, that can help us find her."

Gage and his beer came out from behind the drums, and Johnny leaned over Buzz's shoulder. "Her name is Megan Beemer," I said. "Did you happen to see her?"

"No," Burke said.

"Wish I had," Thomas said. "She is fucking hot."

"Lot of people heard us that night," Buzz said, wandering over to a cooler and pulling out a bottle of Bud. "Can't expect to remember one chick out of the bunch."

I decided not to bust the boys on the beer just yet. Finding Megan was way more important than a juvenile drinking charge. But it bothered me to know Buzz didn't give a damn whether I busted him or not. He was dismissive. Cold. Snakelike.

"Look closer," Shelly said. "Try to remember. She's a pretty girl. You guys pay attention to those, don't you?" She smiled. If I had been a teen boy looking at that smile, I'd have melted.

These guys didn't melt.

Buzz, looking bored, peered at the photo. "Yeah, she's a babe. Not one of the babes I screwed that night, though. Probably."

He laughed, and looked around at his two-man entourage while they laughed, too.

"You think we did something to her?" That was Gage, twirling a drumstick.

I jumped in. "Why do you say that?"

"Um," Gage said, dropping the stick. "Well, you know, you're fucking here, aren't you, asking questions and shit?"

Shelly shook her head. "We are not accusing anyone of anything," she said. "The girl has vanished, and the last place anybody knew, she was listening to a band in a Columbus warehouse Saturday night. You played in that warehouse in Columbus on Saturday night. We just want to find her, that's all. We hoped maybe you'd seen her, or talked to her, or saw her with someone."

"She probably ran off with a guy," Buzz said, sneering. "Hot babe like that? Probably done it with a dozen guys, and one of them convinced her it was love." He turned the last word into a four-syllable monstrosity. "Happens all the time. But none of us fucked her."

Shelly inhaled sharply, but didn't lose her cool. "Fine. None of you remembers seeing her. But we have reason to believe she left with someone from Mifflin County after that show, or maybe came up to Mifflin County afterward. So, do any of you recall seeing any classmates there? Or anyone else from Mifflin County? Another student, maybe, someone who came to hear you play? Or the girl might have run off with an older guy, for all we know."

"Or a girl, or a woman," I added. "Or a group."

"Hot," Gage said, nodding and leering.

"Nope."

"Nah."

"No fucking way."

"You didn't see or talk to any classmates there?" I waved my hand around impatiently. "No one at all?"

Buzz snorted. "Talking to people isn't really something I do voluntarily."

The other two shook their heads.

"OK," I said, figuring we weren't going to get anything from these boys. "I gotta ask. Were you yelling 'turd blossom' in that song?"

Buzz looked suddenly pleased. "Yeah!"

I sighed. "What the hell is a turd blossom?"

Buzz doffed his yellow headband and twirled it on a finger. "You've heard of the phoenix, right? Great bloody bird of fire that rises up from the ashes of its predecessor's total immolation?"

After a few seconds it dawned on me the kid wasn't going to say more until I said yes or no. So I answered. "Yes. I can read. I even do it sometimes. I know what a phoenix is."

"Good for you," Buzz said, raising his beer bottle in a mock salute. "OK, so a turd blossom plays off that idea, right? It's like a beautiful flower, rising up out of the shit that is life. A ray of hope in the midst of Shit City. An incongruous and unlikely blossom rising up, like a phoenix, out of the manure that we all have to wallow in all the fucking time."

Buzz stared at me, his eyes popping and his Adam's apple bouncing. I think I was supposed to say his lyrics were the work of genius. Instead, I said, "Oh."

"Yeah," he said, then he took a big swig of beer. "It is way more of a hopeful song than what I usually write. I mean, it's like some yin to balance the yang of our other stuff, like 'Sausage Head' and 'Dung Puppets.' But we're like trying to balance shit out, you know?"

"Fucking cool, man," Burke said. He hit a low, growling note on the bass. I am pretty sure it was the only note he knew.

"Drumbeat fucking rules on 'Turd Blossom,' man," Gage said. "Fucking rules."

"Fucking rules," Buzz said, reaching out and grabbing Gage's hand for a frat-boy shake. "Fucking rules. When you hit the right tempo. Not like what you did just now."

"Fuck you."

"OK," I said. "This is your home, right, Buzz?"

"Indeed."

"Your parents here?"

"Mom's at work, waiting tables at Briscoe's. Never met Dad. Think Mom only met him once."

"OK. Turn the damned music down so your neighbors can enjoy their turd blossom life. If any of you recall seeing anyone from Mifflin County at your little party, call me." I proffered a card with my phone number on it. "If you remember anything else that might be helpful, no matter how minor it is, give me a call. And if I have to come back out here because of the noise, I am going to hit you with so many charges you'll not rise like a blossom from the shit that is life for months."

We turned to go.

"Wait."

It was Buzz, speaking through the mic so that his one word reverberated between the trailers.

We stopped, turned, faced him.

"I remember seeing one guy from around here at the party—saw him in the toilet," Buzz said. "Pissing a lot of beer, man. A lot of beer."

I asked who.

"Jeff Cotton."

I knew the name, and wished Buzz had seen someone else. "The linebacker."

"Yep," Buzz said. "Local hero."

"Was he with the girl?"

"Didn't see no girl. I think Jeff prefers boys. Or dogs." Beavis and Butt-Head, behind him, snickered in unison.

"OK," Shelly said. "Thanks. Call if you think of anything else."

We walked back to the truck. Light rain started to fall. "I hope this short-circuits their amps."

"You don't like their music?" Shelly smiled as we got back into the truck. "Their manners suck, but I liked the music."

"That," I said, "is not music." Behind us, the bass and drum kicked up again, but at lower volume. "It's going to take a lot of Waylon Jennings to erase that turd blossom shit from my mind," I confessed.

"Waylon who?"

"Jesus. Shoot me."

Shelly laughed. She gave me ten seconds to wonder how the hell anyone could not know who Waylon Jennings is, then continued. "You think they know more than they let on?"

"Probably," I said. "And I will tell you right now, talking to Jeff Cotton ain't gonna be even a little bit of fun."

"No?"

"No," I said, firing up the truck. "Jeff is a football stud, hits like a frickin' truck, and everyone in this county loves him. Ohio State is looking at him. Michigan is looking at him. UCLA is looking at him. To make things worse, his dad is a total nutcase and probably owns more guns than our sheriff's office."

"Lovely," Shelly said.

"No. Not lovely. Not even in the neighborhood of lovely. Ain't seen lovely in years."

CHAPTER SEVEN

Tuesday, 3:55 p.m.

WE ROLLED THROUGH Jodyville's single traffic light, took a right and then a left and hit Big Black Dog Road, which leads out past where I live. As we passed cornfields and barns, I filled Shelly in on Brian Cotton.

"Jeff's dad is like a lot of folks around here. Loves God, loves guns. Thing is, he doesn't like much of anything else. Doesn't like liberals. Doesn't like reporters. Doesn't like courts. He especially doesn't like cops. We're all jack-booted thugs, you see, paid by an evil government to stomp on American freedoms. We want to take away their guns, put Christians in jail and all that."

Shelly inhaled sharply. "I see. Damn. I guess I missed those training sessions."

"Me, too."

"Brian Cotton sounds like a whole lot of fun, Ed."

"He's not. He's really not."

We zipped past half-harvested fields, kicking up dust and scattering crunchy leaves. "A lot of people out here feel that way, the way Brian Cotton does, at least to some degree," I said, "and sometimes I can see why. At least a little. I don't trust the government I work for a whole lot myself—sometimes, anyway." I swerved to miss a rabbit who apparently had accepted a daredevil challenge from his bunny friends. He bolted into the road from the right, and I braked just enough and drifted a bit to give him leeway. From the corner of my eye, I saw his white tail vanish into a ditch.

"Whoa! I can't believe you didn't hit that little guy," Shelly said.

"You get a lot of practice sharing the road with wildlife out here," I answered. "Anyway, OK, I'll admit it. I don't understand it at all how some of these people feel about cops and the law and all that. I really don't. Most folks out here, though, are nice enough. They'll treat you nice, smile and all that, raise money for a neighbor in need. If you stay away from talking politics or God, you can get along with them just fine, for the most part, even if they know you're a cop. And a lot of them are just good, churchgoing people who support the police, raise money to help us out with community stuff like sports leagues and school resources, that kind of stuff. I don't want to paint all the people here as a bunch of zealots. But Brian is . . . Brian is special."

"How so?"

"He leads a group called the Mifflin County Patriots. About a dozen members, and he's the boss. They write letters to the newspapers and post all over Facebook about how the government steals your money, the cops just act as the enforcers for the evil government, taxation is a crime and a sin, the government is illegitimate, your preacher is bastardizing the true word of God, etcetera."

"Great."

"And they'll show up at an ice cream shop all toting their big guns, just to remind everyone else they have a right to carry them."

"Sort of like waving their dicks around?"

I laughed. "You could put it that way."

"Sounds like a party. Should we bring booze?"

"Yeah." I pointed down a dirt road that led past a two-story farmhouse. "I live out that way, by the way."

"That's your house?"

"No, that belongs to my landlords. My palatial estate is further back, by that pond yonder."

"That's a lake."

"One might think. Anyway. The patriots group. They meet at the Cotton farm, further out this road, in a big-ass barn. I haven't seen it in person, not on the inside, anyway, but I have seen a lot of aerial images because I am on SWAT here and it is exactly the kind of place where you might need SWAT one day."

"Wonderful." Shelly shook her head slowly and closed her eyes. "Just wonderful."

"It is like a fortress. Plated with armor and shit. These guys host meetings about surviving the race war to come, defending Christians, needing big powerful high-capacity guns to hold off the government and all that. Letters to the editor every week. Great reading, if you are looking forward to the apocalypse or the Rapture. Guarantee you, we will be on surveillance cameras the whole time we are out there, and probably, we'll be blasted on their website an hour later, even if we behave with impeccable professionalism."

"Good to know. I'll watch what I say."

"Doesn't matter what you say, they'll hear an assault on their liberties, or some such shit. You can say, 'Hi, I'm Shelly,' and they will hear 'capitulate to the New World Order, motherfucker!'"

"Jesus." She laughed. "You are making me rethink my whole plan to move to the country."

"Oh, we have some peaceful hippies, too. You'll even see an occasional Democrat. And in the summer, we've got the best sweet corn you'll ever find. That alone makes dealing with assholes bearable."

"I do love sweet corn," she said.

"We are almost there, by the way. Let me do the talking, OK?"

"Hey, this is my case." Her eyes flashed at me, and not in a friendly way.

"I know, I know. But this guy will assume the worst of us, and I am familiar with his rants. I think I know what to say and what not to say. Can't ever make him like us, but maybe we can avoid open hostilities."

"OK." She did not sound happy about it. "We deal with difficult people in the city, too, you know."

"I know. I just speak the language. I think. If I fuck it up, jump in and take over."

She grinned. "Deal."

To our right, an empty cornfield sloped down to a line of colorful trees bordering Black Powder Creek. To our left was a wood-covered hill. I slowed the truck, looking for the narrow dirt lane on the left that would lead up Breakneck Hill to the Cotton farm. I spotted the mailbox, mounted on an oak post and leaning like a drunk, and turned uphill. The truck bucked in deep ruts.

"Holy shit, you were not kidding," Shelly muttered once we topped a rise and the barn came into view.

I think she summed it up nicely. This was nothing like the barns you see on pastoral postcards or painted on planks at a folk-art gift shop. This was more like a World War Two bunker or someplace Mad Max had to bust into. I thought to myself that a machine gun mounted on the back of my truck might have been a good precaution. Or a rocket launcher.

Taller than a two-story home, and almost as tall as the farmhouse behind it and to our right, and covering enough area to comfortably park maybe a dozen school buses, Cotton's barn loomed ominously against the splashy colors of autumn. Metal plates had been riveted to the walls, concealing most of the ancient black wood, but you could just make out bits of the "Chew Mail Pouch" logo between the armor in some spots. Some of the plates obviously came from old vehicles, and in places you could see where three or four truck hoods or car doors had been stacked like sandwich layers and welded together to form a thick barrier. Other slabs of metal had been culled from junkyards, old farm gear, or God knows where. No one had bothered to try painting it a uniform color, so it was a motley of rusty gray, rusty red, rusty blue, and rusty white.

It was ugly as hell, but I was willing to bet it would be tough for big guns to chew through.

I hoped I would never have to find out.

Between many of the mismatched slabs of iron and steel were vertical and horizontal slits, just wide enough to admit a gun barrel. No light poured out from them, and I supposed there were iron shutters inside. I watched them closely, to see if any opened up to let a gun poke out. I pointed them out to Shelly.

Even the roof was covered with armor, and rain and snow had created streamers of rust running down the sloped roof and down the walls. A small forest of antennas topped the whole thing off.

The front doors were wide open, and I could see several refrigerators and storage lockers inside, plus a venerable, mud-splashed Jeep. Above the yawning doors, one of those yellow Gadsden flags hung in weather-worn tatters. "Don't tread on me," it warned, below an image of a coiled snake. A few other identical flags hung here and there. A big one, impotent because there was no wind, hung from a flagpole behind the barn.

Above the main doors, a second doorway was closed. It had been built as a means to haul hay bales up to the loft, but if I was a paranoid nut waiting for social Armageddon, I'd put a machine gun up there. I was willing to bet Cotton had.

"Just for the record, I support the Second Amendment," I told Shelly. "I just wish we could weed out the dumbasses. Watch out for someone up there."

"I hear you."

I parked my Ford between a John Deere tractor that belonged in a museum and a couple of ATVs. "OK, let's both smile pretty and keep calm. Don't panic."

"I don't panic, country boy," she said.

We got out of the truck.

I was about to holler hello when I saw Brian Cotton emerge from the white farmhouse—I'd describe the house, but it's pretty god-damned ordinary compared to the barn. Cotton held a Winchester pump-action shotgun, the kind that can handle eight rounds. He wasn't aiming it at us, but he had a finger on the trigger in a way that made you want to pay real close attention. It was a 12-gauge, and I doubted it was packed with birdshot. I had no doubt the guy had much more sophisticated weaponry on the property, but the simple, old-fashioned gun in his hands was more than capable of putting big holes in cops.

A dog, more like a bear, really, but it looked like a dog, trotted out from behind the house and took up a position as Cotton's wingman. I guessed its weight at a hundred pounds or so, but it was a big, tan shaggy beast and that made such a determination difficult. I could not begin to tell you how many breeds were represented in that mutt, but I suspected one of them was *Smilodon fatalis*. Yes, I know that's a cat, but still. Whatever it was, it was big enough to hurt us, and it bared fangs and growled low. It stayed by Brian Cotton's side, though, ears up as if awaiting a command.

Brian bared fangs, too.

Brian was a tall man, taller than me, with wide shoulders and a salt-and-pepper beard. Hard gray eyes didn't blink, and he did not smile. What hair he had left was salt-and-pepper, too. He wore jeans and a blue flannel shirt that had seen better days. I guessed his age at around forty. He seemed to be in very good shape, and moved quickly. Apparently, Hollis High's star linebacker benefited from some very good genes.

Shelly and I both held up badges, but I didn't get a word out. "You will get off my property right now. I know you, Runyon, you government thug," Cotton said.

"Sir, we are not here for any kind of trouble," I said, presenting what I hoped was a friendly smile. I held my hands up, palm forward. "We are trying to help a teen girl, and we think Jeff might be able to help us."

He gave us a crystal glare that was rock-solid evidence he was not going to believe a damned thing we said, ever. "Jeff don't know nothing about a teen girl," Cotton said. "He's a good boy. You've got no right trying to mix him up in anything, and I do not recognize your authority."

"We're not trying to mix Jeff up in anything," I said. "And we're not here to tout any authority. We didn't get any warrants or anything, not looking to take anyone into custody. Just hoping he can help us, that's all. She could be in big trouble, the girl we're looking for, and we just want to find her and help her, honest. Jeff may have seen her just before she disappeared. We just want to talk to him."

"Can you put the gun down while we talk, sir?" Shelly said it softly, gently, but Cotton's eyes still widened.

"It's my gun and this is my land and I will carry my gun if I want to," Cotton said. "Especially considering you two came onto my land and you are packing guns, aren't you? You gonna disarm yourselves, huh? I am not disarming myself under these conditions, and again, I do not recognize your authority."

I shot Shelly a glance, hoping she would take it to mean she should shut the hell up. "Mr. Cotton, we are not here to accuse Jeff of anything, or to deprive you of your Second Amendment rights. But we have reason to believe Jeff was at a party where the girl was last seen, and we are hoping he will remember seeing or hearing something that will help us. She's sixteen. You don't want anything bad happening to a sixteen-year-old girl, do you?"

"I surely do not," Cotton said, without softening his tone one iota. "But Jeff don't know nothing about it, I am sure. And sixteen-year-old girls shouldn't be partying, either, should they? Looking for trouble, if you ask me. Not up to me, or my son, to worry about her."

"Did Jeff go to Columbus on Saturday?"

"It is a free country, or so I keep hearing, and Jeff is sixteen. That's a man in my eyes. I don't ask him where he goes. But he ain't mixed up in whatever the hell is going on, and he ain't talking to no government thugs."

"Sir, we just—"

"No!" He said it loudly, emphatically, but the gun in his hands didn't move. The dog by his side moved, though. Its head lifted, its ears popped up, and the growl that fought its way through the big teeth rose in volume. "You leave my boy alone. You leave me alone. This is sovereign ground, my sovereign ground, and you do not come around here without my permission."

I stepped backward, toward my truck, locking my eyes on Brian Cotton's. "Mr. Cotton, please ask Jeff to call us if he saw or heard anything that might help us find the girl. That's all we're asking. OK? Pretty blonde girl, with worried parents and all that."

I didn't wait for an answer. I turned my back to him and walked back to the truck. I walked slowly, because I did not want him to think I was scared. I didn't want me to think I was scared, either.

Shelly got in beside me while Cotton glared at us. The dog jogged around in circles, sniffing at the ground where we had stood.

Shelly blew out a gust of air. "Jesus. That guy is sort of intense. The dog, too."

"Yeah, and they both have our scent now, too. It actually went better than I thought it might, though," I said, firing up the truck. "Thanks for letting me take lead on that. You get to go back to Columbus eventually, but I have to live here."

I turned the truck around, and we headed down the hill. We were up high, and could easily see across the Black Powder Creek valley where the football field lights were flicking on and off in sequence, being tested because there was a home game this week.

"Well, I am an idiot," I said. "I know where we can find Jeff Cotton. He's at football practice."

"Let's go," Shelly said, looking over her shoulder to see if spooky Brian Cotton was watching us leave.

He was. So was the dog.

"Jesus, Shelly, I hate being called a jack-booted thug."

"I'd like to kick the fucker's ass," she said. "But to be fair, he called us government thugs, I think. I was paying more attention to the big dog, to be honest."

"Me, too. Being professional and all ain't easy."

"Damn straight. Is father like son, in this instance?"

"We shall see, Detective. We shall see. But the way football fans around here see it, he could knock my truck over if he got up to speed and put his shoulder to it."

"Jesus Christ."

CHAPTER EIGHT

Tuesday, 4:46 p.m.

THE QUARTERBACK, IN a white T-shirt hiked up from his belly by his wide shoulder pads, got the throw off just as Jeff Cotton's red-shirted shoulder collided with his hip. They both hit the ground, and I half expected a crater. Whistles blew. A coach threw his hat on the grass and stomped it. "Jeff, goddamn it, don't hurt our guys!"

Jeff Cotton stood up, towering, and extended a hand to the QB, Joshua Webb, who was getting up much slower. Josh jumped up and down a couple of times, did a quick step to the right, then to the left, and flashed a pair of thumbs-up. "I'm fine, Coach." He looked and sounded like he meant it. Both boys bumped fists and yelled hoorah.

Downfield, players in white celebrated the completed pass with what I assumed were meant to be dance moves.

"Nice job getting that pass off, Josh!" The coach was happier now that it seemed his quarterback was unhurt, and was hollering across the field at his guys. "Good cool head, way to go. Front line, what the fuck was that? You might remember you are there to block. You know how to block, right?"

Several heads lowered, like the linemen were all looking for something on the ground.

The coach wasn't done bellowing. "Jeff, slow the hell down. We need Josh as much as we need you. OK?"

"Sorry," Jeff Cotton said. "I just play full tilt."

"It's why we love ya," the coach yelled.

Shelly and I sat in the stands. At the other end, a couple of girls watched their phones instead of the action on the field.

The squads played four more downs, and Jeff Cotton had two sacks in that brief span. He was big, like his dad, but leaner. He was scary strong and scary fast. I figured the only way to beat a kid like that in a fight was to cheat.

Once the final whistles blew and he removed the green helmet, though, he was like another kid. Handsome in a friendly, goofy way, with brown hair cut way shorter than most of his teammates. He guzzled from a water bottle as we approached.

"Jeff Cotton? Detective Ed Runyon. This is Detective Shelly Beckworth. Got time for a couple of questions?"

"What about?" He waved at a teammate, who followed the rest of the undefeated Big Green to the showers. Josh Webb, however, stopped to pat Jeff on the back. He was taller than Jeff Cotton and more slender, and he looked a bit like a youthful John Lennon. He had a busted lip, bleeding a bit. He wiped the blood away, and it looked bruised, like an older wound had been reopened. I wondered how many times Jeff Cotton had plowed the QB into the turf.

"That was a hell of a rush, man, and no worries from me, OK? I can take a hit."

"I know," Jeff answered. They did some sort of ritualistic hand-shake-fist bump combo that was too fast for my merely human eyes to follow. Then Josh walked away to talk to one of his receivers, who was tying a shoe.

The rest of the team ran, accompanied by the clatter of football pads, the slaps of high fives, and the drill-sergeant hilarity of their coaches. Jeff turned his attention to us. "Dad says I don't have to talk to cops. Your authority ain't in the Constitution, he says."

"Well, we are hoping you will talk to us," Shelly said, flashing that smile God created to subdue sixteen-year-old boys into mind-numbed compliance. "We are looking for a missing Columbus girl. She was last seen at a party Saturday in Columbus. Were you at a party Saturday in Columbus?"

"Yeah," Jeff said. "I went to see a band."

"Whoa," Josh Webb butted in. "You talking about Soul Scraped's gig? Man, I wanted to go to that party, but couldn't get away from chores."

I turned, and wondered why the QB was still hanging around. "This is a private conversation, if you were not at that party."

"Oh," Webb said. "OK. Sorry." He ran off.

Jeff ignored his friend and glared at us. "So why do you want to talk to me?" He squirted the rest of his water onto his head.

"Something may have happened there, Jeff." I tried to sound patient and nonchalant, which was just the opposite of how I felt. I wanted to find this girl. I wanted to find her alive. I wanted very much to not find her the way we found another girl, in another time and place. I tried to punt the image of that girl—naked, bloody, nailed to a wall and dead way too young—out of my mind.

That did not really work, despite what the Buddha might have said once upon a time.

Jeff shrugged. "OK, yeah, I went to a party to see the local band. We beat the Dusters on Friday, dude, so it was a great weekend to party."

"I know."

Shelly jumped back in. "So you were at the party, at a warehouse, where Soul Scraped performed?"

"Yeah, I was there. Look, my dad would be pissed that I'm even talking to you guys, OK? I mean, I got rights. You got a warrant or something?"

"We're just talking, Jeff," Shelly said. "We are not accusing you of anything. We just hope you can help us." Shelly pulled the photo of Megan Beemer out of the folder. "Did you see this girl at the party?" She handed the image to Jeff, whose eyebrows arched when he looked at it. He had his crazy father's gray eyes.

"I think I would have remembered her," he said. "She looks yummy."

"Take a good look, be sure," Shelly said. "It's important. She was at that party. Hasn't been seen since."

"I hope you find her," he said, "but, I'm sorry. I can't help you."

I took a step closer to Jeff. "Who went to the party with you?"

"Just me," he said. He didn't seem to notice my crowding him a bit. And why should he? He was taller, faster, and stronger, and everyone in the county knew it.

"You didn't take a date?" Shelly made it sound as though that was the most preposterous thing she had ever heard.

"No date," Jeff said. "Between girlfriends. Sort of, anyway." He made it sound like the normal state of affairs.

"No buddies?"

"No. I went alone."

I rubbed my chin. "How did you hear about the party?"

"I heard Buzz was playing. I like his band."

"Really?"

"Yeah, dude. They rock."

"Hmm." I figured there was no accounting for taste. "Did you see anyone else there from Hollis, or anywhere else in Mifflin County?"

"No," he said. "Shit, you guys are looking to pin something on me, right?"

"No, Jeff," I said. "But we have reason to believe she came up this way after the party."

"Dad was right," Jeff said, banging his water bottle against his helmet. "Shit, man, Dad was right. You guys look to pin stuff on patriots, don't you? You are scared of the patriots, the true freedom fighters."

"Jeff..."

"Screw this," he said. He turned and ran toward the high school. For a big guy, he was fast. There was no chance I could catch him if I was so inclined, and I actually run pretty well.

Shelly sighed. "Cops are certainly not popular around here."

"Nope. No, we are not. Let's go drink."

CHAPTER NINE

Tuesday, 6 p.m.

WE HAD THE place mostly to ourselves, and Tuck had reluctantly put on some Kristofferson for me while Shelly and I sat in a secluded corner, beneath a mounted bass that had been caught in the pond I lived by. Not by me, though.

Tuck had made many improvements to turn what had been a grimy dive into a decent little bar and grill with very respectable cheeseburgers, and the wide variety of music was one of them. No one ever seemed to want Kristofferson but me, though, and it was a sign of friendship that my metalhead buddy played it at all. Well, he did consider it an upgrade to the steady diet of Brooks and Dunn and Lady Antebellum many of his country-oriented customers preferred. As a poet himself, Tuck was willing to admit Kristofferson could turn a phrase.

Shelly tried to be polite, but I could tell old-school outlaw country wasn't her thing. And I will admit that Kristofferson's voice is an acquired taste. Shelly was nursing a lager, while I was on my second IPA. Kris was singing about how loving her was easier than anything he'd ever do again. I wasn't thinking about love, exactly, but Shelly had somehow gone from cute as hell to downright intoxicating, in my estimation. Maybe it was the beer. Maybe it was her eyes. Maybe I didn't care. Anyway, wanting her was easier than it had been earlier.

We'd talked a little bit about our pasts, how I became a cop because my dad and grandpa had been cops and I never considered any
other option, and how she became a cop because she was a wee bit
of an action junkie.

After that, we got into detective fiction. "I like Ed McBain and
Sue Grafton," she said. "Always entertaining."

"Give John D. McDonald's Travis McGee a try. Not the most re-
alistic stuff in the world, I guess, except when it is. Always worth
reading, though."

We both came down in favor of Raymond Chandler, and op-
posed to Agatha Christie. We split on Mickey Spillane. Once we got
beyond crime fiction, we disagreed completely on Joseph Conrad.

"Conrad? Oh God, no," she said.

"Read 'Youth' and get back to me," I insisted.

"Not happening."

After that, our talk had returned to the missing Megan Beemer,
and how nothing we'd learned today had turned Shelly's slender
thread of a lead into anything stronger. The case had gone exactly
nowhere. But several teens from here had gone to that party, and it
was a connection worth exploring.

Shelly shook her head. "The kids, all of them, seem evasive."

"Teens talking to cops always seem evasive."

I wanted it all to be coincidental. I wanted Shelly's partner to call
her and say he'd found Megan Beemer alive and well someplace very
far away from here. I wanted this case to go away and leave me alone.

I tried to shake off the tenuous connections. All we knew for sure
was some kids from Mifflin County had been at the same party
where Megan was last seen, and that she'd met someone from Hicksville. The fact of several Mifflin County license plates showing up in
the lot could be explained by Soul Scraped performing at the warehouse. A lot of young people here followed the band, it seemed. I'd

looked them up online while waiting for our beers. They had a following. I had no idea why.

The Soul Scraped website was still showing on my phone screen as Tuck passed by. "Damn, man, I like those dudes."

"Are you serious? They sound like Les Pauls and Ludwigs crunched up in a blender."

"You have no taste, Ed." Tuck pursed his lips, the way he does when a lecture is coming on. "These guys try to do something with their music, you know? They stretch themselves. I like the lyrics. They take chances. I even thought about having them play at this place some Saturday night, except they are all underaged."

I shook my head. "I will shoot you if those kids grow up and play in this bar, Tuck." A man's got to have standards, and I didn't want to drive farther than Tuck's to get a beer. A bar you can do a wobbly walk home from is a thing not easily discarded.

"I can't afford to run a business with just you as a customer, Ed, and I sure don't want to listen to your country shit every night."

"You prefer 'Turd Blossom,' is that it?"

Tuck shook his head, and the beads clattered. "Ain't heard that one, but I like the juxtaposition. Very zen." He wandered off.

Shelly grinned. She had been poking around on her phone while Tuck and I talked. "I told you those boys had talent. My partner has had no luck in Columbus, by the way, and nothing from his buddy in Ambletown." She sighed. "I am starting to hate this case."

"Me, too."

I was feeling unsettled, and trying to fend off memories of New York, and a dead girl in the Bronx. I told myself we had no real reason to believe Megan Beemer had come to harm. It was just as likely she had run off with a guy. Or a girl, for that matter. But Shelly's brows had furrowed every time I mentioned that possibility, and it was clear she didn't believe it. Nothing they had learned about Megan Beemer in Columbus made her a likely runaway candidate, she said.

I waved at Tuck for another brew, and hoped to hell that if something bad had happened to Megan, it had happened in someone else's damned county. I had seen my share of young tragedy, and had spent too many nights in cold sweats, dreaming of being some odd mixture of total failure and avenging demon. I did not want to be either.

Tuck placed a new glass before me, and I drained about half of it in a swallow. Shelly gave me a hard look. "Last one," I said, doubting it was true. "Promise."

"I drive us back to the S.O. and my car," she said. Her face said she would not take no, or fuck that, for an answer.

"Deal," I said. I paused dramatically. "Do you have to drive to Columbus tonight?"

She looked at me, shrugged, grinned. "Yeah. I was afraid of this. Look. One, I am not easy, OK? I take my time."

"Not a carpe diem, love the one you're with kind of girl, huh?"

"No. Also, two, I play for the other team."

"Michigan fan?"

She laughed. "No. Hell, no. O-H!"

"I-O!"

We clinked glasses, drank, and locked eyes over our beers. Her eyes were perfect, but the expression in them was not promising.

"I'm a lesbian, Ed."

"Oh."

"Yeah."

"OK."

"Sorry to disappoint."

"I'll get over it. Is there a lucky girl?"

"There is, expecting me home tonight."

"Well, then, no hard feelings. Drinks are on me."

"I buy next time."

"Deal."

Tuck added the bill to my already outrageous tab, and we headed out to the truck to the sounds of Kristofferson musing about how he'd let Bobby McGee slip away somewhere near Salinas, Lord. If Kris had been there physically, I'd have flipped him off for mocking me. Tuck had shut down Kris and cranked up AC/DC before we even got in the Ford. The band was on a highway to hell. Shelly and I were bound for Ambletown.

Shelly drove, and had no trouble handling the truck. We talked, mostly just repeating ourselves about the case because I had pretty much made things awkward. We decided that I would continue poking around, and would hit Chalmers High School up near Nora the next day, and she would stay in Columbus unless I came up with something solid. Back at the sheriff's office, she got into her silver Mazda and headed toward I-71.

I headed back toward my pond-side trailer off Big Black Dog Road. I was feeling surly, and the Steve Earle disc I was playing was not helping matters. His songs were surly, too. I shut off the music.

I rumbled down the dirt lane that led through the trees and on to my trailer. The towering oaks and maples still had enough leaves on them to blot out most of the sky, so the stuff showing in my headlights was all I could see and the roar and rattle of the truck was all I could hear. The rest of the universe might as well have not even existed. I was just drunk enough to wonder if it really did. Maybe this was all a cosmic joke, and young, pretty girls just sometimes vanished, and gorgeous women preferred other women to me, and it was all just part of the joke.

Yuk yuk yuk.

I pulled into the clearing, parked, stepped away from the road, took a leak, and stared up at the stars. It really is dark out here, I thought. Kind of a mirror for what was in my head. It was dark in there, too.

I wished to hell Shelly had been up for a bit of distraction. I could hear Kristofferson in my head, growling "Help Me Make It Through the Night."

I zipped up, mad at myself, and headed inside and flipped on the light. It was cramped in the trailer, of course. I have a living room area with a sofa that pulls out to a bed, although I seldom bothered. There's a shower and bathroom area toward the back and a kitchen area that sort of separates the two. Most of the space that isn't taken up by furniture was taken up by stacks of books. Twain and Conrad, and enough cheesy crime novels to open my own bookstore. I thought for the millionth time about quitting the sheriff's office and opening a bookstore. You don't make a lot of money with a bookstore, because almost no one fucking reads anymore, but you don't often get shot at or called a jack-booted thug. Or a government thug, or whatever the hell Brian Cotton had called us. Seducing lesbians probably wasn't any easier for booksellers than for cops, though, so there probably was no point in switching careers just yet.

The trailer wasn't much, but it was isolated and I could fish for bluegill or bass for my weekend breakfasts, and could play my battered Martin guitar and sing without anyone to complain about the noise. Jim and Olive Langstrom liked the idea of having a cop living on their property, and I liked the cheap rent and the feeling of leaving the rest of the world behind when I was there. It was a good deal.

Most of the time, anyway. This night, the trailer felt more like a cocoon, a place to hide away, transform, and emerge later as something else. Something that wanted to smack people around, pound faces, and demand to know what the hell had happened to Megan Beemer.

I reached into the cabinet above the tiny stove. I took down the bottle of Knob Creek, the unopened bottle that had been up there for three years, and put it on the pullout table. I had emptied a similar bottle just like it on that last hellish night in the Bronx, the night we'd found a pretty girl nailed naked to a goddamned wall, surrounded by graffiti written in her own goddamned blood. I'd driven west that night, leaving NYPD behind and sipping bourbon from that bottle the whole way. I'd woken up in Ohio, parked near a creek forty feet from what passed as a road and wondering how the hell I'd gotten there. I was astounded I had not killed anyone on that nightmare drive, and astounded that I didn't seem to care that I could have killed myself, too.

I stared at the bottle I'd taken from the cabinet. It was untapped, virginal. I'd bought this bottle not to drink, but to serve as a reminder, and a test of strength. Every day I didn't open it, I won and the darkness lost. The bottle had served that purpose for three years.

Now, here it was, sitting on my pullout table next to a shot glass that I did not remember grabbing, with me hovering over it. I could taste it already, even though the seal was still on the bottle. I sat next to it, gazed at it, trembled a bit.

Goddamn it, I thought. *Goddamn it.*

I turned away and grabbed the Martin. My dad had given me the guitar when I was in high school, and showed me a few chords. It usually relaxed me. I stepped outside into the dark and sat on the steps. I strummed "Blue Eyes Cryin' in the Rain," singing softly, until it occurred to me that Megan Beemer had blue eyes.

Fuck.

I started checking out Megan Beemer on Instagram. She had a little brown dog, named Candy, and she kissed it right on the mouth. She liked to dance with another girl, named Molly. She just couldn't deal with all the folks who wanted brown people to stop trying to come to our country, and to hell with anyone who mocked "the alphabet people," aka LGBTQ humans.

A good kid. I hoped to hell we would find her alive.

My phone buzzed. Linda's name was on the screen. I snatched the phone as though it were a lifeline.

"Hello," I said. "You are up late."

"Yeah, a bit," she said. "I am on Big Black Dog Road, actually, wondering if I should drive down your lane."

I laughed. "Are you psychic?"

She laughed, too. It was a good laugh. "Maybe, a little. I am mostly observant, and a tad buzzed, and reminiscing, and horny. It was good seeing you today."

"Come on down," I said.

"Two minutes," she said before hanging up.

I took the guitar inside, turned on a light outside the trailer, and stepped outside to wait for her in the breeze. The wind carried scents of fresh-cut grass, the pond, and the remnants of burnt leaves. I could hear crickets, and the occasional barred owl. The stars were diamonds mounted on black velvet. It all looked and felt better than it had a few moments before.

I wondered if having Linda stop by was a mistake. She likely would say she'd noticed something off in my voice or behavior when I visited the school. She probably would ask me what I was thinking. She probably wanted to fix me.

I didn't have the patience for that. I just wanted someone to help me make it through the night. Kristofferson would understand.

I saw her headlights, and they grew and grew until they lit up the mulleins and cattails surrounding the pond. She shut off the VW engine, and climbed out. My porch light showed she was wearing a white Jerry Garcia T-shirt, faded jeans, and tennis shoes. She said not a word. She just walked right up to me, wrapped her arms around me, and jammed her tongue into my mouth. She'd been drinking red wine.

"Well," I said a few seconds later. "Hello."

I followed her inside. Damn, she looked good.

She went straight to the fridge and pulled out a couple of IPAs. "I should have known you would have no wine," she said.

"Sorry. I could taste some on you, though. You been to Tuck's?"

She smiled. "Of course."

Mystery solved. Tuck had told Linda about my swing and a miss with Shelly, and Linda was sweeping in to learn all the gory details.

She knew where the bottle opener was, and a moment later we were standing face-to-face, drinking.

"So," I said, "what brings a gorgeous redheaded hippie girl like you to a cramped little hillbilly trailer like this?"

She smiled, green eyes shining. "I came to borrow some books. Honestly? A couple of things." She put down her beer and snuggled up for another deep kiss. "One, you looked pretty doggone good today, and I remembered a lot of very, very good things."

"Me, too." I put down my empty bottle.

"Two, I knew you would make a pass at Miss Cutie Detective and crash and burn big-time."

"Yeah?" I kissed her, and dropped a hand to her ass. "Being psychic again?"

"No crystal ball required," she said. "Just the kind of observation skills you detectives are supposed to have. Sherlock would be chastising you about now."

"What did I miss?"

"That lady cop was checking me out today way more intently than you were, mister detective. Hell, if you had turned me down tonight, I was gonna call her."

"Oh, really? I have her number."

"Don't pretend you wouldn't totally want video of that." She pulled my face into hers, and our mouths and tongues wrestled. I stopped worrying about whether this was a good idea or not.

"So," she said, once we'd surrendered to the need to breathe, "I propose one damned good night. No worries, no expectations on the morrow, no guilt, and no long, probing talks. Let's just have fun."

She locked her mouth on mine for a good twenty seconds, then dropped to her knees and began undoing my belt.

"I think I can manage that," I said.

"You'd better," she said.

*   *   *

Wednesday, 3:07 a.m.

Linda slept beside me. I tilted my phone so the light would not disturb her.

I was checking Facebook and Instagram, hoping to see a new post from Megan Beemer. "Hi, everyone, it's me, just checking in. Lost my phone, so that's why I haven't been on here for a couple days, lol. I am home now, though! Missed ya!"

There was no such post.

A half hour later, I checked again. Same result.

I resisted checking another Facebook account, for another girl. I knew there would be no fresh posts there.

* * *

Wednesday, 7:45 a.m.

The sun was barely peeking through the trees when the aroma of coffee woke me. Linda was singing softly, dancing slowly, already showered and dressed.

I hugged her from behind. "That was fun."

"It was kind of what you needed."

"Yeah, but how did you know?"

"It's kind of what you always need," she said. "And, frankly, it was pretty much what I needed, too." She turned, kissed me well and deeply, then handed me a mug of coffee. "I gotta go teach kids to appreciate Jane Austen."

"Have a beautiful day," I said. "Keep your eyes and ears open about that missing girl for me, OK?"

Her eyes narrowed. "I knew this case would get to you."

"I'm fine."

"Fine?"

"Yes." I saw no need to mention that, despite Linda's best efforts at wearing me out, I'd dreamed about that damned case in New York. The Briana Marston case. The case that almost broke me.

"Call me if you need to," Linda said. "Any time."

"I will." I kissed her, and patted her on the rear as she left. I turned to head to the shower.

My bottle of bourbon had vanished from the table.

Damn it, Linda. Always trying to fix me.

CHAPTER TEN

Wednesday, 8 a.m.

"DUDE, WE GOTTA talk."

"Do. Not. Keep. Calling. Me. About. This. Shit."

"Fuck you, dude. It was you got us into this mess. I don't need fucking cops asking me shit, OK?"

"Lady cop is one hot piece."

"Jesus, yeah, she is hot. She is also a fucking cop! Got it? What the fuck we gonna do?"

"We are gonna calm the fuck down, quit making a bunch of phone calls because goddamn it they might be checking that shit, OK? And we are gonna calm the fuck down and realize they ain't got shit, and they ain't gonna get shit. OK?"

"You sure?"

"Yeah."

"You fucking sure?"

"Yeah. They got nothing."

"OK. You sure?"

"Jesus."

"OK."

"Bye."

"Bye."

CHAPTER ELEVEN

Wednesday, 8:05 a.m.

"Hey, Ed! You doing alright?"

Even through the shitty phone speaker, I could hear the concern in Detective Tom Atkinson's voice. One of these days, I was going to have to call my old colleague when things were going good, just to convince both of us that things sometimes were good.

"Yeah, doing OK, I guess. Just wanted to check something."

"Sure, man. What?"

"Professor Donald Graser."

"Oh, fuck, Ed."

"Professor Donald Graser. Is he still in prison, or did some fucking parole board or psychiatrist let him out?" Graser was not really a professor. He was a self-taught philosopher, able to quote pretty much any religious text you had ever heard of. He liked to parse words, flay ideas, skin concepts and peer into what he called ultimate truth. He was nuttier than a PayDay bar.

He was the son of a bitch who had nailed Briana Marston to his fucking wall, and then later tried to convince us it didn't matter because what the hell did morality even mean, really? We were all just fucking descendants of goddamned bacteria.

"Ed, the professor ain't ever getting out. Trust me."

"You know that for sure?"

"Absolutely. And so do you, damn it. He hasn't been in long enough to even have a parole hearing yet, and the judge denied three attempts to move him to a psychiatric facility. He is in the general population, where I hope he is forced to bend over daily."

"OK."

"Why are you worried about him, Ed?"

I turned onto the highway. "I got a case here. Missing girl. Reminded me of Bree, I guess."

"Oh," he said. "Yeah, it is tough, I bet. I think about that case, too, though I try not to. Very ugly, sticks with you. But believe me, the professor ain't your perp on this new thing of yours, whatever it is. Seriously."

"Yeah, I know. I just . . . You know?"

"I know. Listen, I gotta run. We are hitting a gang today, grabbing a guy who killed a nun. Wish you were here to have my back, Ed. I always liked working with you."

"Glad I'm not there, Tom. Good talking to you. Be careful, man."

"You know it."

"Bye."

After the call, my head was boiling with memories.

Briana Marston had been very much like Megan Beemer. Young, smart, pretty, blonde. All the school clubs, dated the jocks, starred in the school musical.

Her case, we all thought, involved just another teen who had skipped away with a boyfriend because her parents thought her too young to be so serious about a guy. We had her poster on the dingy bulletin board in the squad room, along with a couple dozen others. We all looked at those, tried to memorize names and faces, carried info with us. Uniforms asked around, kept eyes open, and compared every young girl they ran into hooking or running drugs or getting locked out of a car to the faces on the wall and in their computers.

But most of us figured this girl had just run off with a guy, even though she had recently broken up with her beau. The boyfriend was not a suspect. He was still hanging out at home every night, with his nose glued to an iPad. We all figured maybe the girl had a new boyfriend, one she hadn't talked about. Friends said there had been a college boy who showed interest, but they had not met him and could not remember his name and weren't sure Bree was into him anyway.

She didn't seem the type to go all drama queen and run out, to end up selling herself just to get by, or to get high. And there had been no sign of her being taken by force. She had so many clothes in her closet, her parents could not honestly say whether she had packed and left or not. No favorites were missing, though.

So we figured she would call home, or turn up on the beat somewhere, and in the meantime we detectives went on investigating our confirmed homicides and drug rings. "We're doing all we can," we assured Bree's parents, and we thought we were.

We should have known better.

When we found Briana Marston, she was nailed to a wall. Crucified. Spikes through her palms, through her ankles, blood running down to the squeaky floor and flies flitting across her frozen face. Cabalistic bullshit scrawled all over the walls, in her blood. Patrolmen had gone there to investigate a report of screaming, then called us when they found her.

I left New York that night, wondering if any of the other faces on the dingy bulletin board would be found hanging on a goddamned wall somewhere. Wondering if I could have done more. Wondering if I had put some real time into that case if Bree would still be alive.

And knowing that I never wanted to see anything like that again.

My boss had tried to talk me out of quitting, but I was already kind of drunk when I called him from somewhere on the road back to Ohio where I had never seen any nightmarish shit like that. I remember him asking me, "How we gonna save any of them, Ed, if the good guys get sick to their stomachs and run away?" I felt shame, because what he said made sense, but not as much sense as never seeing that again.

That's how I ended up in Ohio and in therapy. I was angry at the world because parts of it were horrible and I couldn't fix it all, the counselor said. I was blaming myself for things that were not my fault. I needed to forgive myself for not having time and ability to investigate every case with my full time and devotion, for trying to decide which cases to pursue diligently and which to put on the back burner. And I needed to forgive myself for sometimes being wrong.

It took a lot to bring me around. It took Linda. It took therapy. It took pills. It took meditation. It took time. But I got a job, a place to live, and, eventually, my old guitar from my dad's place. I had passed through. I even made it through the professor's trial and my own testimony. That surprised me, but I did it.

It had not been easy, either. I was well aware of the stares from the guys who had tracked the bastard down and brought him in while I was off somewhere in farm country. But I endured that, and made it through.

And now there was another pretty missing girl, and all that anger was boiling inside me again. Fears were creeping out of the shadowy closets where I'd carefully hidden them.

My call to Tom had been a ridiculous move, of course. I knew the bastard professor was in prison. I knew he was not connected to this Beemer case. I knew it, intellectually. But I had called Tom anyway. Why?

Fuck if I know.

Maybe it was the nightmares. I had woken up hearing the son of a bitch professor laughing while us big-time NYPD detectives prioritized cases, finding reason after reason after reason to chase this homicide or that narcotics ring, all the while pushing Bree Marston's case into the background. That's what I heard in my dreams, anyway. I won't tell you what I saw.

I had taken my time working up a brave face before climbing out of bed and hugging Linda. I don't know why I bother hiding my worries from her, because she always unearths them anyway, but I do.

And then I had bucked myself up, gotten dressed, and headed to work. Yay me.

Next, of course, I had called an old friend about a case that was closed, and had nothing to do with anything I was working on, just because I needed to confirm what I already knew in order to shut down a fear I knew was not real.

I grabbed a disc at random and shoved it into the player.

Willie Nelson started singing "Crazy."

I shut it off, and laughed and cried all the way to work.

CHAPTER TWELVE

Wednesday, 8:17 a.m.

AFTER A LONG restroom stop that involved much splashing of cold water onto my cold face, I headed toward the squad room. Sheriff Daltry waved me into his office. His stony glare said I wasn't going to like this.

Inside the spartan room, where the only personal touch was a painting of a very white Jesus next to a portrait of Ronald Reagan on the wall behind a desk uncluttered by paperwork, the sheriff sat. He indicated I should sit, too. I did.

"You feeling OK, Ed?"

"A might sick, honestly, but I will get through the day."

He stared at me a while, as if he was pondering a mediocre diner dish and trying to decide whether to send it back or just go ahead and eat it. Eventually, he scratched his head.

"Well, you look like shit. You are a good detective, Ed. You are. But I gotta tell you, showing up for work with beer on your breath ain't good for anything."

"I was off duty, John, you know that. I got called in, remember?"

"Yeah, I remember." He leaned forward, locking his fingers together and laying them on the desk in a manner of grave concern. "We call detectives in on their days off a lot. Comes with the job. I hear you were at Tuck's last night, drinking again."

"Jesus, Sheriff. It's my time, right?"

"Yeah, but it's my headache," he said, sharply. "And you look like hell today. I gotta run for reelection, Ed. That won't be easy if some damn reporter or some damn liberal Democrat smells beer on your breath at a crime scene. What if fucking Farkas walked in here and smelled a brewery on your breath? That shit would be on the front page."

"I get it. You're a man of the people."

"Damnit, Ed, just slow down, OK? And buy some goddamn breath mints."

"Yeah, sure."

Daltry stared at the ceiling for a second, an indicator that he was switching topics. "Anything on that missing girl from Columbus?"

"Not really. Some kids from here were at the party where she was seen last, but that's about as thick a thread as we've got. Shelly is back in Columbus, and I'm going to poke around more here, but all we really have so far is a bunch of kids who don't much like talking to cops."

"I hope she turns up safe and sound after a few days of cuddling up with a handsome boy somewhere," he said.

"Me, too." I stepped out and headed to the detectives' office.

I fired up my computer, and the email told me Daltry had signed off on my report concerning the gay-bashing skinny guy at Tuck's. Bob Van Heusen. Guitar picker out of Columbus. The same Columbus where Megan Beemer was last seen at a warehouse, listening to a rock band. I suddenly found myself wondering why a guy like Bob Van Heusen was drinking beer in a Jodyville bar on a weekday afternoon, and decided my trip to Chalmers High School would have to wait.

I dialed the jail. Oscar answered. Oscar smells bad, usually, but you can't tell over the phone, so what the hell.

"Hey, Oscar. This is Runyon. We booked a guy named Van Heusen yesterday, after a fracas in Jodyville. He still in the pokey, or did he make bail?"

"We still got him."

"Good. If a lawyer comes to spring him, stall. If another jurisdiction wants to extradite him, stall. I want him in the interrogation room in an hour, OK?"

"Yes, sir, we'll get him there. And his lawyer ought to be here before long. She called yesterday."

"Thanks, Oscar."

Next, I called Trumpower. "That skinny guitar picker had a motorcycle, right?"

"Did you read my report?"

"Not yet."

Trumpower sighed, loudly and dramatically. "Detectives. Too busy spending their big paychecks to read my hard work and sterling prose. Yes, he had a motorcycle. We impounded it, pending his release on bail by some goddamned do-gooder judge."

"Great. Case number is in your report?"

"Of course it is, overpaid detective-type person."

"Thanks, Trump."

"Don't call me Trump."

"Sorry. Habit."

"Fuck that guy."

"Amen. Irwin, then. Anybody comes after that vehicle, it's evidence."

"Understood."

I looked up Trumpower's report, got the case number, and called the impound lot to make sure that cycle went nowhere without my say-so. Then I called the lab at Ambletown PD, and told them to go over Van Heusen's bike with every goddamn bit of science they could muster. They asked if I had a search warrant to do that, and I told them I would have one within minutes. I called Judge Brennan, who does not fuck around, and he said the warrant would be on my desk before I could take a dump.

It was delivered within ten minutes. I actually did take a dump in the meantime.

My phone rang before I got away. "Detective Runyon," I said.

"You were at my home yesterday, talking to my boy?"

"Can you tell me who you are, ma'am? I interviewed a lot of people yesterday."

She sighed. "I am Kim Norris, and you talked to my son at my home yesterday, him and his friends."

"Yes, I did. I talked to Buzz and his friends about a party they were at, where a girl disappeared. Did he mention anything to you about a girl from Columbus?"

"Is he in trouble?"

"We're just trying to find a missing girl," I said. "We hoped the boys would remember seeing or hearing something that would help us do that."

"He's not in trouble? Doing pot or . . . or . . . heroin, my God, he's not doing heroin?"

"We have no reason to suspect anything like that."

"Oh, God, thank God." I could almost hear her shaking through the phone line.

"He's not—"

"I work two jobs, waitressing," she said.

"I know, Ms. Norris. It happens a lot, but—"

"I'm never around," she said, sobbing. "And cops come out there, and it's just telling them to quiet the music down, but you are a detective and that's never happened before."

"Right, but we were not there because of any—"

"Really? No drugs? Nothing like that?"

I sighed. "You should know the boys drink beer when they practice."

"But no drugs?"

"No. No drugs."

"Thank God."

"Ms. Norris, did Buzz or his buddies say—"

She hung up on me.

I grabbed a file folder and headed to the jail. It was connected to the sheriff's office by a narrow, sterile corridor. The jail guys had my man in the interrogation room waiting for me.

I had to wait twenty minutes because Van Heusen had invoked his right to have an attorney present. I scanned the guy's priors. Lots of fights, a few pot busts, a DUI. Nothing worse.

Trumpower and Daltry were in the viewing room, watching Van Heusen through the one-way. I joined them and we made small talk while awaiting the attorney.

"Skinny, ain't he?" Trumpower shook his head. "Needs a fucking hamburger."

"Ugly, too," Daltry added.

A phone buzzed, and I stepped out into the corridor to meet the lawyer. The woman who showed up to represent Van Heusen was familiar to me, a tall and bespectacled black brunette named Gretchen Pearson who did a lot of public defender work. I filled her in on why I wanted to talk to the client she had not met yet, she asked me a few questions about why we arrested him in the first place, and then she went in to consult with him.

"Tell your buddies in the viewing room to turn off the fucking speakers and don't watch us," she said.

"Of course," I said, and then I did that. Trump, I mean Irwin, and the sheriff complied.

A few moments later, Pearson opened the door and I walked in.

Van Heusen sat at the coffee-stained table and glared at me as if to say he wished he'd stuck his damn knife in my neck and twisted it. I gave him a smile that said if he'd tried that, I'd have shot him in the head. I think we understood each other.

The lawyer sat next to Van Heusen, ready to take notes and prepared to intervene if I asked this guy anything she did not like.

I dropped the photo of Megan Beemer on the table without saying a word. I wanted to gauge his reaction. He responded to it the way I respond to TV commercials. He just sort of blanked it out.

"Do you recognize her?"

He glanced down at the picture. "No. Why?"

He was no amateur at interrogation. I leaned forward. "She vanished at a party in Columbus. We have reason to believe she came up to Mifflin County. You're from Columbus. You came here to Mifflin County."

"I didn't bring no teenybopper with me."

I stared at him.

"I mean it. I came here alone." He scratched his left arm. A rat was tattooed there. It was jerking off. I don't know why.

"Why did you come here?"

He glanced at Gretchen Pearson. She nodded at him.

"Indian summer and I had a Harley and a day off," he said. "It's pretty around here. All pasteurized."

"All what?"

"Pasteurized. Lots of trees and nature and that kind of shit."

"You mean pastoral."

"That sounds like church, but whatever." He scratched his nose. A scab fell off.

"So you were just out joyriding? Soaking up the countryside?"

He ran a finger across his mustache. The cologne smell had washed off. Now he smelled like sweat and urine. I wasn't sure that was actually worse than the cologne. "Yeah. I work weekends, mostly, and I have my fun through the weekdays."

"What do you do?"

"I play guitar."

"In a band?"

"In any band that needs a guitar. I mostly sit in; some band loses a player or some singer needs a backup band in a hurry. A working band can't afford to lose a gig just because a guitar picker is in jail or broke his finger, right? The show must go on, right? They call me, and I play and get my pay. I can do Jimmy, I can do Nugent, I can do Clapton, Frehley, any of those guys."

"Don't have a band of your own?"

"People like the way I play. They don't like me."

"Why is that?"

"Taste in music, no taste in people, I guess. Anyway, I don't like people, either, so who the fuck cares? It all works out."

"What bands do you usually play with?"

"Do you need my client's entire work history, Detective?" Pearson looked mean.

"It would help, actually," I said. "But I asked a pretty simple question."

The guitar man shrugged. "I played with Changed Agent, Dinner for Rick, Unhallow, Orange Dog Whiskey, bunch of others."

He had not mentioned Soul Scraped.

"Did you have a gig Saturday?"

"Yeah, backing this short little blonde named Allison who thought she was fucking Joan Jett or something. Had a nice voice, and a nice ass, but she was a bitch. We played at a place called Zeke's, on High Street close to campus. Shithole. Ain't been open six months. Probably won't last another three."

"Got a last name and number for her, this Allison?"

"Yeah, in my fucking cell phone, which you guys got locked away somewhere. Zeke's number is in there, too—he knows I played at his place."

"Ever play with a band called Soul Scraped?"

"No."

"Ever heard of them?"

"No."

"We have your bike, Mr. Van Heusen. We are going to check it for evidence. If this girl was on this bike, ever, we're going to know it."

He shrugged. "Do what you gotta do."

"Do you have a warrant to search the bike?" The lawyer's eyebrows arched.

"Indeed, I do." I pulled a copy from my folder and slid it across the table toward her. She looked at it.

She gave it back. "They have a warrant," she told her client.

"It's OK," Van Heusen said. "I don't know that girl, and she wasn't on my Harley."

"I am done here for now," I said. "I will leave you here to let you explain to your attorney how you pulled a knife on me."

I stepped into the hall and closed the door behind me. I walked into the viewing room.

Daltry pulled up his belt. "You think this guy was involved with your missing girl?"

"No."

I went to the vending machine in the break room and bought a Snickers. My phone rang at the same moment my candy bar plopped into the pickup tray. It was Debbie. "We got a nibble from Facebook on Megan Beemer," she said.

"Really?"

"Girl named Ally Phelps—says she saw her yesterday morning in Jodyville. Says she was running, looked scared."

"Where is this girl?"

"At Hollis now. You probably can catch her at lunch if you hurry. She lives over the store in Jodyville, if you want to get her after school."

I did not want to wait. "I am on my way to the school now."

"Farkas called, too. Wants to know about the girl case."

A reporter? Fuck that. "Did you tell him no comment?"

"I emailed him the reports, told him that was all he was getting until we had more to release."

"Good. If he calls back, don't tell him where I am."

"Do I ever?"

I went through the squad room on my way to my desk to grab my keys. Baxter tried to flag me down. "Mr. Green called again. About the tractor."

"He can wait."

"He says he thinks his son-in-law sold the tractor to a guy in Wadsworth."

"The son-in-law's a saint. An idiot, but a saint. He didn't steal it. Green can wait."

Baxter sighed. "That is a weird case, Ed. Don't know what to make of it. It looks like an egg but smells like a chicken."

"Huh?"

"Just don't make sense, is all. Big thing to steal, was in the barn in the morning, gone in the afternoon, hard to hide. I seen that tractor, Ed, it's a real nice one, '59 Allis-Chalmers with—"

I halted, turned, and leaned on Baxter's desk. "I do not give a shit about a fucking tractor. I have a girl in trouble, and I'm going to find her, OK?"

"Jesus, Ed. That tractor's worth some money, and been in Mr. Green's family for years."

I swallowed hard. "Sorry, Bax. I'm sorry."

"OK." His eyes were still wide, and his Adam's apple bobbed up and down like a yo-yo.

"Look, do me a favor, Bax. You want to be a detective, right?"

"Yeah. Working up to it."

"And you know way more about farm equipment than I am ever gonna know, right?"

"You do have trouble telling a combine from a shit spreader and such, so yes."

"Take Mr. Green's case. It's all yours."

"Really?"

"Yes, grab my reports, just take over."

"I am supposed to go on patrol." He glanced at the wall clock that was always fast. "In twelve minutes."

"Patrol up by Mr. Green's house, or wherever he thinks the damned tractor is," I said. "If that is not your beat today, trade with someone. Find the tractor, the sheriff will like you. It will be your ticket to the big time. You'll be a detective."

His eyes widened further, but he was smiling. "OK! Thanks, Ed!"

"Sure. Find that tractor and I will buy you a beer."

"Great! I have one idea I can—"

"Find it without ever talking to me about it again, and I'll buy you two beers." I ran to get my keys.

I was in the truck within five minutes, tearing through a light rain with the windshield wipers going at a slow country ballad tempo. I called Shelly Beckworth.

"Might have a lead. Girl here says she saw Megan alive, in Jodyville, yesterday morning. On my way to talk to her now. Want to listen in?"

"Hell, yeah. Skype me. I'll text you the contact info."

"OK."

Fifteen minutes later, I was sitting in a tiny conference room at
Hollis High School, waiting for a secretary to fetch me Ally Phelps.
I had a small voice recorder on the table. My phone was propped
next to it on an improvised stand made with a couple of huge paper
clips, and Shelly Beckworth's cute but unattainable lesbian face
stared from my screen.

"Think this is the big break we need, Ed?"

"I hope so. I truly do. We'll see."

"Yeah."

Shelly had that "don't get your hopes up too high" expression I've
seen on lots of detectives. I suspect I had it, too.

It wasn't a long wait. "Ally," the secretary said, "this is Detective
Runyon."

"And this," I said, pointing to my phone, "is Detective Shelly
Beckworth, from Columbus. I am helping her find a missing girl,
the girl you say you saw yesterday. Thank you for calling us."

The girl glanced at the floor. The secretary, who looked rather like
the short waitress on *Cheers*, lingered. "Close the door behind you,
please," I said, "and see that we are not interrupted. Thanks."

She complied, begrudgingly.

Ally Phelps was a waif, a freshman dressed in jeans and a T-shirt
and topped with wild black hair streaked with yellow. Or maybe it
was wild yellow hair streaked with black. I couldn't tell. The T-shirt
was adorned with a demon, who was either trying to swallow a cat
or coughing one up. It was tough to figure out which. Once I fought
for a glance beyond all the mascara, I saw that her eyes were brown.
One might describe her overall aesthetic as "pissed at the world."

"Sit down, please," I said. "Again, thanks for calling us."

Ally did not say hello, nor did she look at me. She sat at the table
and gazed at the photo of Megan Beemer.

I slid it across the table to her. "That the girl you saw?"

"Yes," Ally said, sharply. "Definitely." She stared hard at the photo, as if trying to memorize it.

"Tell us about it," Shelly said from the phone. "What did you see, and when?"

Ally cleared her throat, and spent at least ten seconds trying to decide whether to aim her eyes at me while she talked, or at the phone. She finally settled on staring at Megan's photo. "It was yesterday morning, on my way to school."

"So, about seven thirty?" I started taking notes, even though the voice recorder was working fine.

"More like seven forty. I am always running late," she said, shrugging. "I catch the bus at the middle school, ride over to Hollis."

I nodded. "OK. What did you see, and where?"

"I saw this girl," Ally said, pointing at the photo. "She looks stuck-up."

"What makes you say that?" Shelly leaned toward the screen.

"I don't know. She just does."

"OK." Shelly leaned back.

"Just tell us what you saw." I tried to look more patient than I felt.

"I saw her."

"Where?"

"Running into town."

"Where into town?"

"Down the road from where I live."

"Running toward your place? You live over the store, right? So, into town, then she was south of you?"

"Yes, running toward our apartment," she said, glancing at the ceiling. "Guess that's south, but she was on the other side of the street."

"OK," Shelly said. "Did you see where she went? Did she run into a building? Get in a car?"

"I don't know," Ally said. "I saw her, then a bit later she was gone. I did not see where she went."

"Are you sure? It's important."

"That's what I saw," she said.

"Did she look scared?" I asked.

"Yeah. She wasn't exercise running, like her type does," Ally said. "She was scared running, you know?"

"OK." I pictured all this in my mind. If Megan Beemer had entered town as Ally described, she'd come running from the direction of the trailer park, where Soul Scraped filled the world with really loud poetry. Buzz and company practiced their act less than a mile away from town.

"What was she wearing?" I sat with my pen poised, and glanced at the phone. Shelly extended a hand to indicate she'd let me continue to ask the questions.

"Um, just clothes, you know."

"I don't know. It could be important. Try to remember."

"Well, it was a hooded jacket, some sort of school jacket, I think."

"What color?"

"Red."

"A red school jacket, like a fleece jacket?"

"Yeah."

Megan's school colors were blue and gold, and she hadn't worn a fleece jacket to the party. I shrugged. "Like an Ohio State jacket?"

Ally's eyes widened. "Yeah, like that."

Great. Half of the people in this state own Ohio State jackets. I have three.

"Anything else? Like a purse, or a ring? What kind of pants was she wearing?"

The girl looked as though I had asked her to explain quantum mechanics. "I don't know. Jeans. She wore jeans."

"New jeans? Old jeans?"

"New. Dark blue. But ripped, you know, on the thighs? Not really ripped, like you'd actually worn them a long time. You buy them that way. If you think you are cool."

"Your jeans are ripped."

"Because my mom can't afford to fucking buy new ones," she snarled.

"OK. Calm down. Anything else about her you noticed, Ally?"

"Boots. Very clean ones. Black, halfway up her calves. Like, really expensive boots."

Those did not sound like proper running shoes to me. "OK. Did you see anyone chasing her?"

Ally stared at me for three seconds. "No."

"Are you sure?"

"Yes, I am sure."

"Anyone following her in a car? Anyone watching her?"

"No."

"Other kids around? Did anyone else see her?"

"No. No."

"No other kids on their way to school?"

"I was running late," Ally reminded me. "Other kids were already at the school."

Shelly jumped in. "Do you know Buzz? Gage? Johnny?" She apparently had created her own decent mental map of Jodyville and the surrounding area during her visit. There's not a lot of Jodyville to memorize.

Ally glared at the phone. "Yeah, everyone knows them. Everyone knows everyone here."

"Do you know them personally, though?"

"I used to hang out with the band some. Not anymore."

I asked, "Why is that?"

"I don't know."

"Were you a girlfriend to one of them?"

She stared at me before answering my question. "Sort of. Went out with Buzz some."

"Some."

"Yeah. Just some."

"OK."

"Why do you care about that?"

I looked at the girl. "Those guys were at a party, where this missing girl was last seen. Were you at the party?"

Her lips tightened and quivered for a heartbeat or two. "No. Not invited."

"But you and Buzz used to hang out."

"Look, you guys are looking for a girl and I saw her, OK? Why the fuck do you need to know who I know or any of that shit?"

"Whoooooaaaaa, Nelly," I said. "We don't care, really. Honestly. We just want to find the girl, OK? And if you know Buzz, we'd like to know if maybe you heard him say anything about this girl, or any girl, OK? You said you saw her running from the direction of the trailer park, Soul Scraped practices there, and they all were at a party in Columbus, OK? Dots seem to connect. So, do you recall Buzz, or Johnny or Gage, talking about a girl from Columbus, or meeting a girl there?"

"No," she said. "I have not talked to Buzz in a while. And I don't really like the other guys. And they don't like me."

I stared at her a while, hoping she would say more. She didn't crack.

"Anything else you saw that might help us?"

"No. Is she like rich or something?"

"Why do you ask?"

"Just wondered. Columbus, big city, everybody looking for her."

"OK." I ignored her question. "Did you mention what you saw to anyone? Other students, teachers, your parents, anyone?"

"No. Why would I?"

I shrugged. "Weird thing, isn't it? A strange girl in town, running scared. People usually talk about such things."

Ally grinned, rather bitterly. "I don't really talk to people."

Buzz, the poet lyricist of Soul Scraped, had uttered similar words.

"OK," I said. "Thanks for talking to us, anyway. Shelly, do you have more questions?"

"Not for now. Probably later, though."

I collected Ally's phone number, gave her my card, and sent her back to class. The secretary peered through the open door, as if she might be able to see what we talked about.

I picked up the phone.

"What do you think, Shelly?"

"I am . . . not sure."

"Those weren't the clothes she was last seen in," I said.

"Yeah, but she might have borrowed, if she's been with someone a couple days. And she was wearing boots to the dance."

"True. Ally struck me as off-kilter, though," I said. "When she described the clothes, I'm wondering if she was telling us what she imagined a stuck-up rich girl from Columbus would wear, and not something she saw."

"I had the same thought," Shelly said. "She did a lot of editorializing about a girl she supposedly did not know."

"Agreed. But at the very least, I think Ally believes Buzz knew Megan Beemer."

"Yep. And I want to know why she thinks that."

"Me, too."

CHAPTER THIRTEEN

Wednesday, 1:10 p.m.

I WAS EATING tacos at my desk and checking out Ally Phelps in our records. There was not much there. Bax had caught her smoking a joint behind the middle school about a year ago, and she'd sworn it was the first time she'd ever done that. She'd told a cop in Ambletown the same thing when she caught Ally about two months after that. Both cops had let her off with warnings, because who the fuck really has time to do paperwork for a single joint these days?

Ally had no other interactions with law and order in the database.

I was still listening to the Phelps girl's interview when my phone beeped an alert at me. "Attn: SWAT. Hostage situation, 726 Oak St., Nora, Ohio. Man with gun; locked in home; female hostage." The scanner across the room issued the same message before the alert vanished from my screen.

"Goddamn it," I growled at the universe. I did not want to go out on a SWAT call. I wanted to press this lead we had from Ally Phelps. I wanted to find Megan Beemer while she was still alive. If she was still alive. But SWAT calls were not optional.

Unlike those guys on *Hill Street Blues*, Mifflin County did not have a full-time team of officers trained in special weapons and tactics, waiting and training and ready to roll the moment trouble reared up. We had a team made up of officers from several departments, mostly from Ambletown PD and MCSO but with a couple of guys from village departments. We trained as often as we could, then jumped whenever an alert came. And unless you were actively in pursuit of a suspect, exchanging gunfire with someone already or deep undercover at a drug buy, you fucking showed up when the SWAT alarm came.

I stopped a moment at dispatch, in such a rush I scarcely noticed Debbie had her hands quite full with calls and dispatches. "Debbie, see if we can get road patrol out to the trailers south of Jodyville, near Black Powder Creek. See if anyone else besides Ally Phelps saw Megan Beemer."

Debbie nodded and kept pushing buttons on her communications console. If I had annoyed her, she didn't show it. A good dispatcher has to be quite the multitasker. "Will do, Ed. And you be careful out there. I hate SWAT calls."

"Me, too. Thanks."

I dashed out to my truck and opened the locker in the back. I removed the Kevlar body armor and strapped it around my torso, thighs, and upper arms. Then I tossed the helmet and radio into the cab and climbed in after it. I'd grab the Remington Model 700 rifle from the SWAT command center vehicle at the scene. For now, it was time to pop the flashing light on top of my truck, fire up the siren, and get north to Nora as quickly as possible.

I took back roads to the two-lane highway, then gunned it. Even as I focused on not side-swiping any of the cars and trucks that pulled off to the shoulder so I could pass, I kept seeing a pretty blonde girl in my head. Sometimes it was Megan Beemer, but sometimes it was Briana Marston. Bree had died at the professor's hands while we New York cops were busy doing other things, working other cases. I could easily imagine Megan Beemer being killed right now, while I was driving north to perch on a rooftop and maybe shoot a guy who was threatening his wife.

Intellectually, of course, I knew my job at the moment was to help save lives in Nora and that cops weren't supposed to pick which lives to prioritize. But my own little version of the classic Trolley Problem was rolling through my head, because I was human and humans do that shit. Should I let the runaway trolley car continue down the track and kill five people lashed to the rails? Or should I pull the lever and divert the trolley to a different track, where just one person would die?

Should I go to Nora and do my job there, or should I rush to the trailer park in search of Megan Beemer?

My head said one thing, duty said another, and all the while I was aware that my mind was not really in the game.

The radio, set to the SWAT band, gave me an update while I was still two minutes out. "Negotiator in contact with suspect," said Captain Jim Bowman, the Ambletown PD officer who commanded our merry band of highly trained experts. "If you are coming in hot, I want sirens off, flashers off."

I turned off the noise and lights. I could see Nora in the distance, a small collection of homes surrounding a crossroads, with a gas station and a diner that used to serve really good hamburgers before the owner died and the place shut down. I noticed the church steeple, too, and figured it had a commanding view of the whole village. That would be my perch.

I stopped briefly at the intersection to make sure no bicycles, tractors, trucks, or dogs were crossing my path, then bolted on through and banged a left on Oak Street. At 726, I braked to a halt behind an ambulance, on standby. The command vehicle was across from the two-story dirty blue home with the big picture window that was going to be the center of my universe for however long it took us to get this situation resolved.

I donned my helmet and rushed to the command van. An officer handed me a Remington, and I did my safety checkdown. Muscle memory and training seemed to be kicking in, I told myself—but Megan Beemer peered at me from the mind shadows.

Captain Bowman trotted up. He ran his finger and thumb against his hawk beak of a nose, as if he had a headache. "He's talking to Millie, Ed, but he hasn't surrendered yet. S.O. has no prior calls here, so we have no idea what to expect. Young couple—he's laid off and she's a part-time waitress. No kids, thank God. I want you up yonder," and he pointed to the church steeple across the intersection. "He seems to be sticking to the lower floor, near as we can tell. You train on that window," and he pointed to the picture window, "and hope for the best. Pastor is expecting you."

"Aye." I jogged toward the Nora Congregationalist Church.

A man in a cardigan and faded jeans met me at the door. "This way, Officer, this way."

He did not tell me his name, and I did not ask. He pointed me toward a side door. "Ladder in there, it is old, but do not worry, it is solid and it will hold. I will be praying you don't have to shoot, Officer."

"Pray for a girl named Megan, too."

He looked confused, but nodded. "Of course, Officer."

"She's missing. I am supposed to be looking for her." I started up.

"I will pray for her and for you and for everyone involved here today," the reverend said.

I hoped that would help.

I strapped the rifle across my back and climbed up through the dust and streams of sunlight pouring from above. On the way up, I thanked God that I was a good shot and thus working from a distance. I was not one of the guys who might be ordered to approach the home to spy through a window, or storm the house, or even crouch behind a squad car close by and get hit because sometimes bullets find a way to rip all the way through a squad car or ricochet from a utility pole or some other damned thing.

It was an odd prayer of thanks, I guess, and certainly more selfish than the pastor's. I was feeling blessed because I can shoot people in the head from a distance, and I felt a bit guilty at having those thoughts. But if there is a God, he is smarter than me and I trusted him to sort it all out. I kept climbing.

At the top, I opened a hatch and clambered out. I was under a roof mounted on four sturdy corner posts, with a large gray bell hanging in the center. I freed my rifle, took my position, and peered through the scope.

Things were not good.

My radio crackled. "Report, Ed."

"Angle is good, for picture window, and OK for upper floors. Light is bad, Captain. I can make them out through the picture window, two figures, moving around, but indistinct. Some window glare. Thin curtain, too. I think that glass is mighty damned thick, enough to deflect a shot."

"Roger."

He would not order me to shoot under such conditions. Still, my vantage was a good one, and I could serve as an observer. I could see the front, side, and most of the back yard. And if the guy bolted and needed to be shot, I could do it from here unless he ran west, behind the house. Other guys were positioned there. We had the place surrounded, and there was nowhere for this guy to go. Except hell.

But the odds of me taking the guy out through the window if it came to that? Zero. I prayed Millie Martin, the hostage negotiator for our county and two adjacent counties, would be able to talk this bastard down from whatever the hell had ramped him up.

I peered through the scope. The window glare would clear up in a few minutes as the world turned. Part of Millie's job was to play the fish, give us time to assess and overcome such obstacles, and I had no doubt the captain had passed my report along to her.

Wind was minimal. That was good, if I had to shoot.

Beyond the glass and curtains, the two shadowy shapes were close together. I could not be sure, really, which was the crazed man and which was the female hostage. I knew, though, that neither one of them was Megan Beemer.

"Fuck," I said, cursing myself. It was not my duty right now, right here, to worry about Megan Beemer. It was my duty to concentrate, observe, and be ready to shoot this son of a bitch dead if needed. A million things could go wrong here. He could shoot the woman. He could start shooting through the window at the cops surrounding his house. He could come outside, gun to his hostage's head, and try to coerce his way through the net we had him trapped in. He could just come out, guns blazing, and attempt "suicide by cop." Or he could come up with some new wrinkle we'd never seen, because why should everything go by the book? Have you ever seen the book? It's a fucking thick book, and the one thing you know for sure as a cop is that not everything is in it.

I was supposed to be ready for anything.

I tried focused breathing, something a counselor had taught me after I'd been bullied into seeking real help in warding off the mental paralysis that followed the Marston case. In through the nose, out through the mouth, don't force it, just be.

That started to feel like a distraction itself, so I spat a gob into the air and told myself to make sure the crazy guy inside didn't rush out the front door and kill one of my fellow officers.

This went on for two goddamned hours.

"Still talking with Millie," the captain said. "He seems to be calming down a bit."

"Go, Millie, go," I whispered. Millie Martin had a psychology degree and could shoot like a pro, so it was good to have her on hand no matter which way this went down.

If I had wanted, I could have looked around and predicted what I would see. Cops, blocks away, keeping the curious at bay. People craning their necks, maybe looking through binoculars, definitely lofting their cell phones and shooting video. Farkas, from the *Gazette*, would be out there somewhere, too, hoisting his own cell phone and definitely shooting video. If I had to shoot the guy inside this house, it might very well end up on goddamned Facebook Live.

But I did not look around. I peered through my scope, watching the shadows inside the house, trying not to peer into the shadows of my mind.

Time kept unfolding. Once the earth had turned a bit, the window glare vanished. I could now see two figures, close together, and now I could tell that one was a man, holding a gun to the head of the other, a woman. The man, the taller of the two, was talking. Maybe he was talking to a phone lying around. He did not have a phone in his hand. He had a gun.

"Captain, better sighting now. I have a shot. Still worried about the thick glass, but if they separate, I have a shot. If we can break the glass first . . ."

"Roger, Ed. Stand by."

A part of me just wanted to shoot this asshole and get back to searching for Megan Beemer, but I did not say that aloud. I am a professional.

The shapes inside the home separated.

"Stand by," the captain said.

The woman rushed to the front door.

"Hold your fire."

She came out, a shaking, shambling, disjointed brunette mess.

The man inside turned about, slowly, like a merry-go-round winding down.

"Hold your fire."

Two officers emerged from behind a squad car and gathered the woman up. They led her to cover, quickly. They practically had to carry her.

Inside, the man spun faster and faster until he whirled like a dervish, his long dark hair streaming. He was shouting, kicking furniture, waving his arms.

Then he ended the situation. He bit down on the barrel of his gun, and his head burst open.

The woman screamed when she heard the gun's thunder, and tried to tear herself away from the officers restraining her. She tried to run back in there.

"Jesus," I said to myself.

They finally got her behind the command vehicle.

"Hold your positions," Captain Bowman said.

Two officers crept, slowly slowly slowly, toward positions on either side of the picture window.

"Woman confirms, no one else inside," Bowman said over the radio.

"I had a good view," I told the captain. "No way he survived."

"Roger."

One of the officers by the window risked a peek inside, then he signaled with a thumbs-up.

It was over.

I closed my eyes, and tried to control my breathing. I was not very proud of some of the feelings battling in my head. I was relieved that I did not have to kill anyone today, but I was angry at this guy. I had lost four goddamned hours in my search for a missing girl, just so this asshole could kill himself.

CHAPTER FOURTEEN

Wednesday, 7:30 p.m.

I KNOCKED ON the trailer door three times before the gray-haired gent answered. He leaned on a cane, and smiled at me. "Can I help you?"

l flashed my ID. "Detective Ed Runyon, Mifflin County Sheriff's Office. I am looking for a missing girl, and we have reports that she might have been in this area." I put the ID away. "Can you look at a photo for me?"

"Sure," he said. "Come on in. I am Dave Gentry. The kitten is Thomas Skittles. Coffee?"

I was checking the trailer park south of Jodyville because few people had been around during the day when road patrol tried. Ally Phelps had told us she had seen Megan Beemer not far from here, and Buzz and his friends played what they called music behind the last trailer in the row. I had missed a lot of legwork time because of that SWAT call, and this seemed like the most promising way to make it up.

"No thanks," I said in reply to his offer of coffee.

"Your SWAT friends had some trouble up in Nora today," he said.

"They sure did." I did not mention I was there, because that would just take time. I took Megan Beemer's photo from the folder I carried. "Have you seen this girl around here?"

He sat in a rocker, and the gray kitten leapt into his lap and stared at me as though I were the least consequential thing in the universe. I did not really care what the cat thought. I had lost a perfectly good girlfriend in high school just because I didn't like cats, and I still held a grudge.

Mr. Gentry took the photo from me and stared at it, while I looked around at the photos and souvenirs that dotted his crowded trailer. This guy was a Vietnam War vet. A much younger version of him smiled at me from a bridge over a jungle river.

"I see you are a veteran," I said. "Thanks for your service."

"Thanks," he said, pointing at another photo. "That's my plane there, F-4 Phantom II. Did a lot of air support missions, landed more than once with bullets in my fuselage. I do not miss those days."

His gaze returned to the photo I had given him. "I have not seen her, no," he said, after a long look. "Pretty girl. Read about her in the paper. So sad."

"Heard any of your neighbors talk about seeing her?"

He chuckled. "Oh, they leave me alone. Me and Thomas Skittles here, we're mighty dull." He stroked the cat.

"Did you happen to step outside yesterday morning, about the time kids were headed to school? We have a witness who puts the girl in this area about then."

"No," he said. "I sleep in, most days."

I nodded. "You ever go outside to yell at the band down the row here, Buzz and his friends? Maybe they have girls around sometimes?"

"No, I don't bother them. They are just having fun, and I don't hear all that good anyway. I take the hearing aid out of my ear and I can't even tell they are playing."

"It ain't exactly music, so you are not missing much."

"I suppose not. But hell, my mom and dad hated the crap I listened to, you know? That's how it should be, I guess."

"Seen any strange vehicles lately, heard anyone come or go at odd hours?"

"No, not really."

"OK, well, thank you for your time, and again, for your service." I pointed at one of the photos, him hoisting a can of beer with other guys wearing flight jackets.

"Vietnam was a shithole." He shook his head. "Total shithole. Things are better now." He smiled.

"If you recall anything that might help me find the girl, call me here." I held up one of my cards and placed it next to his phone.

"I sure will, Detective. Thank you for your service, too. And if anything bad happened to her, that girl you're looking for, why, when you catch the fucker, you call me. I still remember a trick or two. I'll make the fucker squeal like a pygmy goat."

I looked at him. He was grinning. But he looked serious, too. Deadly serious. The guy who had dropped bombs in Vietnam while taking enemy fire was back, and I wondered if the hands that gently stroked Thomas Skittles were strong enough to strangle.

"I know how you feel, sir. I know how you feel. Have a good evening."

There was no answer at the second trailer, or the third. I was working my way toward Buzz's place. Apparently, the band was taking the evening off.

At the fourth trailer, a woman opened the door seconds after I knocked. She had a pistol in her hand, aimed at my face. But she moved it, aiming for the sky, before I could even touch my own gun.

I raised my hands and remembered to breathe.

"You're not Dave," she said.

"The old guy over there?" I nodded toward her neighbor's trailer.

"Fuck no. Sorry." She tossed the gun away, somewhere behind her, then spun around and vanished within the trailer.

I drew my gun, crouched, and peered inside the trailer. She seemed to be alone. She had her back to me, leaning on a countertop next to an open bottle of vodka and a pitcher of what probably was orange juice. An empty glass sat precariously close to the counter's edge. Her shoulders quaked, and I guessed she was sobbing.

I stepped inside, and the scents of tobacco and vodka hit me immediately. Everything was dusty, and it smelled as though she had a dog, but I didn't see a dog. I saw her Cobra Arms Freedom .380, though, on a couch that showed springs poking through the fabric. I moved to place myself between her and the gun.

"I thought you were Dave," she said quietly.

"No," I said. "I am Detective Ed Runyon, Mifflin County Sheriff's Office."

"Well, shit. Knew this was coming." She spun around and faced me, her reddened eyes wide and staring.

Now that I wasn't staring at a fucking gun, I noticed that she was blonde, skinny, wearing a huge T-shirt and nothing else. She probably was between forty and fifty years old. I saw no needle tracks on her arms, and no drug paraphernalia anywhere within sight. But she was trembling, and her lower jaw shook like a flag in a brisk wind. The scent of warm screwdrivers rode on every exhalation.

"You came to bust me, right? Dave say I was hooking?" The words were heavily slurred, with incomprehensible noises inserted between the words I could understand.

"No," I answered. "I don't know Dave. I came to ask you questions about a missing girl who was seen near here."

"Jesus." She shook harder, closed her eyes tight, and slumped against the counter, almost disrupting the pitcher. I holstered my weapon. "Can you tell me your name, please?"

"Don't wanna."

"You aimed a gun at me, so I am going to get your name one way or another."

"Tess Baldwin," she said. "OK? Guilty. Blowing guys for money, OK?" She poured vodka into the glass, then tipped orange juice into it. "Because why in fuck should I grab some extra money, right? Use the one goddamned skill I have to make a living, right?"

I sighed, and retrieved her gun. I emptied it, then stuck gun and ammo into my jacket pocket. This was going to turn into a long stop, another distraction from the Megan Beemer case. I wanted to just turn and go, but this woman was clearly unstable, very drunk, and waiting to kill some guy named Dave. Or maybe herself. Booze and guns don't mix.

"I don't actually care about what you might be doing here or know anything about it," I said. "You are not in trouble, not from me. I am looking for a missing girl. She was seen around here." I fished the photo out of the folder, and held it out to her. I wasn't certain Tess Baldwin could even see straight, let alone remember anything she might have seen before, but I had to try.

She looked at me for several seconds, her eyes unfocused, then she took the photo. She stared at it a long time. Finally, she handed it back. "Ain't seen her."

"You sure?" I slipped the photo back into the folder.

"Sure." She picked up a tiny purse from a grimy counter near the sink. She pulled free a cigarette and lighter. Seconds later, she was inhaling deeply. She released a cloud of smoke and said, "She ain't blowing guys around here? Don't need competition." I think she intended it as a joke, something to ease the tension, but her voice cracked hard and tears started flowing.

"She vanished. After a party. In Columbus."

"Well, I ain't seen her. She ain't here."

"Not with Buzz and his band?"

She shook her head. "No, not those boys. Fags. Well, maybe fags. Seen girls with them sometimes. Not that one."

"You are certain? It's important."

"Yeah," she said. "Sure. Pretty. That girl."

"Yes," I agreed. "So, who is Dave?"

Her forehead creased. "Fuck Dave." She started shaking again. "Jesus. Cops. He's gonna shit. Gonna kill me." She started looking around. "My gun. Jesus."

"I confiscated your pistol. You are not in any condition to—"

"Gimme my fucking gun!"

"You are not killing Dave tonight."

"Fuck Dave!" She grabbed at me, and I spun her onto the couch. Her landing was harder than I'd intended.

"Calm down," I ordered.

"Not killing Dave! Killing m-m-m . . ."

"Tess."

She covered her face with quaking hands. "Killing m-m-me. Myself. Can't . . . can't . . ."

She began sobbing, hard, and fell over on the couch.

I pulled out my phone. I told Carolyn, the night dispatcher, what had happened, and that I needed a road patrol to assist, and an ambulance, and asked her to arrange an emergency committal at the hospital for a drunk, possibly high, detainee.

"You busting me, are you?"

"Yes." I sighed. I wanted to be out there hunting Megan Beemer, not dealing with this woman's messy life. But here I was, unable to just walk away. "I am placing you under arrest, attempted assault on a police officer—"

"I thought you was Dave!"

"—firearms under the influence, possibly more." I tried to look her in the eyes, but her head was shaking hard. "You are going to the hospital. You are going to get help."

"No."

She uttered the word "no" three more times before I finished reciting her rights.

"You spoke of killing yourself. That means you need help, whether you want it or not." I could have added I knew that from experience, but decided not to.

"Fuck."

We stayed there, her sitting and crying and me pacing and awaiting the cavalry, when I heard the roar of a heavy engine outside. The vehicle braked hard and shut off.

"Dave," Tess said, fear filling her eyes. She stumbled to the front door and peeked out. "Dave."

"Wait here."

I stepped outside. A broad-shouldered man who seemed made up mostly of beard and sweat stepped out of a rusty blue Chevy pickup. I glared at him. "Are you Dave?"

"Who the fuck are you? Just get laid, did you?" His fists clenched, and he strode toward me. "What did she charge you?"

I flashed my badge. "Detective Ed Runyon, Mifflin County Sheriff's Office. Who are you?"

He halted suddenly, raised his hands. "Hey, man. Just visiting."

"I am here on official business," I said, putting my badge away. "Who are you, and what brings you here?"

"I just . . . I know the woman who lives here." He pointed at the trailer.

I waited a few seconds, to see if he would mention any concern about showing up here to find a cop, or maybe ask me if Tess was OK. He didn't.

"I asked your name," I reminded him.

"Dave. David Conley. Live in Ambletown."

"State your business," I said.

"I just wanted to see her, is all. No business." He edged back toward his truck.

"Well, I do have business here. Do you come out here a lot? Have you seen a blonde girl around here lately? Pretty. High schooler."

He shook his head. "No, man. No girl."

"Then you can stay here and interfere in official police business, or you can turn around and go." As I spoke, I memorized his license plate.

Blue and red lights flashing from the road got his attention. The road patrol was coming.

"Shit, man," the bearded guy said, "not looking for trouble." He headed back to the truck, and I watched to make sure he didn't reach inside for a gun. He climbed inside, cranked the key, and the truck started with a roar. Dave did a quick turn and headed for the road.

I should have asked him more questions. I should have tried to figure out why Tess Baldwin feared him, why he was so eager to leave once I announced I was a cop. But this was already eating up time I could be spending on the search for Megan Beemer, and I could bust this guy later if I needed to. Tess Baldwin would be tucked away safe, at least for a while. I noted his plate number in my phone and went back in as the road patrol rolled up. The woman was still sobbing on the couch.

"Dave left in a hurry."

She nodded.

"Does he have some reason to worry about cops? Does he hit you?"

She nodded. "Shoves me." She lifted her shirt and showed me some bruises on her belly. She showed me some other stuff, too, but did not seem at all concerned about that. "Threw me at the counter. Mad because I'm a hoo . . . hoo . . . hooker."

"Do you want to file a complaint?"

She shook her head. "No."

Deputy John Gavin announced his arrival while still outside, then walked in. He removed his hat to reveal a buzz cut worthy of the Marines. "Heard you had a gun pulled on you?"

"Briefly. She thought I was someone else." I explained the situation to Gavin as quickly as possible, and we both heard the ambulance pull in. Gavin went out to fill them in.

I turned back to the woman. "If we were to search Dave's home or vehicle, would we be likely to find some pot or some other illegal substance? Maybe stolen goods? Anything I could lock him up for?"

She looked at me. She stared for about thirty seconds before nodding slowly.

"Then we will search his place," I said. I managed to slowly get what she thought was Dave's address out of her. His last name was Bannon, not Conley, she said. "OK. While we deal with that, you are going to the hospital, to get checked out."

"I am fine."

"You are drunk and talking suicide." I reached out a hand to help her stand as the paramedics came in.

"I am fine," she said slowly, although she nearly fell while trying to stand. She threw up a little.

"Stretcher," one of the paramedics said. They unfolded it and I helped get her onto it.

"Fuck," she said. "Fuck. Fuck."

They took her out. The Vietnam pilot peered at us from his doorway. Gavin headed toward his cruiser to follow the ambulance, but I halted him. "John, a minute?"

"Sure, Ed."

I gave him Dave's name, address, and plate number. "She says this guy beats her, and that's why she was waiting with a gun. I have that in my pocket, by the way—I'll bag it and you can take it." I headed toward my truck for an evidence bag. "In the meantime, I'd like you to get a warrant, based on an anonymous tip from a citizen, or get Bob to do it, and search this guy's place. She says he's got pot, maybe other drugs there." I finished bagging the confiscated gun and ammo, grabbed a pen and filled in all the info on the bag, and handed it all to him.

"I can do all that, Ed, set up a search and all, but aren't you going to be in on that?"

"I have a missing girl to look for, so help me out. I don't have time to follow up on this now, but I would not mind seeing this Dave guy in the pokey for the time being."

He looked a little put out. "OK, I will."

"Thanks. I know I am pushing some stuff off on you. I'll owe you one. I'll write up my report on this tonight. Probably late."

"Fine." Deputy Gavin returned to his cruiser with the woman's gun. I glanced at the time and cursed the minutes ticking away.

I looked toward Buzz's trailer. Lights were off, and no one was peeking out to see what was going on with all the cops and paramedics.

I went over there and knocked anyway. No one answered. I walked around the trailer, peeked into windows and saw nothing. I checked the four-wheelers parked nearby, but none were warm.

"Fuck," I muttered.

I walked back to my own truck, started it up, and aimed it away from the sheriff's office. I knew I should go follow up on this situation with Dave Bannon, or Conley, or whatever the hell his name was, but I was going to leave that to others. With luck, they'd find enough on the guy to run him in while maybe, just maybe, Tess would sober up and get things under control. A cop can dream, anyway.

But I was going to let this be someone else's problem. Megan Beemer was still missing, and I needed to get back on the hunt.

CHAPTER FIFTEEN

Wednesday, 9 p.m.

"Dude, get your ass over here!"

"Why?"

"Things got worse. Just get over here!"

"How much worse?"

"Way fucking worse, man! Get over here now!"

"Why don't you text me this shit?"

"Cops can find the texts if they want, that's why. Jesus."

"They can?"

"Yes! Jesus, did you text about this?"

"No."

"Did you?"

"No."

"You better not."

"I won't. Fuck."

"Get over here. We gotta do something. And we gotta do it now."

"What happened?"

"Ain't saying it over the phone. But it's bad."

"Bad?"

"Real fucking bad. Just get your fucking ass over here now."

CHAPTER SIXTEEN

Wednesday, 11:36 p.m.

I DOWNED A shot of bourbon and toggled the laptop screen between photos of Megan Beemer and Briana Marston. It had not been merely my imagination. The two looked eerily similar. The same blue eyes. The same blonde hair. The same smiles.

I reached for the bottle of Knob Creek, purchased on my way home, and poured another shot. "Up yours, Linda," I muttered as I lifted the shot to my lips. I considered sending her a bill for the bottle she'd stolen.

I should have been asleep already, or at least trying. Instead, here I was outside my trailer, sitting at a picnic table and testing my Wi-Fi's limits, scrolling through photos of two girls. Every now and then I browsed Google to see whether Professor Donald Graser had slipped his prison bonds and started killing girls again. I found myself typing his name again and stopped, slamming my palms against the table surface. "Fuck," I said.

I knew it was my own irrationality, fueled by bourbon, that made me try to connect these two cases. Yes, the girls looked alike, but you could find equally pretty, blue-eyed blondes in any high school in America. The only other connection between the case that had sent me running from New York and the case I was working now was me—the guy who had been too busy with other police work in the

Big Apple to find Bree before Graser had slaughtered her. And here I was, worried that Megan Beemer would meet a similar fate because a county detective's work is never done.

"Fuck," I growled, hurling the empty shot glass. It splashed into the fog-shrouded pond, and the frogs went silent for a moment. I started rehearsing a speech in my head. "I am leaving SWAT, Sheriff. Find another sniper. I am done with that and with stolen tractors and with fucking Career Day speeches and fairgrounds security details and hookers and wife beaters and every fucking thing else until I find this girl."

I thought it sounded good in my head. But then again, I was drinking straight from the bottle now because I had thrown my fucking shot glass at some goddamned frogs, so what the hell did I know?

CHAPTER SEVENTEEN

Thursday, 7:38 a.m.

THE PHONE BUZZED while I poured coffee and tried to forget haunting dreams.

"Hey, Bob," I said.

"Hello, Ed." Bob Dooman's voice is one of the deepest I've ever heard, a Darth Vader voice, cultured and refined and somewhat creepy. He sounded like he should be lecturing on Shakespeare, or quasars. "Listen. We have a dead body, south of Jodyville, in Black Powder Creek not far from the bridge. Might be the girl you and that Columbus cop are tracking, might not. But it's a teen girl, blonde, naked."

"Damn. OK, Bob, on my way."

"Yep." He gave me the precise location. It was not far from my place at all, and not far from the Cotton farm. Buzz and his band were fairly close to that spot, too, but from the opposite side of the river from the Cotton place.

I rushed to grab a shirt, and felt dizzy. I had known this would happen, goddamn it. I leaned against my closet door, closed my eyes, tried to get it together. Then I hurried out to my truck, dialing Shelly.

"Hi, Ed." She sounded groggy.

"Hey. We have a body. Teen girl. Blonde. In a river."

"Oh, no," she said. "Shit."

"Yeah."

"On my way."

"I will text you the location. Remember I showed you where I live? Same road, further out, but not far from there."

I rushed to my truck. I had left the Knob Creek bottle on the picnic table. There was a distressingly small amount of whiskey left in it. I could not quite decide if I found it distressing because it meant I had drunk a lot, or because it meant I would need to get more.

I fired up the truck and roared toward the road, ignoring the wave from my landlord. He was carrying a spinning rod toward the pond to catch some bass. I was going to see if Megan Beemer was dead.

The location, a wide bend in Black Powder Creek, was just three miles or so farther down Big Black Dog Road. I hurled past the driveway that led up to Cotton's armored barn on Breakneck Hill on my way to the crime scene.

I drove a little faster than was strictly prudent. My teeth hurt from clenching my jaw. I knew this had to be Megan Beemer. I'd failed again. Intellectually, I knew the odds were that she had died before I'd ever heard of her. If this was indeed her, she had most likely been killed Saturday night or Sunday morning, on the heels of the warehouse party, and then dumped here, long before Shelly showed up in Mifflin County.

That girl, Ally Phelps, said she had seen Megan alive Tuesday morning, but my instinct told me Ally was not a reliable witness. She had seemed confused, evasive. Maybe she was lying. But if she really had seen Megan, then maybe the girl had been alive while I was stuck on a SWAT call, or almost getting shot by a drunk hooker, or arranging for someone to bust a guy named Dave. Maybe history had repeated itself.

The shadows in my brain told me I'd failed again. Just like they told me I'd failed Bree. I'd spent a good deal of money on counseling and antidepressants trying to convince myself that I had not failed Bree, that bad things sometimes happen despite the best efforts of cops, that it was not, in fact, all my fault.

For a few years there, I believed the counselors. Now, I wasn't so sure.

I punched the roof of my truck. I might have left a dent, but didn't look to see. I knew I'd scraped blood from a knuckle.

Bob Dooman was waiting for me when I rolled up.

"Thank God it's harvest season," he said, wiping a handkerchief across his dark brow. Bob kept his head shaved smooth, and the beads of sweat on his dark pate reflected the morning sunshine in a way diamonds could only envy. He pointed across a field. "Jerry Coontz was working this field, riding high in that goddamn thing"—he paused to point at a harvester—"and because he was sitting up high, he saw her in the river. Fortunately, it's not too misty this morning or he'd have missed her."

Jerry Coontz sat on the ground by one of his combine's massive wheels, holding a worn John Deere cap between his knees, while Trumpower listened to him talk and took notes. I knew Jerry only slightly, but enough to know he was a decent, friendly guy, the type who would be hit kind of hard by finding a girl's body in the river.

We were crossing a harvested portion of that cornfield now, walking toward the river, which for some goddamned reason was called a creek on maps. We passed by a trio of road deputies and a couple of Ambletown cops who were there to make sure no curious bystanders followed us. We trod upon the stubble left behind by the combine, on ground that was just moist enough to give way a little beneath our shoes.

I eyed the ground, but didn't see any kind of track that hadn't been made by the combine, deer, dogs, or the forensic team near the bank below. Those people had waited patiently up on the road until Dooman had given them clearance, and then they'd walked single file.

There wasn't any evidence in the field for them to trample, though. This probably wasn't where she had gone into Black Powder Creek, which currently was high and swift. She'd most likely gone in upstream, and only God knew where. But there was a bridge across the two-lane highway, not far upstream, and within sight of the trailer park where Buzz and his cohorts played their angsty rock music. They could have reached that bridge, easily, and tossed her in. Of course, hundreds of other people could have done so, too. A high school linebacker. A guy on a motorcycle. Anybody.

A line of skeletal maples and oaks stood between us and the river, and I heard what I thought was an animal scurrying about. Turned out that was just a dry, dead leaf, spinning about in a swirling wind and scratching the naked branches. The still-standing corn to our left rattled dry leaves in the breeze, too. It sounded as though we were surrounded by rattlesnakes, or things trying to scratch their way out of graves.

That unsettling thought turned out to be the perfect prelude for what awaited us on the riverbank.

"She was caught under that tree there, in those gnarly branches," Dooman said. He pointed toward a maple that had been undercut by the current long ago but was still fighting gravity. It leaned across the river, its branches drooping into the water like a kid's fingers dangling from a raft. Jason Melograna, our MCSO crime scene photographer, was practically doing yoga trying to get an angle on the spot.

"No tracks or anything here, and Baxter, bless him, swam over to the other bank. He did not see any tracks or anything over there, either, and he's a hunter. So I don't think anyone shoved her in there. I think she drifted from upstream and got caught." Dooman's voice was even, steady. He was a veteran cop, not given to emotional displays. Not given to the kind of anger I could feel boiling in my gut. "We are not far downstream from the state bridge—might have been thrown in from there."

"Not an accident, then."

"Don't think so, Ed. You'll see."

I did see.

There she was, just this side of the riverside brush and trees, having been hauled out on a stretcher. She was nude, on her back, deathly pale, weeds entangled in her hair, mud marring her skin, red scratches all over her white body, a rusty red that had to be blood staining her blonde tresses. Her forehead was broken, cracked, raw.

She looked too goddamned much like another girl, in another town, who had died in a horrible way because we did not find her in time. I tried to blink that memory away. It didn't work.

Rick Danvers, the county medical examiner, knelt on one knee beside her. He was near retirement, bald and skinny, and looked out of place no matter where he was, but he was good at his job. Several paramedics stood nearby, soaked from the waist down. They had hauled the girl out of the water. They had to be freezing in the autumn breeze, but they weren't going anywhere just yet. They would carry her up to the ambulance when Danvers was done with his examination.

"Hi, Rick."

Danvers looked up upon my greeting. "Hello, Ed. You bust a knuckle?" He pointed at my hand, bleeding slightly from the punch I gave my truck roof.

"Minor scrape, getting out of my truck."

He reached into a case and pulled out a Band-Aid. "Cover it up. That's an order."

I complied. "I'm working a missing girl case," I said, pulling a bunch of facts remembered from Shelly's file into the working part of my brain. It wasn't easy. I had to tell myself to focus. "My girl is a teen blonde. Has a butterfly tattoo on her left shoulder."

"Well," Danvers said, and I probably could have chimed in and finished the sentence for him, "this is a blonde girl with a butterfly tattoo on her left shoulder. And I would estimate age at fifteen to eighteen."

"Monarch butterfly?"

"I would say probably, yes," Danvers answered. "I don't know butterflies very well, though. I don't want to roll her, but I have an image on my iPad. Just a sec." He flipped back the cover from the device lying on the ground beside him and started tapping the screen and sliding fingers across it.

Dooman inhaled deeply. "Fuck, Ed. Gotta be her."

"Yeah," I said. "The Columbus cop is on her way."

"Sad thing," Dooman said.

"Yes," I said.

"Here is this girl's butterfly," Danvers said, showing us the image on his screen. I'd seen the same image on Megan's Instagram photos, only brighter, not dulled by death and cold river water.

"That looks like hers," I said. "Not official confirmation, obviously, but it's hers."

Dooman sighed. He was the senior detective, and I was supposed to defer to him, especially on the big cases, and with all the press this was going to generate, this was a big case. But Bob is a good man, and he wasn't going to swoop in and take charge on a case I was already working. He looked at me. "What can I do to help?"

I spat. "I have a guy in the pokey. Bob Van Heusen. Plays guitar in any rock band that'll have him, and none of them will have him in anything but short doses. He is based in Columbus, where my girl was before she disappeared. I would love to know when and where he was born, what he was doing Saturday night, how he votes, what he reads, how long his dick is, the whole fucking shebang. Mostly, I want to know how he ends up in our goddamned countryside at the same time as this dead girl."

"You got it," Bob said. "Sounds like a big coincidence, and you know how I feel about those."

I stared at the girl. "We have other coincidences." I filled him in on Soul Scraped, and Jeff Cotton.

"Shit," he said upon hearing the local football star's connection. "That is going to be delicate. I'll read your file on the case, get caught up."

"Thanks," I said. "The Columbus cop, Shelly Beckworth, it's really her case. I'd like to stick with her and talk to all the kids. None of them knew anything last time, of course, but we didn't know the girl was dead at the time. We'll try to shake a little more out of them now."

"Good," Dooman said. "Got a working theory?"

"Not really," I said. "Not yet, anyway." The closest thing I had to a theory was that I might just beat the killer to death and toss his carcass into Black Powder Creek.

I glanced across the river, through the trees, and watched cars roll slowly down the highway. I could just make out the state bridge, and through the trees I could see the trailer park where Soul Scraped practiced songs about turd blossoms. I turned to Rick. "Anything you can tell us before this girl gets hauled to Columbus for an autopsy?"

"Not a lot. She was tied up at some point. I see what seem to be rope burns, or maybe wire, on her ankles and wrists. Looks like she struggled against them. A lot. Her forehead took a damn heavy blow from something—whatever it was it was, long and fairly sharp. That is probably the blow that killed her, but she took a couple other blows, too, to the face and the back of her head. Bruising to the face." He pointed. "Other blows to the back of the head. Those were done with something smaller, I'd say. I see what might be rust flakes clinging in the biggest wound, to her forehead, although the river flushed it pretty good."

"Sharp weapon, you say?"

"Edged, I would say, but big, and damned heavy, regarding the principal wound. It hit her hard. Maybe an axe. Or a machete, even. Of course, it might even have been something she hit when she was tossed—or when she dove—into the river, although at first blush I consider that diving hypothesis unlikely, given the multiple wounds. I'm just trying to keep an open mind to all possibilities until I do a thorough examination."

"Understood."

He nodded. "You might want to check upstream at any likely entry points, though. We'll know more from the autopsy."

"OK. Any idea when she was killed?"

Danvers sighed. He hates being pressed for information before he's finished with all his scopes, knives, and test tubes. "Well, I can't say for certain yet—need to do some lab work and a post-mortem, of course—but I've seen bodies pulled from rivers before. I'd bet, at this point, anyway, she went in last night, maybe yester-day afternoon at the outside. But not long ago, most likely last night. Can't say that definitively, though, until I examine her more closely."

"Of course." I nodded. Last night, or yesterday afternoon. Hell, she might have been killed while I was out playing SWAT or staring down the barrel of Tess Baldwin's pistol. She might have been dumped into Black Powder Creek while I was getting drunk and trying to keep two separate cases from tangling in my mind.

Jesus. It really did happen again.

I stared at the dead girl. I could see the potential, the life that she might have led, in her cold, sleeping face. I shuddered. All I could think of in that moment, all I could conjure into my brain, was an image of me gunning down the son of a bitch who had done this thing. This was not the way the universe was supposed to work.

If she had died yesterday or last night, it meant Van Heusen was off the hook. He had been locked up tight. It also might mean Ally Phelps had told us the truth.

I looked at Bob Dooman. He was impassive.

"The guitar man was in jail, so if she went in last night it wasn't him," I said. "But there still might be a connection, so I still want him checked out."

"Yes," Dooman said. He looked toward the road. "I think I see your detective from Columbus."

I followed his pointing finger and saw Shelly Beckworth trudging down the sloped cornfield. She must have busted the speed limit big-time.

"Yes, that's her." I seized the opportunity to get away from Dooman's good example of the stoic detective and trotted toward Shelly. A couple of vans belonging to the Ohio Bureau of Criminal Identification and Investigation fell into line and parked behind her Mazda, and a cadre of people emerged from the vans and started donning field gear.

I was huffing a bit from my jog when I got to her.

"Who is the black Adonis?" Her eyes were locked on Dooman. He was built like a linebacker, but preferred playing cello. Women tended to notice him.

"I thought you were gay?"

"I am, but, damn."

I marveled at Shelly's apparent ability to compartmentalize. She was upset about this development, too. I could see it in her face, but she was not letting it rule her. She was going to do her job.

I thought I had learned that skill, too. Maybe I hadn't.

"Is it her?" She looked at me with an expression that said she already knew.

"No official ID, of course, but it's her. I reached around my neck and tapped my shoulder. "Butterfly."

"Fuck." She took a few seconds to process that, then continued. "We got the phone forensics back, by the way."

"Anything useful?"

"No. She didn't take a single photo or text anyone during that party. Didn't arrange any meetups beforehand, didn't add any boys' names to her contacts, or girl names, either; didn't follow anyone new on social media, didn't call anywhere. Nothing useful at all."

"Shit."

We walked toward the river, and I filled her in on what we knew so far. Then I introduced her to Bob and Rick.

Shelly got right to business. "Anything more you can tell us, Doctor Danvers? For instance, did her head wound occur before she went into the water, or after?"

"Science takes time," Rick said, winking. "But I can tell you this. The crack in her head," and he paused to point at the horrible gash, "was more than sufficient to kill her."

Shelly nodded. "Any idea how long she has been in the water?"

Rick smirked. "I already told Ed, probably went in last night. Can't say for sure, though. I am good, but not that good." He picked up his iPad. "But not long. I will know more after a full autopsy, of course. I am thinking about buying a T-shirt that says that, by the way. 'I'll know more after a full autopsy.' I'd sell one to every coroner in the state."

"Probably," Shelly conceded. "We'll keep asking pesky questions anyway."

"I am sure you will. I'd like to assist the state lab, if possible." Rick had control freak tendencies.

"I don't object as long as Doctor Melville doesn't," Shelly said. "I have heard you are pretty good at this, so I will ask Doctor Melville myself. I know her pretty well."

Danvers seemed pleasantly surprised. "Thank you, Detective."

Shelly nodded. "I'll take all the help I can get. Any idea where she could have gone into the river?"

Bob pointed toward the bridge. "That would be the most convenient spot, but it could have been lots of places. River's up a bit, moving fast, she could have gone a long way before getting stuck in the roots. But if she indeed went in last night, then probably it was not too damned far from here."

While the coroner and detectives talked, I tried not to think about how pretty girls dying seemed to be a thing that happened all the goddamned time. I tried to ignore the part of my brain that said go buy some more bourbon and let someone better than me fix all this shit. I had not found Megan Beemer in time, but I could catch her killer. I could avenge her. I wasn't going to get drunk and run away this time.

I had work to do, and I needed to settle down and do it.

That's what I told myself, anyway. Another voice in my head laughed at that.

I stared at the body, trying to reconcile the pasty inanimate thing with the vibrant cheerleader from the photos in Shelly's file. I stared, hoping that somewhere among the pale flesh and red scratches and muddy swathes and horrid gashes we would find something that would point me in the right direction. Something that would lead me to her killer.

I knew I would not see such a clue. That was for dreams and fairy tales. But I imagined the eureka moment and envisioned myself sniffing along the trail that led to my fingers on the culprit's throat. My staring wasn't going to make that happen. But I knew the lab people would dig deep and find something. Microscopes, Petri dishes, tox screens, DNA. They'd find something.

The big question, though, was the amount of time that might take. State money is always tight, they say, and the labs are short-handed and overwhelmed. The killer might well vanish in the weeks those tests could take. The killer might get caught, eventually, but it might happen far from here, years from now. I wanted it to happen now. I wanted to be the one to crack it.

Shelly was trying to call her partner, and had wandered away in search of a better cell phone signal. Bob Dooman watched her walk away. "Mmmm . . ."

"Back down," I said, trying to make a show of how calm and cool I was. "You're married."

"I can still enjoy a good show," he said. "Don't matter where I get my appetite, long as I go home to eat."

"She's gay."

Bob laughed. "I don't care. I'm only looking, remember?"

He started wandering up toward the road. The brief levity had pulled me up from my mental swamp, at least for the moment. I wondered if Dooman had noticed my mood and tried to ease the tension on purpose.

I took one last glance back toward Megan Beemer, who was now tucked into a body bag. An EMS crew lifted the stretcher and began the long, slow trek up the slope toward the waiting ambulance.

I watched them all the way.

Then I walked over to talk to Jerry Coontz. Trumpower nodded. "I have his statement, Ed. I'll be on my way."

"Thanks." I knelt by Jerry. The lines on his face seemed deeper than usual, and his eyes were shut. "You OK, Jerry?"

He looked at me. "Who kills a girl, Ed? Who does that?"

"I won't know until we solve this one. But we'll solve it. You've made that easier, I want you to know that. The longer she stays in that river, the less evidence we get. Hell, maybe she even breaks free of the branches and flows on downstream, down to the Jacob Fork, on down to Erie, and we never find anything. Without you, that might have happened, but you saw her, and you are going to help bring the killer to justice. I want you to know that, OK?"

He nodded. "Yes. Good."

"Alright." I looked around. "You farm a lot of fields around here. Those across the river, near the bridge, are those yours, too?"

"Yeah. Don't own them, but I lease them and work them."

"Seen anyone hanging out, driving on the road late, stopping near the bridge, anything out of place in the last couple days?"

"No. Wish I had, but no. I told all that to Irwin."

"OK, Jerry. You remember anything, you give me a call, OK?"

"I sure will, Ed."

"Need a ride home? Don't want you finishing this field today, until we walk the corn rows and all that. I don't think we'll find anything here, because she probably went in somewhere else, but we've got to walk it just the same."

"Trump told me all that," Jerry said, flipping his John Deere cap back onto his head. "Told me he'd give me a ride, too."

"OK, then. Let's go."

Once Jerry was in Trumpower's cruiser, I strolled over to Shelly. "You and me will go see if we can find any sign of a girl being tossed from yonder bridge."

"OK. Let me get some lab people to follow us."

CHAPTER EIGHTEEN

Thursday, 8:42 a.m.

"WE'RE FUCKING FUCKED."

"Calm the fuck down, or fucking hang up."

"They fucking found her. They fucking found her. They fucking found her."

"I know."

"You said they wouldn't fucking find her. It's online, dude. On the news!"

"I know. Don't pay attention to the news. It's bad for you."

"They fucking found her."

"I know. Calm down."

"What the fuck are we gonna do?"

"Nothing. Fucking nothing. They can't pin her to us, man. They can't. We cleaned up, right? Remember? They ain't got shit. Just a dead girl. Bodies get dumped all the time. Could've been anyone, right? Drug dealers dump bodies. They'll figure drug dealers. So we do nothing. And we vouch for each other. Alibis, right?"

"Right."

"Stories are straight, right?"

"Right."

"So calm the fuck down."

"Right."

"OK. Stop the panic calls. Someone will hear you."

"Right."

"And don't freak out if a cop asks you questions."

"Oh, fuck."

"Don't freak out. Don't. They gotta ask questions. Doesn't mean they know anything, OK?"

"OK."

"Believe me?"

"Yeah."

"I'm serious. We're good."

"OK."

"Bye."

"Bye."

CHAPTER NINETEEN

THE SUN HID behind gray clouds as Shelly and I stood on the bridge that carried the two-lane highway across Black Powder Creek. Lab people wrapped in blue overalls fussed over the guardrail, the asphalt, the naked maple branches, and the roadside gravel. Shelly and I stood in the middle of the road, right on the yellow stripe. Deputies north and south of us were turning traffic away. Across the river to the north and east, the investigators were walking the corn rows and the bank, looking for clues.

Shelly did a slow spin. "Nothing to see from this spot but farmhouses, and those are not close. This would be a fantastic place to toss a body in the river. Dark night, I'm guessing not much traffic?"

"We are off, as they say, the beaten path," I answered. "Almost all local traffic on this stretch, very few mere passersby. Big highways pass us by completely."

She thought. Her tongue stuck out just a wee bit, touching her upper lip, and her eyes rolled skyward. "So, she goes to a party, meets up with someone, presumably a guy, leaves with him and ends up in this river."

"Possibly," I said. "And whatever happened, she was bound and beaten, maybe tortured, even. Who would torture her? And why?"

I tried to envision it. An empty stretch of road at night, with a nice long straight stretch of highway so you could see headlights from either direction. Very little traffic in the wee hours. Hell, very little traffic in the daytime. Fog tends to cloak the river here at night this time of year, too, providing extra cover. It had been foggy at my place last night, and probably had been so here, too. It had been foggy Saturday night and early Sunday morning, and the same went for Sunday night and Monday morning and every morning since she had vanished.

The only real danger to a killer dumping his victim here would be campers on the bank below, doing some fishing, or perhaps teenagers pulled off the road to do what teenagers do in parked cars in lonesome places. There were dirt paths on both sides of the bridge that people used to drive down to the bank for some fishing or drinking or whatever. But it would have been easy enough for a killer to confirm whether there was anyone around to inconvenience him before dumping his victim. From the bridge, the killer would be able to see any campfires or lanterns, or any vehicles.

Hell, with a little patience, someone could have emptied a truckload of corpses here, without worrying about witnesses.

One of the lab guys spoke through a white face mask. "Lot of people stop on this bridge?"

I sighed. "Well, not a lot. But people fish from this bridge sometimes. I've seen bicyclists stop here to take a piss or a photo of the river. I've seen tourists stop to take photos of the river, too. And people walk their dogs out this way."

"Thought so," the masked man said. "Lots of evidence of foot traffic, human and canine, but mostly old and mostly scuffs. We can get a few shoe prints, but not much else, and nothing definitive. No signs of struggle here, no blood, no tire marks."

While the lab guy had given that bleak assessment, I had wandered over to the guardrail. I stared down into the murky water. I imagined Megan Beemer's body going over the rail, into the water, drifting with the current until it got tangled in the branches of a leaning tree. I wished I had brought the rest of my bourbon.

"Shelly, come here."

She did.

"Look down there." I pointed at the field to the north, bordering the river. Dark streaks of furrows, in pairs, entwined with one another in the mud, like traces of a snake orgy.

"Four-wheelers?"

"Yes. Kids come here to fish, or to make out, or to camp and drink," I said. "And four-wheelers hit these fields just for fun as soon as the corn is out of them. Big, wide-open spaces, no one nearby to disturb, and loud, mud-churning ATV machines full of horsepower. It's the American way."

"I suppose just about everyone around here has a four-wheeler?"

"Yes, ma'am."

"That won't deter us from gathering tire prints, though."

"No, ma'am. And"—I pointed toward the trailer park—"Buzz has a couple of four-wheelers right up there."

Shelly talked to the lab guys while I pondered the terrain. Our prick guitar player could have brought the girl to Mifflin County, killed her, and dropped her body off this bridge. He had a motorcycle, though, and carrying a dead girl on a motorcycle isn't the easiest trick in the world. And if Rick was right, the girl had been dumped here while Van Heusen was in jail. Not even the Professor could kill girls while he was behind bars. I'd spent most of last night convincing myself of that.

Our rock band of local esteem, Soul Scraped, had been at that Columbus party, and they practiced just two miles from here. They could have driven ATVs from the trailer park straight across the empty field, without ever even going on the road. They could easily have carried the girl here and dumped her in the river under the shroud of fog and night.

Football stud Jeff Cotton had been at that party, too. I stared across the river. Brian Cotton's barn-turned-fortress was maybe three miles from here, up on Breakneck Hill and just off of Big Black Dog Road. They had four-wheelers up there, too. Jeff could have come down from that hill on an ATV, crossed Big Black Dog Road, and crossed the field to this spot. He also could have driven here in a truck, for that matter, and dumped her from the bridge.

Or someone else could have driven here from Columbus and dumped her.

Every damned farm in Mifflin County had one or two four-wheelers. We would examine tire prints, scan the ground down there for blood or hair or semen, and maybe at some point we'd match someone with a motive or opportunity to a tire print that we found in the mud by Black Powder Creek.

And maybe the fucker would resist arrest or put up a fight, and I'd get to break a damned jaw or shoot him in the head.

"Whoa, you OK?" Shelly punched me softly on the bicep.

"Yeah, why?"

"Your jaws were clamped pretty tight there, buddy. And you are making fists."

"Just something I do when I am thinking hard."

"OK," she said quietly. "Let's go talk to our kids and see if they remember a few things now better than they did before."

"Yep. Follow me to Tuck's—we'll leave a vehicle there and go check out the kids together. Figure out our approach that way. Sound good?"

"OK. Let's go."

CHAPTER TWENTY

Thursday, 12:30 p.m.

WE DID NOT make it to Tuck's.

"All units in area, possible OD, Jodyville Market. Repeat, possible OD, Jodyville Market."

Goddamned heroin. That shit was killing people all over Ohio. "Dee Two reporting, I am close. On my way." Trumpower's voice blared right after mine. "Unit Three, en route."

He was coming at the market from a different direction, but our roads converged on the town and he was so close I heard his siren fire up in the distance. I gunned my engine, and soon zipped past the trailer park. I looked for the Soul Scraped guys, and listened, too, but detected no sign of them.

I did hear Trumpower's siren power down, though. I rounded the corner and saw him. He had beaten me to the market.

I screeched the truck to a stop across the street from the store. Deputy Trumpower was already kneeling by someone prone on the sidewalk. I opened a tool chest in my truck bed. "Need more Narcan, Irwin?"

"Always do," he yelled. "Just used my last dose."

I grabbed my own supply. "Two doses here." We tended to run out of the stuff as fast as we could get it, as people all around us overdosed on pain pills or heroin. I ran across the road as Shelly parked behind my truck. "Shelly, got Narcan?"

She nodded and headed toward her trunk. In the distance, I heard an ambulance's sad wail. I hoped we could keep the person alive long enough for an ambulance to do us any good.

I knelt next to Trumpower, who was staring at his watch while checking the victim's pulse. I did not recognize the dark-haired teen boy lying on the sidewalk, but I recognized the blue lips, blue nails, and shallow breathing. I'd seen those symptoms way too many times. I pulled apart the eyelids of his left eye, and his pupil looked like a period at the end of a sentence. A death sentence.

The breaths came shallow, and labored, but they came. "Time for another dose, Irwin?"

"Yeah, been three minutes." The training said to wait three to five minutes, but it is hard to wait five minutes with someone dying in front of you. I ripped open a packet and handed the nasal injector to Trumpower. He bent toward the boy's nose.

Deputy Baxter was taking statements from the handful of people gathered at the scene. "Ought to just let him die," one man said.

That voice came from behind me. I stood and whirled. A chubby fellow of thirty or so with curly blond hair mashed beneath a John Deere cap stared back at me. "How much does that medicine cost me in taxes, just so this fucker can keep partying?"

Deputy Baxter saw my face and turned away, with a glance at me that said "you don't want this on my body cam, do you?"

I was precisely in the mood to not take this guy's shit. Before he could say another word, I had him against the market's big plate glass window. His head did not crack the glass, but not for lack of effort on my part.

"Ow! Let me go, cop! Jesus Christ!"

I strongly considered busting John Deere boy's lip. "I let you go, you keep right on going, you got me? You go and go and go until I don't see your sorry ass anymore, and you hope I never see it again. Got it?"

"Jesus!"

I slapped him. "We don't just let people die, you got me?" I shoved a bit harder, and my eyes were less than an inch from his. He looked like he was about to piss his pants. "You make me sick. Get the fuck out of here."

I spun him away from the window, and shoved. He fell on his ass, rolled as fast as he could onto his knees, and got up. Then he ran. Sort of. The John Deere cap got left behind.

People around me were holding up their phones, probably live-streaming my infraction to the world. I wondered whose side Twitter would take, the fuckhead's or mine.

Someone grabbed my arm. I figured it was Shelly, but when I turned, I saw Tuck.

"What the fuck, Ed?" He tried to say it quietly, but his voice was strained. Shelly stood behind Tuck, scowling at me. The ambulance rolled up just then, its wail making further talk impossible. The siren shut down, and the paramedics sprang from the vehicle and took over the medical chores.

We all stood around, taking turns staring at each other and watching the medics try to pull off another miracle. As they carted the victim away, one of them punched Irwin on the arm. "I think this one is gonna live—this time, anyway. Good job, Trump."

"Don't fucking call me that anymore," Irwin said. "It's Irwin, OK?"

The paramedic rolled his eyes.

We regrouped and decided Trumpower and Baxter could grab the witness statements so Shelly and I could get back to the murder investigation. Shelly looked as though she could not wait to speak to me in private, and Tuck glared at me from the crowd. The discussion among the bystanders seemed to have turned to whether I should be arrested, fired, or given a medal.

I headed toward my truck, but Tuck was on my heels.

"Ed, what is wrong with you?"

"Nothing."

"Bullshit!" He ran ahead and blocked my truck door. "The other day I watched you corral two guys fighting, one had a fucking knife, and you were all calm and zen and shit. In control. Dispassionate, you said. And now I just watched you try to shove an unarmed bystander through a goddamned window!"

"I'll shove harder next time, OK?"

Tuck shook his head. "Jesus, Ed."

"Yeah, Jesus, Ed." That was Shelly, behind me. "What the hell was that? You trying to lose your job? Get sued?"

I inhaled sharply and closed my eyes. "This is not a banner day, OK? I got a bit carried away."

"I'll say," Shelly said, while Tuck nodded.

"Half an hour." I turned to look at Shelly. "Give me half an hour, I'll collect myself, and we'll meet at Tuck's. Then, we will go see the band. OK?"

She stared at me, hard, and I thought for a moment she might slap me.

"Half an hour, then I will give you a chance to explain to me why I should not ask your sheriff for another partner."

"OK."

She returned to her Mazda. I turned toward my truck. Tuck was already walking toward his bar, shaking his head.

Scott Baxter trotted toward me. "Half the witnesses think you are full of shit, Ed, and half think you let that fucker off too easy."

"Sounds about right," I muttered.

"I'm between a rock and a mean pig, Ed."

I didn't try to figure out what Bax meant. "Huh?"

"I gotta report what I saw."

"Oh. Sure. I know. Do the right thing, Bax. It's your job, right?"

"I kind of wanted to punch the guy myself," he said, staring at the road. "But we ain't supposed to do that. He's got a right to express an opinion and all, right?"

"Yeah. Get your statements, Bax. File your report. Be honest. And it's all over the goddamned internet by now anyway. Just write the truth. Don't worry about me, OK?"

"OK."

I got in the truck, and wished to hell there was bourbon in the glove box.

CHAPTER TWENTY-ONE

Thursday, 1:35 p.m.

I STOPPED THE truck in the middle of a gravel road few people even knew about. I tried not to think about the partial bottle of whiskey back home on my picnic table, not very far away at all.

I closed my eyes, sought to control my breathing, tried to let the tension flow out of me, first from my clenched jaws, then from my knotted brow, then from my neck, from my arms, all the way down. I had a job to do. Someone had murdered Megan Beemer. My job was to discover who had done it.

I imagined finding the son of a bitch and shooting him dead.

I shook my head, popped a Doc Watson CD into the player, and started the truck.

As I turned onto a real road and headed to Tuck's, I tried to let Doc's perfect guitar work calm my mind.

It didn't.

The phone buzzed. It was Deputy Gavin.

"Ed, that Bannon guy is a grower. Had about five grand worth of pot all bundled up for sale. He's in a cell now. We'll need you to actually do that report."

It took me a moment to remember the guy who had showed up at the drunk hooker's trailer after she'd aimed a gun at my face. You'd think something like that would stick in your mind, but my mind was not exactly at peak performance.

"Fuck. OK. Yeah. Sorry. Lots going on. How about the woman?"

"Docs say she was very drunk, that's about it, based on early results. They kept her at the hospital, but they are probably going to release her in a few days. Your actual report, if you write it, might weigh into their decision. You planning to charge her?"

I closed my eyes tight. I did not want to deal with this. "No. She was defending herself from expected harm."

"She was drunk and aimed a gun at a cop."

"Give her a stern warning. She mentioned suicide, though. Tell them that. It'll be in my report. I'll get it done soon."

"Ed, I think—"

He was still talking when I ended the call.

CHAPTER TWENTY-TWO

Thursday, 4 p.m.

SHELLY STARED AT me. I had just spent a lot of time trying to explain the Marston case to her, and what it had done to me. We were in a dark corner booth at Tuck's, and she was trying to decide whether to kick me off the case.

"OK," she said, after a long pause. "That was horrible. I can see how that would stick with you."

"Yeah."

"But you have to be in control." She wasn't as cute when she scowled. "I mean it, Ed. What I saw today outside the store, that can't happen again."

"I know."

"I mean it."

"I know." I took a sip of coffee but maintained eye contact. I did not want to get shoved off of this case.

"I can find someone else to show me around, but . . ."

"But?"

"This is personal to you, Ed. I get that. You want to see it through. I get that. It means you are motivated, and so you are not just going to blow my case off, and I can appreciate that. I've had cops in other jurisdictions blow me off. So, two things."

"Name them."

"No more punchy."

"Got it."

"And I am in charge. It is my case. You are the help, not the boss."

"Got it."

Shelly took a long, slow drink of java, then set her mug down with some authority. "I am taking a chance, cowboy. Fuck it up, and I will make you regret it."

"Understood."

"Sheriff's probably going to take the decision out of my hands and suspend your ass anyway when he sees the reports from the heroin rescue. Or, you know, the internet."

"Yep."

"So I might as well get some work out of you anyway, while I still can."

"Thanks. I appreciate it."

"Don't fuck up."

CHAPTER TWENTY-THREE

Thursday, 5:35 p.m.

"THERE'S BUZZ." SHELLY pointed toward our skinny rock star, strolling on long legs across the trailer park gravel and gently rocking his shoulders and head from side to side. He looked like a scarecrow in the wind. The only touches of color on him were his pale face and the yellow scarf that kept his long hair from falling into that face. Everything else was black. There was no point in yelling at him, because he had earbuds in. Those were black, too.

We intercepted Buzz, and his face clouded when his chest ran into my hand. He popped the tiny speakers out of his ears. "What the fuck, law and order dude?"

"That girl we're looking for? We found her."

Shelly gave me a sidewise glance, silently reminding me I was supposed to keep my cool and let her lead. That was the price of staying on the case.

"Well, good," Buzz said. "But I don't know her and don't give a shit."

"We found her dead, Buzz."

He stared at us, his eyes darting between mine and Shelly's. "Well, that's sad," he finally said. "Still, only marginally interested here. I didn't know her."

"You sure?" I stepped toward him. "Rock star wannabe goes to the big city, plays a gig, drinks a little, lots of girls there, drinking too, everybody's partying and happy, you mixed it up with some girls, right?"

"Not her, though. I saw the picture, remember?"

"Weird though, Buzz, because now she's dead miles and miles from where she was last seen, but not very damned far at all from where you and the rest of your Deep Purple band practice your songs."

Buzz scoffed, indignant. "Deep Purple? How fucking old are you?"

Shelly glared at me and tried to keep the conversation from going any further off the rails. "Look, Buzz, you were there, she was there, and now she is dead, and we found her right down there." She pointed toward Black Powder Creek. "And we have a witness who claims to have seen the girl, near here, just the other day. So it is looking pretty bad for you, and I am going to highly recommend you lose the attitude right this second."

Buzz looked at his ratty shoes, then back toward the trailer he'd exited. "Jesus." He looked at Shelly. "Honest, I never seen her before."

Shelly wore a perfect poker face. "If you know anything, and I mean anything, you had better remember it right now. You might have seen something, or heard something, that would help us. It might not have seemed important to you at the time, it might even seem insignificant to you now, but a girl is dead and a family is grieving and we want to give them answers. And we want to find the person or persons responsible. She was killed, Buzz. Murdered. And if you know something and are keeping quiet to protect someone, you will be in deep, deep smelly shit when we find out. And we will find out."

Buzz's head was flinging back and forth and his eyes were on the ground. "I got nothing to do with it. Nothing. And I got enough people in this town thinking I'm Satan's fucking rented luggage boy as it is." His head came up, and his eyes were wet and blazing. "I don't need you bringing me this shit; I don't need you trying to tie me to it."

He ran a hand roughly through his thick black hair, as though he would tear it out, and knocked the yellow scarf to the ground. "Just fucking leave me out of this shit, OK?"

Shelly started to answer, but Buzz was off and running.

"Fuck," I said, spinning around and looking for Buzz's bandmates.

Shelly stepped in front of me, and she looked a bit pissed. "Do you think you could have eased into the accusations just a little bit slower there, Ed?"

"Excuse me?"

"You made it hostile right away, and his guard was up," she said. "If we'd gone a bit slower, a bit less rough, he might have talked more and told us something useful."

"I wanted to rattle him."

"You looked like you wanted to throttle him."

I stared at her. She was right. I had wanted to throttle him. "Fine. You do the interrogations."

"I will. Thanks. That's how it was supposed to be, remember? That's what you promised."

"Yeah. I just really want to nail this one."

"We will. But you gotta smarten up."

"OK."

"I mean it."

"Yes." I looked around. "I don't see our fucking drummer or bass player."

"We can track them down."

"Yeah. I know where we can find Jeff Cotton right now, though." I started strolling toward her car. "Football practice." I could see the glow of the football field lights in the distance.

"You think him before the bandmates?"

"His dad's fortress on Breakneck Hill isn't that far away from the recovery scene, either. And he was there at the party that night, too. Plus, we know right where he is right now."

"OK."

We drove to Hollis High in silence.

Jeff Cotton was easy to spot. He was the bulldozer shoving a big fullback ten yards in reverse before driving him into the turf. A chorus of cursing followed, and a coach rushed out to see if the ball carrier was OK. The runner got up on his own, waved the coach off, and then high-fived Jeff.

We stopped on the sideline next to the head coach, Doug Rimmel. "Coach, I am Detective Ed Runyon, Mifflin County Sheriff's Office. This is Detective Michelle Beckworth, Columbus Police Department. We need to talk to Jeff Cotton."

Rimmel spat a brown tobacco wad onto the grass. "We got a big game tomorrow night," he said quietly.

"We got a big murder to solve," I said.

Rimmel's gray eyes doubled in size, and his bald pate glistened with moisture I had not noticed a moment earlier. "The girl in the river?"

"We think Jeff can help us," Shelly said.

"Is he in trouble?"

"Don't know," Shelly said. "Maybe, maybe not. But he may know something that will help us in our investigation. We talked to him once, but we have some follow-up questions. And it can't wait."

"OK," Rimmel said reluctantly. He blew a whistle with a sound that cut the air like a laser. "Cotton! You're out! Brant, go in at middle linebacker. Hustle now! Slowpokes lose games!"

Jeff Cotton rushed to the sideline with impressive speed. Sweat soaked his jersey. He removed his helmet, and his hair was a wild jungle. But he wasn't breathing hard at all. "I wasn't trying to hurt Donnie, Coach."

"I know, I know," Rimmel said. "And he's a big boy, he can take a hit. Still, though, just tag him next time, OK? We need him as much as we need you."

"Yeah, Coach, OK."

"These cops hope you can help them out."

Jeff looked at us as though we were Jehovah's Witnesses walking toward his front door. "Yeah, sure."

"Everything OK?" Coach Rimmel looked at Jeff, looked at me, stared at Shelly, looked at Jeff again.

"Yeah, Coach, it's cool. I know what they want, it's cool."

"Fine, go talk to them, head to the showers. Brant could use some practice time anyway, and I know you are game ready."

"Thanks, Coach." Cotton headed toward the school building. Shelly and I caught up with him, me on his right, Shelly on his left. We all walked at an easy pace.

"Jeff, we found the girl we were looking for." Shelly said it very simply, without a hint of accusation.

"In the river, dead," Jeff said. "Yeah, it was all over Insta today. Look, I am sorry I kinda blew you guys off last time, OK?"

Shelly nodded. "Are you sure you don't recall seeing her, or talking to her, at that party?"

"I am very sure."

"Are you sure you went to that party alone?" I tried to keep accusation out of my voice. I am not sure I succeeded.

"Yeah, just me."

I grabbed his bicep. It was like grabbing a brick. Still, he stopped, and I looked him in the eye.

"We think there were other Hollis kids there that night. Did you see any, other than Buzz and his band?"

"No," Jeff said.

"We're going to find out who else was there," I said. "If we find out they hung out with you there, it's going to look really bad considering how we found that girl dead right here in Mifflin County and you've been lying to us."

"Whatever, cop," Jeff said. "I told you I went alone, I told you I didn't see any classmates there, I told you I didn't see this girl. I am sorry she is dead. That's a sad, bad thing. But I don't have anything to do with it and I don't know anything that'll help you out. If you will excuse me, I gotta go wash sweat and turf off my hide."

Cotton took off running at a pace neither Shelly nor I were eager to duplicate.

Shelly drew in a deep breath. "Well?"

"I'm wondering why Buzz didn't seem to know anything about the girl being found, while Jeff says it was all over the internet."

"I'm wondering about that, too."

I called dispatch and got Debbie. "Any noise complaints?"

"Um, yeah, that Jodyville band again. You psychic?"

"Yep. Reading your filthy mind right now."

"Fuck you, Ed. Oh, thanks for shoving that fatass at the heroin thing. He deserved it."

"Thanks."

"Victim is alive, I hear."

"Good."

"Sheriff's pissed."

"Not surprised."

It took only a few minutes to get to the trailer park. I had Willie Nelson singing "Red-Headed Stranger" in my head, sort of an inoculation against whatever shit Buzz and his friends might be playing when we arrived.

We rolled up, and heard Buzz screaming Rumpelstiltskin, or some damn thing, against a machine-gun rhythm of drums and bass, but with at least four chords this time. I jumped out of the Mazda, rounded the trailer, flashed my badge, and approached swiftly. They stopped. Shelly stood beside me as Buzz, Johnny Burke, and Gage Thomas stared at us. Buzz had replaced his yellow bandanna with a red one.

"Jesus," Buzz said. "You guys planning to just crawl up my ass and move in? What now?"

"Wanted to talk to Johnny and Gage, too," Shelly said, before I could make things more hostile, which I really wanted to do. Then I remembered who was in charge and clamped my mouth shut.

"It's a murder case, guys," Shelly continued. "Serious business. If you saw or heard anything that night she disappeared, we need to know."

"We were on the stage," Johnny said. "Bright-colored lights on us, all that. We couldn't even see the fucking audience."

"You took breaks, though, right? And mingled, and partied a little?" Shelly's tone and voice made it clear she knew there was no way such hot young guys didn't mix with the girls at their show, and Gage, at least, bought it.

"Well, yeah," he said, sheepishly. "I got some, and the other guys got some—"

"Gage—" Johnny glowered at him.

"But none of us got her, I swear," Gage Thomas finished. "I saw the picture, OK? You don't forget a girl like that. If I had seen her, I'd have tried to nail her."

"I would have nailed her," Burke said.

"And if I had nailed that, I would totally not forget," Gage added.

"Did you see any other Hollis kids there? Or local faces, for that matter, grown-ups, even?"

"No," Buzz said. "No," said Gage and Johnny, a split-second later.

"None at all?"

"I told you guys about Cotton. That's all I know. Look, lady, we were busy playing, you know?" Buzz spat. "We saw Jeff, we told you that. Heard some shouts in the crowd, go Big Green, shit like that, so there probably were other people from Hollis there, but we didn't see them."

"We'll find out if you are lying," I said.

"You'll make shit up if you have to," Buzz said. "Gotta pin it on someone, right?"

"You on Twitter, or Snapchat?"

Buzz looked at me as though I had asked him if he fucked puppies. "What?"

"I want to follow. I'm a fan."

Buzz stared at me. "Social media is for morons, the lowest common denominator, the lizard brain, the cesspool of so-called humanity." He spread his arms wide. "No, I am not on fucking Twitter, or fucking Snapchat, or fucking Facebook, or fucking Instagram. I am too goddamned smart for that shit."

"C'mon." I led Shelly away, while the band fired up some ungodly riff behind us.

"I am starting to hate this case," Shelly said.

"Welcome to the club."

Shelly aimed the Mazda toward Tuck's. "I got a thing tonight," she said. "Anyone else we can talk to before I head south?"

"No," I said. "I can see who else was there on my own and get back to you."

"OK," she said.

She dropped me off at the bar. "A little less Clint Eastwood tomorrow, OK?"

"I'll give that a try," I said. I turned toward the door and wondered if Tuck still had bourbon.

Linda put a beer in my hand as soon as I walked through the door.

"You stole my damned bourbon," I said.

"Yep," she said. "I like you better minus bourbon."

"Bitch," I said, taking a swig of the Commodore Perry.

"Come sit," she said. She led me to a corner table. Jay-Z was playing on the jukebox. I considered shooting the damned thing, but Tuck was trying to run a nice business and I had caused enough problems for one day.

Linda and I stared at each other across the small, square table.

"I am a grown-up," I said. "I get to decide what I drink, and how much."

She sighed. "Ed, when you first came here you were pretty damned messed up, remember? You never really told me about it, at least not all of it, but you told me enough, and I don't want to dredge shit up, but I know that missing girl case back then messed you up pretty bad. And here you are with a new missing girl case, and she's been found dead, too, and Tuck told me about the OD thing at the store ... and ... damn it, I am allowed to care about you. I don't want you going back where you were, mentally, when you came here."

"I am not going to."

"Good."

"I'm not."

"Good. Bourbon was your crutch back then, remember?"

I stared at her, but said nothing.

"Remember?"

"Yeah," I said.

"So I took it. Sue me. I care about you, mister."

I swigged the beer. "It's OK. I can get drunk on this."

She sighed. "Yeah, don't I know. But it won't be the same drunk, the depths-of-despair drunk, the Poe-on-a-bender drunk. Still, I think you should slow down on the IPA, too."

"You want to do all my thinking for me? That'll save me some time and fuss."

"Damn it, Ed." She fumbled around in her purse and took out a pack of cigarettes and a lighter.

"When did you take up those again?"

"Right after I decided I needed to steal your fucking bourbon," she said. She lit her cigarette and inhaled deeply.

I shrugged philosophically. "OK, so we all have our crutches."

"I guess," she said. "And you are going to have to realize I am a better crutch for you than bourbon."

"You are more fun than bourbon," I said, watching her drag on the cigarette.

"Goddamn it, Ed, I am not talking about being your little sex toy. I care about you, whether you realize it or not and whether you like it or not. You have people who care about you. I care. Tuck cares. Nancy cares—that's why she is always trying to drag you to church."

"I know."

She took another drag. "I know how it is. You want to live in a universe where pretty young girls don't end up dead. We all want that, but the rest of us can separate ourselves a bit from harsh reality. But you can't. Most of us, the rest of us who are not cops, that is, if we don't know the girl anyway, can read about the case in the paper, tear up a bit, feel sad, toss some thoughts and prayers out on Face-book, make a charitable donation or two, and then get on with life. But not you. You are in a job where you can't ignore the fact that bad things happen. You have to face it, head-on, and do something about it. And the realities of the universe collide with your image of how the universe ought to behave every fucking day."

"You been reading Buddhist scriptures?"

She smiled. "Yes, actually, and meditating every goddamned day. You should, too."

"Who has the time?" I drained my glass.

"Make time," she said. "But don't wallow. Don't beat yourself up because you can't make everything fucking perfect. OK? You do good work. You tilt the scales toward the side of justice. You make the world a slightly better place. But you can't make it a perfect place, OK? It ain't ever going to be perfect. We can only nudge it a little closer to perfect. That is the best any of us can do."

I raised my glass and waved at Tuck, realizing I had already surrendered to Linda's arguments and decided to bypass the bourbon. I looked into her eyes as I waited for my next beer. "I feel a lot of rage, Linda. A lot of rage."

"I know." She sipped her beer and lowered her eyes.

"I want to find whoever did this shit and tear them apart. I want to cut them, and shoot them, and break them, and . . ."

"I know."

"Who could do that? Who could take a girl like that, and . . . and . . ."

"I know."

"You don't know. You're like a fucking hippie angel or something," I said. "You don't know that kind of anger, that kind of rage. You don't picture yourself with a gun to their heads, drilling bullets into their brains, gutting them . . ."

"Hey . . ."

"Ripping them . . ."

"Hey . . ."

Tuck set the beers down, and I caught the brief meeting of glances between him and Linda. He wondered if he should take the beers away, and she told him no, though neither of them said a word.

"Baby, I know you hurt," Linda said, after Tuck headed back to the bar. "I know the world isn't what you think it should be, and I know you think you are supposed to be some kind of goddamned Superman . . ."

"Batman," I said.

She laughed. "Batman, then. But you don't have a Batcave, or an Alfred, or a Batmobile, or a Batplane, or a . . . a . . ."

"I get your point."

"You've got me. And you've got Tuck. And you've got to stop blaming yourself because bad things happen and you can't always stop them."

"OK."

"OK?"

"Yeah."

"Well then, drink up, me hearty, yo ho. I want to take you home and show you the beautiful side of life."

"I could use a little of that."

"Me, too." She tamped out the remainder of her cigarette. "Let's go embrace life and fuck hard, mister."

"You have a dirty mouth for a schoolteacher."

"Meh. You should hear my students."

CHAPTER TWENTY-FOUR

Friday, 8:30 a.m.

I BARELY ACKNOWLEDGED Debbie's hello on my way into the squad room the next morning. I did catch her look of concern.

Dooman caught me in the hall. "Your guitar man sells a lot of weed, on the record, and maybe harder stuff off. I have not found anyone who saw him with a blonde teenager that night. And forensics hasn't found anything to put her on that bike, dead or alive. Any other angle you want me to work?"

"Ask Detective Beckworth, OK? It is really her case."

"OK." His voice dropped to a whisper. "I hear you got a little rough yesterday."

"I was provoked."

"Not what I heard. And not what I saw online. Don't get provoked again."

"Got it."

"Good." He passed me and took a peek down Debbie's blouse on his way out. I turned toward the squad room, but Sheriff Daltry waved at me from his office door. "Ed."

I nodded and followed him in.

"You know I understand how it is out there," he said, trying to fake sympathy. "It is dangerous work, cops take a lot of crap, I know all that."

"Yes, sir."

"And if you need to blow off some steam now and then, well, hell, I did road patrol for quite a few years, back in the day. I know how it is. Hell, you had a drunk woman aim a gun at you. That's some stress, right there."

"Yes, sir."

His eyes narrowed. "But we do not blow off steam in a crowd. We do not blow off steam in front of witnesses. We do not blow off steam in front of a dozen people with cell phone cameras."

"Sheriff, that guy—"

"That guy is a taxpayer, and a voter. And from what I read in Baxter's report, he was just saying what a lot of other taxpayers and voters are saying, too."

"Jesus, Sheriff, if this is just about getting you elected again—"

"This is about you keeping your goddamned job, Ed. If I lose you, I don't know if the commissioners will let me replace you now, if ever. How we got two goddamned Democrats on the board I will never know."

"One of the Republican candidates bought a lot of porn," I said.

The sheriff glared at me. "Not proven."

"Voters seemed convinced."

"Fuck, Ed, just straighten up, OK? I have invested serious time in keeping Swammer—Jim Swammer, that's the guy you roughed up—from filing a lawsuit. Not sure I convinced him; time will tell. I told him you'd just left a murder scene and were all worked up. That seemed to cool him off a bit. He ain't a bad guy, Ed. Little girl like that gets killed, he can see how that would rattle you. So he might simmer down. He might not. But one thing is for damn sure—I have been ducking Farkas and reporter calls ever since you fucked up. I have told people that the videos they're seeing ain't telling the whole story, and if they saw all the footage it would show you were provoked. But I know there ain't more video that shows that. I'm just blowing smoke up their asses."

"I know."

"If that smoke don't calm them all down, I will not hesitate to kick you in the nuts and feed you to the wolves. Do you understand?"

"Yes, sir."

"Good. Jesus," he said, wiping his brow on his sleeve. "Remember last year, we played softball with those kids? That was the kind of internet I like, Ed. Not this roughhouse shit."

"Right."

"You hit a home run in that game."

"Yeah."

"No more roughhouse shit, and you don't say a goddamned word to the goddamned press. Now go catch bad guys."

"OK."

I got out of there as quickly as I could.

I was on my third cup of coffee, and my second text from Linda after ignoring a dozen voicemails from reporters, when my cell phone buzzed. It was Shelly. "We have some forensics action, Ed."

"Yeah?"

"Yeah," she said. "Helpful stuff, too, I think. One, not all her injuries were inflicted at the same time. Some are at least a day or two older."

"Huh." Had she been held captive and tortured?

"Two, she'd had sexual intercourse, and recently."

"Rape?"

"Not conclusive, no vaginal tearing or anything like that, but she had been bound, so . . . maybe rape. Probably rape."

"Jesus." I could feel my blood burning.

"Three, and this could be a break for us, she had some yellow fiber caught between her teeth, and strained muscles around her mouth and jaws. They think it was from something used to gag her."

"Fiber identified?"

"Not yet. This is pretty fresh, all preliminary. But they are working on that."

"Let's have them check that against forensics on Van Heusen's motorcycle."

"Yeah, they are on that. But," she said, "the coroner's prelim shows the time of death most likely Wednesday night. Van Heusen was in jail then. Did they find shit on his bike?"

"No, not really." I sighed. "He still could be connected, though. I don't know. Maybe he had help. Maybe he brought her down here and other guys took over, some shit like that."

"Maybe," she said.

"Just seems weird, a Columbus guitar picker and weed merchant up here in Jodyville at the same time a Columbus girl shows up here dead. Can't help trying to connect those dots. Meanwhile, you know the last time I saw yellow fiber?"

"Around Buzz's head."

"Fuck yeah. I am going to go grab the skinny bastard."

"We. We are going to go grab the skinny bastard. My case, remember? I am in the parking lot."

CHAPTER TWENTY-FIVE

Friday, 9:30 a.m.

WE SHOVED OUR way through a crowded hallway, then pulled an assistant principal and a couple of teachers from a writhing mess of legs and arms to find Ally Phelps trying to claw the eyes out of Buzz Norris.

Once we'd disentangled them, I had Buzz by the arms and Shelly had the Phelps girl against a wall. Buzz was still snarling and Ally was still wailing, and none of it was comprehensible. I put a little pressure on Buzz's elbow. "Be still, Buzz."

Shelly whispered something into Ally's ear, and the teen quieted down. There was nothing quiet about her eyes, though. They shot venom at Buzz.

"What is this about, Ally?" Shelly's voice was calm, and she glanced my way to see if I was likewise calm. I tried to look all Buddhistic, despite the gangly teen boy straining to free himself from my grasp.

"He . . . killed . . . that . . . girl!" Barely audible sobs filled the void between words.

"Like hell!" Buzz tried to twist away. I pushed his elbows closer together behind his back, as though I were using pruning shears. He winced, muttered "Jesus!" and his knees nearly failed him.

"Don't do that again," I said. "You will get your say. For now, settle down."

He did.

"You fucked her, and you killed her!"

"Ally," Shelly said, "we'll talk about this. Be quiet for now."

"He—"

"Quiet."

Ally settled down.

"We are going to take both of you to the S.O. and talk this out, OK?" Shelly made it sound like a negotiation. I thought we had enough to drag Buzz in right now, whether he wanted it or not, but it was Shelly's case, and she was playing it cool.

"OK," Ally said. "Drag it out of him."

"Do I have a choice?" Buzz spoke through clenched teeth.

I leaned toward his ear. "What do you think the right choice is, Buzz?"

"I'll go."

"Good."

He stood still. I let go of his arms and called for a couple of squad cars, one for him and one for her. I took Buzz into the principal's office while Shelly kept Ally busy somewhere else. Principal Reed waved students back to classrooms. He looked as though someone had peed on his cat.

While we waited, I scanned Buzz's pockets. No yellow scarf or bandana. "You want a jacket or something? It is chilly out. We can go to your locker."

"I'm fine."

"You sure?"

"Yes."

Fine, I thought. *We'll get a warrant. We'll check your locker, and your trailer, and your car. We'll find your yellow headband, and we'll have the science guys do a little fiber analysis. And if we get a match, I just might break your fucking arms.*

"Why does Ally think you killed Megan Beemer?"

"I want a lawyer."

"We haven't arrested you."

"I want a lawyer."

He stubbornly maintained that position until Deputy Trumpower came to give him a ride. I paused when I saw Shelly, Ally, and Deputy Erskin Holloway emerge from the auditorium. Holloway was staring at Ally's ass. I flicked his ear and shook my head. I do not really like Deputy Holloway much.

Shelly handed me her keys. "I am going to ride with Ally. You drive my car, OK?"

"Sure."

CHAPTER TWENTY-SIX

Friday, 11:42 a.m.

BACK AT THE sheriff's office, Shelly arranged for separate interrogation rooms while I filed search warrant requests. I listed all sorts of stuff on the warrant—drugs, weapons, girls' clothing, makeup, any and all items that might be connected to that warehouse party—and I listed vehicles that might have hauled instruments and amps to the gig, a truck Gage's brother owned, and cars that Buzz and Johnny drove. The warrant included checking the ATV tires for matches against the tracks and mud we found by Black Powder Creek. What we wanted most, though, was a yellow headband. Any yellow fabric, really. Anything connected to Buzz that we could give the lab team, to compare to the fibers caught in Megan Beemer's teeth.

I envisioned the girl, straining, biting at the cloth that silenced her, then envisioned myself pounding the shit out of Buzz. I was still envisioning that when Shelly walked in. "They are set. Let's do the girl first." She paused and stared at me. "You are clenching your jaws again."

"Am I?"

"Yes, Detective. You've got to relax; this anger is not healthy."

"I'm just processing it, that's all. I'm fine." I punched Buzz one more time in my daydreams, and wiped the blood from his face on his black T-shirt. Then I tried being a professional. "Warrant request is filed; Dooman will handle that end of it."

"Great. Let's go." She did not look enthusiastic, despite her words. I made a mental note to bury my rage. I did not want her going to the sheriff and getting me kicked off this case.

Ally Phelps was drinking a Diet Coke and tugging on her Supergirl T-shirt to better hide her boobs. Shelly plopped a recorder onto the table, turned it on, and stated the girl's name, her name, my name, the location, the date and the time.

"Ally, you really think Buzz killed that girl, Megan Beemer?"

"Yes."

"Why?"

"They were there, at the party where she vanished, right? And now she's here, and she's dead, right down the road. And she's just the type of pretty bitch who . . . I mean, sorry, she's . . . she's dead . . . I shouldn't call her a bitch, right? But she is . . . was . . . she was so pretty. And Buzz likes the pretty ones. I'm not pretty enough, but she . . ."

"You told Buzz what you suspected." Shelly talked quietly, without judgment.

"I told him I knew he killed her."

"How did he respond?"

"He called me an ignorant, boring whore. Said I was making shit up because I was jealous."

I could not help myself. I jumped in. "Ally, do you have any evidence, any reason, other than the fact that Buzz and this girl attended the same party and she was found here, any other reason at all, to suspect Buzz killed Megan Beemer?"

She glared at me.

"Anything?" I glared back. "Anything solid?"

Her eyes leaked, and she shook her head.

"Are you sure?"

She nodded.

"OK." I looked at Shelly. Shelly nodded. I got up and left. I called Bob Dooman for a progress report on the search warrants.

A few minutes later, Shelly met me by the coffeepot. "She is on her way home. Not with that Holloway pervert."

"Good."

Shelly poured a cup. "So, what do you think?"

"I think Miss Phelps left out a very pertinent, relevant, and damning detail, and I am wondering why."

"You noticed that, too, huh?"

I got myself a cup of coffee. "Yeah. Pressed for evidence against Buzz, she seemed to completely forget about her report to us earlier."

Shelly nodded. "So, you think she lied about seeing Megan."

"I do." We started walking down the hall. "Her story about seeing the girl seemed out of whack, anyway. Like she was describing the girl she thought Megan was, rather than a girl she'd actually seen."

"Yeah, true."

"I think it is possible that Ally saw the news about Megan's disappearance on Facebook, connected some dots, and convinced herself that the boy who used to woo her had found himself a pretty blonde in Columbus."

"Maybe," Shelly said. "Maybe. Doesn't rule Buzz out, though. Or his friends."

"No, it doesn't," I answered, "and there's that yellow fiber from Megan's mouth."

Shelly sighed. "Right. So everybody's still in play as a suspect. Heard from Dooman?"

"Yeah, just a minute ago. They found a lot of scarves and bandanas and shit in Buzz's car, and at his trailer, including four yellow ones. Those are headed to the lab now."

Shelly sipped her java and looked at me after we sat at my desk. "Let's hope we get a match. Did they find anything else? Pot? Drugs? Signed note confessing to the murder of Megan Beemer?"

"Nope. But they are still searching. Maybe we'll get lucky."

"Damn."

I shared her disappointment. A stash of weed or a gun or suspected stolen goods would have given us a solid reason to hold Buzz while the lab did its magic. But all we really had was some yellow cloth and the testimony of a not-so-trustworthy teen girl.

"Jesus," I said, almost knocking over my coffee cup as I placed it on my desk.

"What?"

"Shelly . . . add another suspect to our list. Ally Phelps."

She shook her head and grinned. "No, Ed. No."

"Think about it, just a second, OK? Remember your Shakespeare, a woman scorned and all that."

"Ed, I looked her up after we talked to her before. She doesn't even drive. We can't place her at the party scene."

I nodded. "Yeah, I looked her up, too. But she doesn't have to drive, does she? Maybe she has girlfriends who drive, or a new guy or something."

She considered this while sipping coffee, and I could almost hear the gears in her head. "I remain skeptical. Lay it out for me."

I waved a finger like a conductor as I thought out loud. "Let's say Buzz went to the gig in Columbus, met the girl, and brought her back home."

"OK."

"Then Ally gets wind of this. Maybe someone tells her, maybe she goes to see Buzz and catches him with Megan, or whatever."

"Well," Shelly said, "I've seen shit like that, but Ally is a munchkin. I don't see her beating the hell out of Megan who was bigger, older, and more athletic."

"Ally and some girlfriends, maybe," I said.

"Ally seems a bit reclusive by nature, if I'm any judge," Shelly said, "but we haven't looked into her friends or anything."

"Or boyfriends," I added. "Maybe she got some guy to do her bidding."

"I think this all sounds melodramatic," she said. Then she sighed. "It's an avenue we can pursue, though."

"Agreed."

My phone buzzed. It was Dooman. I listened for a minute then said, "Thanks." I paused dramatically and stared at Shelly. "We have a match on tire prints. Two four-wheelers behind Buzz's trailer match tracks we found below the bridge."

"That is something solid to go on." Shelly put her mug down. "Next interview."

"Hell, yeah. Let's go talk to the genius behind the hit song 'Turd Blossom,' shall we?"

"Let me do the talking."

"Don't worry," I said. "I am not going to beat the shit out of the little fuck until I am sure we have the right little fuck."

She glared at me.

"I kid. I'm a kidder. A little levity."

CHAPTER TWENTY-SEVEN

Friday, 12:30 p.m.

DETECTIVE BECKWORTH STARED across the table at Buzz, after going through the whole recording machine mantra. Buzz stared at the ceiling, then at the table surface, then at the coffee stain on the wall. Some people claimed it looked like Alfred Hitchcock. I thought it resembled Gozer the Gozerian, but other cops usually looked at me funny whenever I said that. Buzz did not express an opinion.

"Did you kill Megan Beemer?" Shelly's eyes locked onto Buzz's, like she could see between the atoms of his brain to find the truth.

"No." Buzz did not divert his gaze. It was a staring contest between him and Shelly. I watched for quivering lips and shaking hands, but saw neither. Of course, the Professor had been icy cool when we dragged him in for killing Briana Marston back in New York. You can't always tell a killer by sight, even when you are putting the squeeze on him.

"Why did Ally think you killed the Columbus girl?" Shelly kept her voice even, pitched low.

"I don't know."

"Louder, for the recorder, Buzz."

"I don't know! Jesus, am I under arrest, lady?"

"No."

"Because it feels like I am under arrest. You guys think Ally is right! I want a lawyer."

"You are not under arrest," Shelly said. "Yet, anyway. But Ally Phelps made a very serious accusation, and we need to check it out."

"That bitch, that little turncoat bitch!"

"Why do you say turncoat?"

"I want a lawyer."

"You are not under arrest, Buzz, and you said you wanted a chance to talk."

"I said I wanted a lawyer, you made all nice and everything and I said I'd talk, and now I am not so sure I should have agreed to that, so I want a lawyer, a fucking lawyer, and I am shutting up until I get one!"

"How often do you ride your four-wheeler down by the creek?"

He looked as though a light bulb should be floating above his head. "Oh. Oh, Jesus. Fuck. You think, you must think, holy shit."

I'd rattled him, and I wanted to keep it up. "Think what, Buzz?"

"We ride down there all the time! So do other people! Just because you found tracks . . ."

"Who said we found tracks?"

He snarled. "If you didn't find tracks you are too fucking dumb to be a cop. She was found downstream, right? You think she went in there at the bridge. Everyone knows you searched at the bridge. Of course, you found fucking tracks. Jesus! I want a lawyer."

Shelly nodded at me, and we got up and left the interrogation room.

"You pressed him harder than you should have. Once he started talking about a lawyer . . ."

"Yeah, whatever."

"What do you think?" she asked. "Hold him or not?"

"I would love to know about the yellow fibers before we make that call, but lab work is slow." I scratched my head. "And he actually is right about the tire tracks. Kids are down there all the time. We don't have a conclusive age on the tracks we found, Bob said. Could have been there before she went in."

"OK." Shelly shrugged.

"Tell you what, let's release him. You drive him home. Take your time. I'll set up a tail on him, see what he does when he thinks we aren't looking."

"Not a bad idea," she said. "You set that up, and I will give our boy the 'don't leave town' speech."

We parted company. My phone buzzed about thirty seconds later. It was Buzz's mom. She was livid. "You arrested my son?"

"No, ma'am. We talked to him."

"You dragged him out of school! And you have cops going through the trailer, and his car, and . . . Jesus. Is it drugs? Is he on drugs?"

"No, ma'am. There was an altercation, between Buzz and a girl. We talked to both of them and right now we're arranging a ride home for Buzz. Unless you want to come pick him up? I would like to ask you some questions anyway."

"Take him home. I have to work." She hung up.

I stopped in the men's room, my mind chugging on the operation Shelly and I were planning. Deputy Baxter was in there, regaling a couple of other deputies with a tale that had him animated. ". . . and it was just fucking parked on the far side of the hill, not two miles away from Green's fence. Couldn't see it from the road, and it was in among the trees and shit. Miller had his own gear surrounding it, too, had it hid pretty good, but it was right there, and he confessed to the whole thing—he had been wheeling and dealing, trying to sell it in pieces."

"Pieces?" One of the fellows gasped. "Be a shame to tear that tractor up."

"But stupid to sell it whole," Bax said. "Get caught for sure. In pieces, though, it might work like a spanked dog. Lots of guys out there restoring antique tractors, looking for parts."

"Good job, Bax," said one of the guys, slapping him on the shoulder. "Right smart of you."

"Thanks!" Baxter looked up and noticed me. "Ed! Make me a detective, bud! I found that tractor!"

"I don't give—"

"I just asked myself how would I steal it if I wanted to steal it and bam! I had the whole turkey dinner right there. I figured it could not have gone far, right? Antique tractor like that, people would notice—most folks around here have seen it in the parades and at the fair and such. Very easy to recognize. So you couldn't drive it away, not far. You'd need a big flatbed, you'd need to cover it up, just too complicated, right? And the window of opportunity to steal it was pretty small—thing vanished after Mr. Green went to town that morning, was gone when he came back. Had to be a quick job, in broad daylight."

I stepped to the urinal. "Bax, I don't—"

Bax was too excited to notice my mood, so excited he started repeating himself. "You'd need to have your flatbed all ready to go at exactly the right time, and that's just too much clockwork right there. That was the key, Ed. Lots of folks around here know that tractor, a '59 Allis-Chalmers—I mean, it's highly recognizable among the farmers, and pretty well known to most around here. That thing travels any distance on the road around here, someone is likely to notice. And getting it up on a flatbed? That's a fairly big operation there. Seemed weird the thief would have all the gear and tarps he needed at just the right time when opportunity struck, don't you think?"

I didn't think. I finished, zipped, flushed, and went to wash my hands. I was trying to get back on track with my own case, so I missed a few words from Baxter's excited retelling. The other guys stood around, apparently eager to hear it all again. Bax was talking fast.

"So I thought, maybe someone just drove it out of there, but not too far," Bax said. "Green's place is way out there anyway, not many witnesses if you stayed close, so I went and looked at the barn where he kept it. Then I climbed his hill, Gobbler's Knob there, and looked around and I thought where would I drive that tractor from here if I was going to hide it close? And not in my own barn, right? Because that would just suck if I got caught with a stolen antique tractor in my own barn. People looking for a stolen tractor would search a barn, wouldn't they? And I saw Miller Hill, not two miles from there by road and shorter if you go over land, and there's a grove of trees down there on the other side of that hill, and I thought how easy it would be to just notice Mr. Green heading to town and just come right over and get that tractor and take it home . . ."

The audience approved. "Good thinking, Bax. Sheriff happy?"

"Hell yes, he's happy," Bax said. "Mr. Green, too, and me, too! How about you, Ed? You happy?"

I shut the water off and spun on him. "Jesus Christ, Bax! I do not give two shits about Mr. Green's fucking tractor or about your big case. Fuck!"

I left. The room was silent behind me.

Four steps down the hall, I heard a voice behind me. "That was uncalled for, Runyon."

I couldn't tell which deputy had spoken, and I didn't turn around to look.

"Yeah, I know. I'll try to care later."

CHAPTER TWENTY-EIGHT

Friday, 1:35 p.m.

"So, Ed, you gonna tell me what this is all about?"

Charlie Watkins and I were wearing Mifflin County road crew overalls striped with reflective yellow tape. We had hard hats and shovels, and stood shielded behind a county road crew truck parked across from the trailer park. We were digging a hole that did not really need to be dug, but we had a vantage from which I could watch anyone leaving or entering Buzz's trailer, by the front or the back.

"Can't say much, Charlie. Just doing a stakeout, and my truck would be recognized. No good reason for a guy in a truck to just sit here, anyway. So I called you. I really appreciate the help."

"I appreciate the fifty bucks."

We dug our unnecessary hole and drank diet pop. After a while, Shelly's Mazda approached from the direction of town. I watched from beneath the visor on my helmet. Buzz paid no more attention to a couple of guys doing manual labor than any other teenager would have.

I watched Buzz get out of Shelly's car and walk briskly into the trailer. I heard the metal screen door slam, and the trailer shook a bit.

"Boy seems pissed," Charlie said as Shelly turned her car around.

"Yeah."

"He kill that girl from Columbus?"

"Can't really say, Charlie." I was beginning to think I should have come alone. Charlie had been reluctant to lend me the truck, though, because "I am responsible for it, Ed, and what if you get in a goddamned chase or something?" After a bit of haggling, in which Charlie somehow ended up helping with a "real police stakeout," we'd come up with this plan. He and I would set up shop, and his wife would come get him after a while and he'd leave me with the truck. I decided if I ever chose to go this route again, I would just commandeer the fucking truck.

We pretended to dig as a couple of hours passed. No one came or went, and it seemed Buzz had the trailer to himself. His mom was a waitress at a bar in a town called Fiddles, and Trumpower had popped in out of uniform for a beer, at my request. He had called and confirmed mom was there and was scheduled to work all night, and that I was missing out on hot wings and good beer.

"I don't think he's going anywhere, Charlie," I said.

Charlie looked vaguely disappointed. "OK. Wife's driving up, anyway."

"I will drop the truck and overalls off at the garage tonight, or tomorrow morning."

"OK."

I hefted a pair of binoculars out of the truck. "I appreciate it, Charlie."

"OK, Ed. Have a good night."

"Yep. Thanks again."

I headed toward the trees nearby, and Charlie headed home.

Hours passed. I peed twice. In the distance, I could hear the barely audible loudspeaker and the occasional cheers from Big

Green's football game. I wondered if hard-hitting Jeff Cotton had put any opponents in the hospital. That stirred a memory of Megan Beemer's injuries, and that made me wonder if I was trailing the wrong guy.

Or the wrong girl. Where was Ally Phelps tonight?

Eventually, porch lights ignited throughout the trailer park, and I kept my binoculars pointed at Buzz's trailer. I really wanted to know what he was doing in that trailer. I'd half expected him to bolt, but that hadn't happened. Was he in there destroying evidence, something we'd missed in our search? Was he talking to friends to get stories straight?

What the hell, I decided. *Go have a look.*

I doffed the overalls, despite the chill. I did not need those reflectors flashing in porch lights or headlights. I kept low and headed slowly toward the trailer. I dashed across the road, then crept toward a window.

I listened, rather than peeking in. I could hear a TV or a stereo or something. After five minutes of this, I risked a quick glance.

Buzz was watching porn and doing what teenage boys do when they watch porn.

I snuck away, regretting my choice of careers, and headed back to grab the overalls.

I watched a long time. Buzz never came out.

I got in the truck and called Shelly.

"Anything?" She sounded hopeful.

"No, just him watching an orgy on the DVR and jerking off."

"Well," she said. "That's no help. We'll talk tomorrow."

I hung up and started to dial the S.O. but called Linda instead.

"How are you tonight?"

"I don't know," she said. "How are you?"

CHAPTER TWENTY-NINE

Saturday, 8:49 a.m.

"So, have I lost my charms?"

"No." I squinted in the morning sunlight and kissed her. The kiss felt forced.

"Because you seemed pretty preoccupied. And tense. And you still do."

"I'm sorry." Linda was right. I'd called her to see if she could tell me who Ally Phelps hung out with, but Linda had other plans. She had been loving and attentive, and I'd been . . . somewhere else. Going through the motions, as they say. "It's this case. I thought we were onto something. Possibly. Didn't pan out. Then I had another idea, and now that seems stupid, too. Has me sort of fucked up."

She nodded, and locked her eyes on mine, like she was drilling into my mind. "Anything I can do to help?"

"You helped plenty last night." I kissed her again, then rolled out of bed and stepped to the counter to make coffee. I wished I had a bigger place, so the kitchen would be farther from the bed, but the distance was not great and Linda could keep right on talking.

"I mean talk, or listen," she said.

"I know. Really. I am fine."

"You could try counseling again, you know."

"Jesus."

"I am not trying to piss you off."

"I know. I do. But I am fine. I am going to make coffee. And I am going to go to work and do justice and all that stuff and catch the bad guy and everything will be right in the world again. Does Ally Phelps have a boyfriend? Or girlfriends who might help her out?"

Linda's eyes widened. "Ally? She keeps to herself most of the time. I think she prefers Skype or Discord to actual human presence. I know she accused Buzz, and she's wrong about that, by the way, but—"

"I'm not sure she's wrong about that."

"But," Linda said again, her emphasis showing her annoyance at me for interrupting, "I don't think she has a new guy, or any real close friends. Please tell me you do not think she is involved in this."

"I don't know. Maybe involved, maybe not. Cops just have to ask a lot of questions."

Linda glanced at the clock. "Shit, no time for coffee. I am supposed to help set up an art fair today." She started hurrying into her clothes. "I will run home, change clothes, and grab a cup at McDonald's."

"My coffee's better."

"Everyone's coffee is better, but theirs is done." She dropped her bra on the bed and winked. "I'll come back for this later." The flirtation seemed a bit forced. No doubt it was.

"Please do," I said, glad to be done with the counseling talk.

I stood, steaming coffee in hand, and watched her drive up the lane. It was chilly, but not too much so, and mist still clung to the pond. I retrieved my battered Martin guitar from the trailer and headed down to the stump. I sat, placed my cup in the nice little hollow in the ground that always kept it from tipping over, and slowly strummed a G chord. A red-tailed hawk, feathers puffed up, listened from a naked branch across the water.

A few random key changes later, and I was playing "Blue Eyes Crying in the Rain." Then I saw a pair of dead, blue eyes staring up from the mud and muck of my mind and threw the guitar aside. It tumbled with a discordant noise, sort of like "Turd Blossom."

"Goddamn it," I growled, with no one to hear me but the hawk. He seemed unimpressed.

All I'd wanted was a few minutes of peace, with no one trying to drag my feelings out of me or order me to shove them deeper inside. Just a little cool air, pond mist, a hawk's occasional cry, and my guitar. Too much to ask, I guessed.

I reached for the coffee, and realized I'd kicked it over. I got up, picked up the guitar, and found I had snapped off a tuning peg. I squared up like Babe Ruth and swung the damned thing at a sycamore. Broken strings lashed my face, shards flew, and my own wretched scream tore through the fog. The hawk took flight, swooped low, and vanished behind the trees.

I knelt. I tried to remember the coping techniques I'd learned. Focus on breathing, just breathing. I was breathing pretty goddamned hard. I tried to notice my thoughts and just let them go. The first thought was wondering if I could have done something to find Megan Beemer faster. The next thought was that this was all my fault, that I should have not let myself be distracted by SWAT calls and drunk hookers with guns. I knew none of those things had been avoidable, but I blamed myself anyway.

Depression is a lying bitch.

And the third thought? My hands, tight on the killer's neck, my nails digging into flesh until blood welled up, the faceless head bobbing left and right, back and forth, slowly spinning, popping into the air.

Eventually, my breathing settled. I wiped away snot and tears, stepped over the guitar shards, and headed back to the trailer.

I could not save Megan Beemer. But I could find whoever had killed her. And if things got ugly after that?

Fuck it. I'm only human.

CHAPTER THIRTY

Saturday, 10:36 a.m.

THE PHONE VIBRATED. I swallowed the rest of my sausage sandwich and answered. "Runyon."

"It's Shelly. Where are you?"

"Pumping gas into my truck and eating bad food. Where are you?"

"You aren't supposed to use your phone while you pump gas."

"I will issue a warrant for my arrest. Where are you?"

"At the S.O. You didn't answer earlier."

I glanced at my phone. It was 10:37 a.m. I had missed a couple of calls and messages while trying to get my act together. "Sorry. What's going on?"

"I have news about the yellow fibers."

I replaced the gas hose. "Really? On a Saturday?"

"Yeah. Lab guys put a rush on things for me. We got some info."

"Matches something from Buzz?"

"No."

"Van Heusen's motorcycle?"

"No. But it matches something in an FBI database. The fiber comes from a flag, manufactured by Banner Flag Emporium Store."

"That's the most redundant goddamned thing I have heard in a month."

"Yeah, well. That's what they call it. Based in Illinois, some town I can't fucking pronounce."

I replaced my gas cap. "Shit, Shelly. You know where we saw a lot of yellow goddamned flags."

"Yep. With coiled snakes on them. And we saw a lot of steel plate on a barn. And guns. And a big fucking dog. Anyway, my partner is on the phone with the flag company right now, trying to see if we can confirm a purchase by your redneck cop haters."

"Shit. We need to talk about this."

"That's why I am at the S.O. and calling you instead of relaxing with my lady love. Get here quick. I have a warrant rolling already."

"On my way."

I climbed into the truck, but someone knocked on my window before I could start it up. It was Nancy.

I rolled down the window. "What?"

"Well," she said, clearly taken aback. "I was going to ask you if you'd changed your mind about church tomorrow. I invited you the other day, remember? Reading the papers, thought maybe this was a bad week for you. You could use some church. Emmy brought me down here for coffee across the way, and I saw you over here, and . . . well, sorry I bothered you."

She turned to go, walking pretty well for an eighty-year-old.

"Nancy, I'm sorry."

She waved a hand in the air without looking back, and kept going.

"Fuck," I said, turning the key. Stepping on the gas pedal, I rolled into traffic. I would make amends to Nancy later, I told myself. And to Bax. For now, I would forget church—all theology is amateur theology, anyway—and go catch a killer.

On the way, I pondered the best approach. That armored barn on Breakneck Hill was a powder keg waiting to go off. Should we go in quiet and peaceful, and hope for the best? Or mobilize SWAT, the National Guard, a couple of helicopters, and fucking James Bond?

However we went in, though, I saw it ending one way. I saw myself staring into Jeff Cotton's eyes and watching him die.

And yes, damn it, I knew I was not supposed to be thinking this way. I was doing it anyway. Megan Beemer was in my head. Briana Marston was in there, too. Both of them glared at me, blaming me, telling me to fucking make amends.

Amends can get bloody.

The star linebacker was younger than me.

Faster.

Stronger.

I was going to have to cheat.

CHAPTER THIRTY-ONE

Saturday, 10:45 a.m.

"Runyon!"

Sheriff Daltry stood in the hall. He did not look too pleased.

"Yes, Sheriff?"

"That girl has got a warrant, and she is talking about running up Breakneck Hill to arrest Brian Cotton's boy. I told her to slow the fuck down, but I do not believe she took me seriously. She needs to calm the fuck down!"

"I am going to talk to her now."

He inhaled deeply. "I called Jim Bowman—he's already here with a couple of his gung-ho boys. Him and them SWAT guys and the damned girl cop are in the conference room."

"You called Bowman?" Daltry hated Bowman, because Daltry wanted to run SWAT himself, but the commissioners and every mayor in the county had insisted on Jim Bowman.

"Hell, yes, I called Bowman. I don't want this going bad, and I want him under my thumb before that girl has every SWAT officer in Ohio up on Breakneck Hill. Hopefully, Jim will do what he always does and talk for three hours, give her a chance to calm the fuck down. Jesus God. You sure we are on the right track here, Ed? Brian and his crowd, they are noisy, but they are true patriots. Good people, Ed. Good American people. I don't want this turning into some goddamned, some goddamned . . . what's the word?"

"Fiasco?"

"Yeah, that. I don't want a fiasco. I think the risks of something going wrong up there are high, so we had better not poke that god-damned bear unless we really, really have to. Especially seeing as how I know those people up there, good people, and I don't think Jeff is your guy. I really don't."

"We've got good probable cause, Sheriff." I told him about the flag evidence. "And Jeff was at the same party as the girl. And lives not too far from where she was dumped. How do you feel about coincidences like that?"

"Hell, lots of them flags been sold since Obama got elected, and they kept selling after he was out," Daltry said. "Don't prove nothing."

"It's enough of a connection, along with the rest, to talk to Jeff Cotton, and search those grounds."

He stared at me as though he hoped I would come up with some counterargument for why we should not search the Cotton farm. I did not give him one.

"Well, then," he said after a pause. "Brian Cotton is a good man and a friend of mine." Daltry kept his voice low by chewing on ev-ery word. "But he ain't gonna put up with much government intru-sion, you know? If we go up there all half-assed, waving guns and shit . . ."

"I know," I said, trying to look calm and reassuring, but I honestly felt like running up there waving guns and shit. "It is a delicate situ-ation. I have an idea for how to approach it, without a lot of shit blowing up."

"You do?" He looked relieved. "God damn, Ed, I thought I was the only one with any sense. That girl seems ready to just bring in the goddamned National Guard; and you know Bowman. He just loves to show off his goddamned SWAT team."

I did know Bowman, and I was not too worried about him going off half-cocked.

"I don't want a gun battle up there anymore than you, Sheriff. Honest. And neither does Jim."

Bowman stepped into the hall from the conference room. His hawk beak of a nose was pointed up at a forty-five-degree angle, and his arms were crossed in a way that made it seem like he was posing for an official portrait. "Ed? John? We're talking about busting up a fortress to catch a murderer. You might want to get your asses in here." He returned to the conference room before Daltry could bark back. The sheriff and I hustled to join the discussion.

It was almost like the Situation Room depicted on *The West Wing*. Several cops sitting around a conference table, most with iPads or laptops open in front of them. A large flat-screen computer monitor on the wall, with a Google Earth aerial image of the Cotton farm on Breakneck Hill and a cursor dancing to Captain Bowman's touch on an iPad. A separate mounted screen showed Megan Beemer's face, Jeff Cotton's face, and a list of weapons believed to be in the armored barn. It was a long list, and I was willing to bet it was too conservative.

Shelly held up her phone. "Got me a text right here from my partner. Flag company did not want to talk, but when they found out about the girl, well, they talked. They confirmed Brian Cotton is a regular customer of their store."

"A lot of people buy those flags," Daltry said. "Hell, I have two of them myself."

"Flag fibers in the girl's mouth, and flags on Cotton's barn, and Cotton's boy was at the party where she disappeared," Shelly said. "That math adds up."

Daltry huffed. "This is my county."

Shelly nodded. "Yes, and we're all going to work on this together." It sounded very diplomatic, but her eyes said she thought Daltry should get over himself.

Bowman continued. His finger swirled around on his iPad screen, and the cursor looped rapidly around the Cotton barn on the map on the wall.

"We don't know who is at the farm now, and it will be difficult to ascertain," the captain said. "Thirteen men and two women in his little group. There is nothing much out there, as you can see, and no good way to park a car or set up an observation post and see who comes and goes without being seen ourselves. The only thing out there to watch would be Cotton's barn, so any attempt at surveillance is just going to tip them off. If we're out there, they will know it's because we are watching them."

"I agree," I said, drawing a glance from Bowman. He continued before I could say any more. "And they are all bloody well convinced we are going to come in with guns blazing one of these days, anyway. So if we decide we have to go in—and Sheriff Daltry, it is your jurisdiction and your call, entirely—but if we have to go in, I have asked the state patrol to do a flyover." Bowman raised his eyebrows. "With me so far?"

We all nodded, with the exception of Daltry, and Bowman went on. "Just one pass. Any more would look suspicious and probably raise some hackles, but we'll get a look at how many vehicles are there, maybe see anyone out on the grounds and such. We'll shoot photos and videos as we pass, and we will analyze the snot out of those. Compare what the patrol sees to this map and see if anything new has been built up there since Google added this image. The chopper will head on over to the highway like it is doing routine traffic control. If we don't move in too quick, we might not spook them too much. Hell, if we are lucky, it'll just be Brian and his kid there."

"We could use a drone for surveillance, Cap'n." That came from Zach Turner, a fairly new guy from Ambletown PD. Turner was on SWAT because he'd served as a soldier in Afghanistan, and Bowman knew the guy would not panic in a tight spot. "That's what we have drones for, right?"

"You know what happens if a drone buzzes that armored barn, Zach?" Bowman shook his head slowly. "Cotton sees it, goes ballistic, his guns chew up our drone, and you owe me for the lost gear. No, we have to be sneaky. These aren't a bunch of dumbass meth heads. Cotton and his friends probably watch for spy drones all the time. Hell, they probably see them when they ain't there. But a plane or a copter flying over, well that happens from time to time and it could be for any number of reasons. They'll be suspicious, because that's what they are, but a single pass won't be something they've never seen. They'll most likely just jot it down in their notes and complain on Facebook that we are spying on them. But we've never sent a drone up there. That would spook them good, I think. By the way, they don't announce their meetings on Facebook. Already checked. Too paranoid, I guess."

"Jesus Christ," Daltry said. "Are we seriously talking about a raid up there on Breakneck Hill, Jim? Or are you just trying to convince us you could do it?"

"It's my job to know how to crack that nut if we ever have to," Bowman said. "And I do my job, so yes, I can crack that nut if I have to. But it is your call, Sheriff. One hundred percent your call. And if we don't have to crack that nut, well, I am more than fine with that."

Daltry inhaled sharply. "I am glad you recognize that. I think it would be a goddamned, uh, well, a fiasco if your cowboys just raided that place. We'd have a lot of blood on our hands."

"Captain, I agree," I said. "A quiet approach is best. I don't think we should go in all at once, even after the surveillance."

"Amen," Shelly said, drawing a glare from Daltry because women weren't supposed to talk at meetings. If Shelly saw Daltry's dirty look, she ignored it.

"Go on," Bowman said, nodding at her. "It is your case. But that is one dangerous place up there, and if we have to go in, it's my job to figure out how best to do it. But if we don't have to go in, well . . . that's best."

"I know," Shelly answered. "Detective Runyon and I went up there and talked to Brian Cotton. We talked with his son, Jeff, as well, in connection with this case. So we know they might be a bit wary."

"A bit wary is their normal state, Detective Beckworth." Bowman took a sip of coffee. "This won't be normal. They will be ready to shoot."

"Maybe not," I said. "I know the guy—a bit, anyway. I believe Brian Cotton will talk to me, as long as we're not raiding his farm, and I think I know a better way to broach it, anyway. I just think if we go in like fucking Desert Storm, we're going to have some serious carnage."

"So who goes up?"

"Ed and me, Captain. Just the two of us." Shelly's look of determination belonged in a picture, beside the dictionary definition of *determination*.

"Oh, hell no," Bowman growled. "If it goes bad, you'll be a pair of sacrificial lambs."

"That's on us," Shelly said quickly. "And I think it is worth the risk. You can have the cavalry standing by to come rushing in to save us."

Bowman looked skeptical. "Sheriff?"

Daltry slapped the table. "I sure as fuck do not want a bunch of people shot up on fucking Breakneck Hill. I sure as fuck don't. But I can afford to lose Runyon."

I think he meant that as a joke.

"I said there might be a better way, everyone." I spread my hands. "Consider this. We have enough, in my opinion, to bring Jeff in for questioning. He's maybe got a girlfriend, he's got football practice, so he gets away from the barn sometimes. I say we lie in wait for him somewhere, grab him away from his dad's powder keg armored barn, and bring him in for questioning. His dad will be pissed, but his dad will have to come to us if he wants to express his displeasure. We can be ready if he brings an arsenal, or friends, which I don't think he will, but you never know. But let's not go up there on the hill at all if we don't have to."

Heads were nodding, so I kept going. "Once we do that, we can confront Jeff with what we know, see if he cracks, talk to his dad off-site, maybe convince him the best way to clear his kid's name is to let us go up there and search, but have that discussion away from all his goddamned weapons, hell, even hold him on some bullshit charge if we have to, but we escalate slowly, away from the farm, get things under control and then go up and look the place over."

"His buddies might hole up there if they think we are fucking with Brian and Jeff," Bowman said. "Could be a shitstorm no matter what."

"Could be," I agreed. "But it could also be that if we have Jeff in custody, maybe Brian decides to cooperate. At least we get a chance to build up to it, rather than just showing up with a warrant and a bunch of cops in riot gear. Because that would be one hell of a firefight."

Bowman nodded. "What do you think, Sheriff?"

"I think I like it a whole lot more than having SWAT storm up that hill," Daltry growled.

"Well then," Bowman said. "Let's do it that way. If Detective Beckworth concurs?"

"I concur," she said. "I like this plan."

And that, ladies and gentlemen, is how I, the guy who wanted to pull Jeff Cotton's guts out through his navel if he killed Megan Beemer, calmed down all the detatched, dispassionate professionals around me. Believe me, it surprised me more than anybody.

Bowman continued. "And my team can spend time going over details in case we eventually have to hit the place. We can also be on standby close at hand when the actual arrest is made, wherever that may be." He moved the cursor around on the aerial image. "If we ever do have to go in, here's the scenario. We can stage in a couple places at a distance, the Baptist church here, this field here. We stage there. Quietly. A couple guys at a time, unmarked cars, gather and suit up in Burl Chater's barn. Forest camo. Then they go through the woods, very quiet . . ."

"Ninja style," Shelly said, and Captain Bowman smiled at her.

"Ninja style," he said.

"You have been planning this for a while, haven't you?"

"Yes, Shelly, I have." The captain grinned. "Like I said, it's my job."

"Do we have to hear your whole goddamn plan?" Daltry was seething again. "Ed's plan will make this all a moot point, anyway."

"Maybe, maybe not," Bowman said. "My guys are going to be ready for anything, regardless. I assure you of that."

"Well, then," I said. "Let's talk about arresting Jeff Cotton, first. I like the idea of having the cavalry close by when we do that."

"Sure, Ed," Bowman said. "Any idea what he's up to today?"

"I'm checking his social now," Shelly said, tapping away at her phone. "Big Green won last night . . ." She looked up as a couple of guys cheered quietly. "Jeff had pizza after the game . . . Jesus, five sacks?"

"Five sacks of pizza?" That got laughs. I did not see who said it.

"Five QB sacks in the game—Jeff was on fire," Shelly said, then resumed scrolling through Jeff's Facebook. "Here we go. Looks like Jeff has a date tonight."

"Good," I said. "We can catch him en route."

We spent several more minutes hashing out details. Sheriff Daltry leaned toward me. "I am counting on your powers of persuasion, Ed, to keep everything calm once we nab Jeff. A shoot-up involving a bunch of decent God-fearing men ain't anything we need. The boy might be a shit, maybe, anyway, but his daddy is a good man."

"I will do my best, Sheriff." But I was thinking that if Jeff Cotton was our perp, I wanted five minutes alone with him. I really, really did.

The meeting broke up, and everyone scurried off to their assigned roles. I headed to the restroom and checked my phone. Linda had called. Twice.

I called her back. "Hey," I said, trying to sound all casual.

"Your landlord called me, Ed."

"I am paid up."

"He found your goddamned guitar, all smashed to shit."

"So I will clean it up."

I heard her exasperated, nervous laugh. "That is not even anywhere near the fucking point, Ed. What the fuck is wrong with you?"

"I dropped it. It is just a guitar," I said.

"You dropped it all over the goddamned place! And your dad, your dad, Ed, gave you that guitar! You love that guitar!"

"Can we do this later? I have a bad guy to arrest."

"Is that why Bowman is at the S.O.? And a bunch of other cops?"

"Jesus, are you spying on me?"

"I called Debbie when you did not answer."

"Jesus." I laughed, but it sounded bitter even to me. "It's like a network of conspirators. Or a coven."

"Let the other guys do this, Ed. Please. You stay out of it. You are not in a good place."

"This is my job, Linda."

"There are a lot of cops, Ed, and they aren't all . . ."

I counted silently to five. "Aren't all what?"

"They aren't all looking to kill someone because they blame themselves for a girl's death in New York. That's not justice!"

"I have to go," I said. "It'll be fine."

"No, it—"

I ended the call. I had work to do.

CHAPTER THIRTY-TWO

Saturday, 4:30 p.m.

I SAT IN my truck, a mile beyond the Cotton farm on Big Black Dog Road. I was parked off the road and in a copse, out of sight, waiting for Jeff Cotton to roll by. Shelly sat beside me, scrolling through Facebook and Instagram on her phone.

We were not too far from where we'd pulled the girl out of Black Powder Creek. That's where my mind was at the moment. In a cornfield, by a muddy riverbank, staring at a dead girl with a Monarch butterfly tattooed on her shoulder.

Jeff's date lived out on Buggy Road. This was the quickest way for him to get there from the fortress on Breakneck Hill, so we expected Jeff would roll by soon. Our hiding place was good, our plan was good, but Jeff was taking his sweet time. In the meantime, Shelly was searching the social media accounts, searching for more clues.

Johnny Cash was singing through my truck stereo. Shelly pretended not to notice, and I had the volume pretty low as a professional courtesy.

"I'm still thinking Buzz," Shelly said between songs, and I turned the volume down a bit more.

"Yeah?"

"Yeah," she said. "Just a gut feeling."

"Maybe. We'll see. But we did not connect Buzz to the yellow fibers."

"Yeah," she said. "Maybe there is some connection between Buzz and Jeff? Maybe they were in on it together? Not finding much online, though, except that Jeff and his friends really like Soul Scraped's music."

"We should lock Jeff up for that," I said.

"And yet you make me listen to twangy shit." Shelly sighed. "What do you think of Bowman's preparations for this?"

"What, you think it's a little over the top?"

She shrugged. "Maybe."

"Look, if it all goes according to plan that's great," I said, "but a lot of shit could go wrong. God knows how Jeff's dad and his buddies are going to react when we bust Jeff. I think Bowman is right to have everyone on the ready. If it all just turns out to be a SWAT training day, great, but if it all blows up . . ."

"I guess," Shelly said. "It all makes me a little nervous."

She went back to her phone, and I eyed the road, watching for our suspect.

Johnny was halfway through "Folsom Prison Blues" when Jeff Cotton drove past, one hand on his steering wheel and the other holding a phone to his head. I punched off the music and had the mic in my hand and the truck rolling before Jeff's truck was out of sight around the bend. "Dee Two to station. Target is rolling. Repeat, target is rolling."

Debbie's voice answered: "Roger, Dee Two. Backup headed your way."

I followed Jeff Cotton while listening to Debbie talk to Trumpower. He was not far away, and once we heard him say he was turning onto Buggy Road, I rolled down the window and placed the flashing light on top of my truck. "Irwin is coming from the opposite way," I told Shelly. "We've got this son of a bitch in pincers."

"He hasn't spotted your lights yet," Shelly said. "Oh, fuck, wait . . . yep, he's spotted them."

Ahead of us, Jeff Cotton hit the gas. His white Chevy pickup growled and vanished over a rise. Shelly grabbed the mic. "Rabbit is running! Repeat, rabbit is running!"

I accelerated and concentrated on making the curves without hitting roadside oaks.

"I am in place, blocking the road," Trumpower said. "He ought to be in my sights before long."

We passed the field where we'd found Megan Beemer. I hoped her ghost was watching, and would see us drag her killer down.

Jeff Cotton was driving way too fast, and I began to fear that he'd wrap his fucking truck around a tree before I got a chance to wrap his spine around his own leg. My F-150 was hard pressed to keep up, but I floored it and did my best. Shelly, beside me, muttered the names of several saints with machine-gun rapidity and placed her hands on the dash to brace herself.

I imagined Jeff topping a rise, spotting Irwin's truck, and braking so hard he might leave ditches in the road. But the football player called an audible.

Jeff Cotton's Chevy veered off the road through an opening between guardrails. His truck plunged into an idle field overgrown with every weed Audubon ever catalogued. The truck rolled downhill, toward the oaks and maples and sycamores that lined Black Powder Creek.

"What the fuck is this motherfucking fuck doing?" Shelly's voice quavered, because my truck was bucking like a goddamned bronc as I followed Jeff Cotton off the road.

"He's bolting!" I steered around a big-ass rock. "Maybe thinks he can run on foot at the creek!"

"That's stupid!" Shelly closed her eyes as my truck scraped a large rock. I fought to gain control, and once I did, I yelled back.

"Yes, it's stupid! How smart did you think he is?"

But I began to wonder if it really was stupid when my truck bogged down in a low point, while Jeff's stopped a hundred yards away at the line of trees that bordered the creek. I smacked the steering wheel. "Son of a bitch!"

By the time I got my truck freed from the grass and mud, Jeff Cotton was running from his own truck. And he carried a little surprise.

"Jesus," I said.

"Fuck," Shelly replied.

Jeff carried a weapon, and just as he vanished into the trees, I recognized it. As a SWAT officer, I train for this shit, so I was certain.

Jeff had an AR-15.

"Damn, he's going to put up a fight," I said.

"We should call for backup," Shelly answered.

"We've got SWAT all over the place. You let them know," I said, aiming my truck for the gap in the trees where I had last seen Jeff Cotton.

Shelly was still talking into the mic when I braked hard, slammed the gear shift into park, and jumped out of my truck. I had my gun in my hand before Shelly jumped out, too.

A thunderous drumroll echoed in the woods, and my windshield shattered as sparks flew across the hood of my truck. I dove hard to my left and heard Shelly grunt on the other side of my vehicle.

Little geysers of dirt and gravel flew into the air around me as Jeff Cotton kept firing.

I rolled behind an oak that I wished had been about two feet wider as the big gun ripped bark from it. The tree's outer layers ripped open like a zipper, exposing white wood underneath. Sawdust sprinkled my face, but that beat the shit out of bullets.

The salvo paused. I risked a peek. I saw Jeff Cotton aim again.

"Duck, Shelly!" I kept my head down as bullets chewed up my truck.

A sudden silence took over.

"I'm hit!" Even yelling, she seemed calm. "Not bad, though!"

"OK. Calling the cavalry!" I pulled my radio from my jacket pocket and hit the SWAT channel. "Mayday," I said.

"Yeah, we heard," Captain Bowman answered. "We're go."

SWAT had been standing by, with a state patrol chopper over the highway mimicking a traffic air patrol and officers in unmarked cars at various points around the area. The sheriff had argued it was unnecessary, but Bowman had pointed out that Jeff had access to high-powered weapons. Daltry had relented.

I acknowledged Bowman and signed off just as gunfire sounded from the woods. The tree I hid behind threw bark everywhere.

I decided to move, rolling downhill and finding a bigger tree to hide behind. I ate a few weeds in the process, but I needed to see Shelly, to assure myself that she was OK.

Once behind cover again, I stole a glance. She was behind a rock. She had ripped her T-shirt and was using the fabric to bind her right thigh. A good deal of blood stained her jeans. Her tongue was hanging out as she concentrated, and her fingers moved swiftly and steadily. She caught my glance and winked. She yelled: "You like the bare midriff, don't you?" She waved a hand over her belly, exposed by her torn shirt.

"I do," I hollered. "Even on a lesbian." I knew she was trying to make light of her injury, and I had just enough awareness left to try to help her do that. But what I really wanted to do was gun down Jeff Cotton.

His bolting act had convinced me. This was our killer.

"I am OK, Ed. I mean it."

She sounded calm. I believed her.

I took a peek into the woods, but saw no sign of Jeff Cotton. "I think he moved on," I said. "I am going after him!"

"What? Fuck no!"

"I'm doing it."

"No, you wait on backup!"

"Backup is already rolling in. I'm going to get him."

I turned the radio volume all the way down. I didn't need Jeff hearing a squawk or beep once I got to the woods.

Then I rose, aimed my gun, and rushed forward.

"You goddamned reckless shit!" Shelly gave me some covering fire, but I was not sure what she aimed at. Jeff was nowhere to be seen. It wouldn't really matter, though, if the shots made him keep his head down.

I reached the bank, crouched by a maple, and peered at the creek. A brown cloud of mud flowed past me, and I spotted a deep print left by a boot on the bank. I listened for a splash and heard one. Jeff Cotton was wading upstream.

I headed that way, but stayed on the bank, working my way around the trees and foliage. It was slower than I liked, but it avoided loud splashing in the water, and I needed to hear Jeff's movements. It was the only way I had any idea where he was.

I didn't want him to know where I was, either. Maybe he would not know I was on his heels. Maybe he would think I had stayed with my truck. Maybe he would be so focused on moving forward, he wouldn't look back.

These are the kinds of things cops tell themselves when they are moving toward a guy with a gun full of ammo it can spit out all at once.

I wondered what had broken Jeff. He'd been pretty calm in our previous encounters. Now he was running for his life, and apparently ready to take out a few cops on the way.

I stopped to listen for a moment. I could hear Jeff splashing in the creek. He seemed to have slowed down, maybe looking for cover, maybe searching for pursuit, maybe aiming at me this very goddamned moment. I focused, tried to control my breath, and looked ahead. Jeff Cotton was there, climbing out of the creek on the opposite bank. One hand held his AR-15, while the other grasped a young maple.

The wump-wump of a helicopter grew gradually louder. The cavalry was coming.

Jeff reached the top of the bank way sooner than I thought possible, and I knew there was mostly level farmland beyond the trees on the other side.

I could not see beyond the foliage on the far bank to determine whether there was corn standing in that field or not, but it didn't matter much. Once he reached that field, Jeff would quickly be beyond my reach. He was faster than me, and far more agile, so I needed to slow him down.

I raised my pistol and fired three shots. I chopped some branches, and scared the living shit out of a squirrel, but did not hit Jeff. I am a pretty good shot, but hitting a distant moving target in the woods with a pistol isn't a very easy thing to do.

It was a desperate, stupid thing to do. Not the kind of thing a calm, dispassionate cop would do. But I was hardly that at the moment.

I didn't have a prayer of hitting him, but I had gotten his attention, though. Jeff leapt over a root, did an impressive cut, and then dove behind a fallen tree.

I figured this would be the best chance I had to close the gap, so I jumped into Black Powder Creek. The water was thigh-deep here, but clear enough to see the bottom. I ran, to the extent that I could, heedless of making noise because speed was all that mattered now. I ignored the cold. If Jeff could take it, so could I.

Refraction fooled my eyes, and I stumbled on the rocky riverbed. I did a headlong splash as the helicopter whirled overhead and two of Jeff's bullets kicked up water near my left hand.

I staggered toward the far bank, surprised my own blood wasn't streaming into the creek, and hoping the water had not fouled my weapon. I climbed out of the creek, using a big oak for cover, and shook water out of my gun barrel.

Jeff got up and ran, not across the open field, where corn had been harvested recently, but east along the creek bank. He was sticking to cover now that the chopper was circling overhead. I shot a glance upward. The chopper was bucking in the wind a bit.

I ran to close the gap. Both of us were zigging between trees and leaping thorny brush like we were eluding tacklers on a football field. South of me, I saw flashing lights on the road as SWAT guys roared in. I knew the same thing was going on to the north as well, though I couldn't see it from where I was.

I should have been listening on the radio. I should have been feeding information to the surrounding team members. I should have been helping them zero in on Jeff Cotton.

But I was not doing that. I wanted to catch this son of a bitch myself. Violent images filled my head.

Jeff stopped, whirled around, and opened fire. It was a burst of three that missed me by a good three feet, because Jeff just shot without looking.

I dove behind a rock, not quite big enough to be called a boulder, and realized I was lucky to be alive.

"We need to talk, Jeff!"

Down the slope below me, Jeff Cotton peeked from behind his cover, an ancient fallen oak. "Fuck you, cop!"

"I have a warrant to bring you in for questioning. Just questioning, it says, but you've complicated the shit out of things here, Jeff." I thought I sounded a lot calmer than I really was, but I did not have time to pat myself on the back.

Jeff answered with two more bursts of bullets, some of which ricocheted off my precious rock.

I had fifteen rounds left in my gun. Jeff certainly had a whole lot more than that.

"Fuck you, man!" He punctuated that with another round of gunfire. "Fuck you!"

"Why'd you kill her, Jeff?" I fired two shots, then rushed to crouch behind a tree when he ducked. I moved pretty fast. Adrenaline can do that.

We were maybe twenty yards apart now.

I had thirteen rounds to go.

"I didn't kill anyone, man! You got it wrong!"

"Drop the gun and you can explain it to me."

"You are gonna set me up," he said, sobbing. "It's a setup!" Jeff was low to the ground behind his tree, but I could see his gun, the barrel now pointing skyward. I thought for a moment he was going to shoot at the helicopter. I glanced up and saw a rifle aimed at Jeff from above.

Jeff was crying louder. "I didn't kill anyone! Not anyone!"

I rose, stepped forward slowly, gun at the ready, my eyes locked on the tip of his rifle. I was ready to dive if it moved, or shoot him if I saw the least bit of him.

"You can't win here, Jeff. No way. You are surrounded by now, plenty of cops with plenty of guns. I don't care what your dad has taught you, this is not a fight you can win. Let's just talk, Jeff. You will get a fair shake." An image of Megan Beemer's corpse filled my head, then Briana Marston's, and I suddenly hoped Jeff would make a dumb move.

"I didn't kill her!" He was sobbing harder now. The gun lifted, slightly, then the barrel dropped behind the tree he used for cover. "I didn't!"

My eyes went back and forth, between the spot where the end of his gun barrel had vanished and the spot where I thought his face would emerge if he decided to fight. I saw that face in my mind, and imagined my bullets turning it into pulp. Megan and Briana cheered me on.

But he stayed behind the tree.

I heard men crashing through the woods from several directions. They were moving fast, no doubt having a clear picture of the tactical situation thanks to the eyes in the sky, but with no help from me.

"We can do this peacefully, Jeff. Drop the gun. Come out with hands up. We can go talk."

I did not want to talk. I wanted him to lift the gun, to emerge from cover, to open fire and fully justify my killing him. I wanted that very, very, very much.

"You can't blame me for that girl's death! That ain't justice!"

His gun rose. So did he.

He started to aim the rifle.

I aimed for his chest.

Gunfire exploded from the sky.

I heard Linda in my head. "*That's not justice!*"

Jeff's gun erupted. Bullets whizzed by my head.

I shifted my aim to his knee. His fucking knee. I returned fire.

My bullets, three of them, ripped into his right leg.

Bullets from the sky, a staccato triple burst, slammed Jeff in the shoulder.

Jeff's gun dropped from his hand, and he spun like a wobbly top. He fell, clutching his shattered knee as blood burst through his fingers.

I rushed forward, and stood on his gun, my pistol aimed at his head. Ten rounds left.

The chopper held its place above, wobbling in the wind and the sniper peering down at me, the luckiest son of a bitch alive. Lucky, because I should have been really fucking dead.

Jeff Cotton was lucky, too, because I really wanted to shoot him in the face. He was writhing, bleeding heavily from the knee and less heavily from the shoulder wound, a shallow cut. It had been a difficult, hurried shot, aimed from a moving vehicle in the air at a moving suspect on the ground. I was sure the man up there—Ty Parker, a damned good shooter—had aimed at Jeff's head. Jeff should have been really fucking dead, too.

But here we were, Jeff and I, neither of us dead, and me aiming a gun at his face.

It wasn't the witnesses in the chopper above or those emerging from the woods that kept me from pulling the trigger. It wasn't any sense of right or wrong.

It was Linda.

I kept seeing Linda's face, and hearing her words. *"That isn't justice!"*

Was it mere coincidence that made Jeff's words mirror hers in that crucial moment? Or was some God trying to keep me from leaping into the abyss I'd been peering into?

I had no goddamned idea. I only knew that I'd really wanted to kill this fucking kid, and that I could have, and should have, because he was sure as hell trying to kill me . . . and yet I hadn't.

I'd stared into the abyss, but I had not jumped in.

"Fuck! It hurts!" Jeff clutched his knee. My shots had shattered some bone. His lower leg seemed to be attached to the thigh at the correct angle, though. He ignored the shoulder completely.

"You will live," I said. "Goddamn it, but you will live. You have the right to remain silent . . ."

I heard footsteps in the woods behind me. "Under control, Ed?" It was Irwin Trumpower.

I was still aiming my pistol at Jeff Cotton's face. Ten rounds left. But, yeah. Under control. "Yeah. We're good."

I stepped off of Jeff's gun. Trumpower took it up. Irwin stared at Jeff's busted knee and wondered why it wasn't a busted sternum. Training said I should have killed the kid who was trying to kill me, instead of trying a low percentage shot like going for his knee. Hell, he could have killed me ten times after I shot up his leg, if he hadn't dropped his rifle.

I didn't answer the questions I saw in Trumpower's eyes.

"That Columbus cop," Trumpower said. "She's going to be OK. Tore up her clothes, made a bandage. She's tough."

"Good," I said. "Yeah, she's tough."

"You OK, Ed?"

"Yeah," I answered.

I was not OK. I wanted to shoot this bastard who had killed a girl. But I could not do that, after all.

But at least it was over.

CHAPTER THIRTY-THREE

Saturday, 8:33 p.m.

BACK AT THE S.O. I had showered to wash away the muck and thorns and blood from the events at Black Powder Creek. I had a fresh shirt and undies from my locker, even a pair of tennis shoes, but a road guy had to lend me some jeans. They were a bit too wide in the gut for me, but they were clean and dry.

I stared at myself in the mirror, poked at a fresh scratch on my cheek and decided it was not going to start bleeding again, then asked myself whether I had screwed up by letting Jeff Cotton live.

I knew the answer, of course. Cops are supposed to take suspects in alive if possible. Judges and juries decide which suspects deserve death. All that math changes, though, when a suspect points a gun at you. A cop is allowed to defend himself, and his brother and sister officers. The way to do that is to shoot to kill.

I had shot at the kid's knees, and I was struggling to figure out why.

The problem was, of course, that I still wanted to kill Jeff Cotton. I'd seen enough of butchers killing pretty young girls, and I was a cop and I was supposed to make that shit stop. The fact that I could not make it stop, that no one could ever make it stop, didn't matter to me. Part of my brain blamed me for what had happened and ignored the facts.

The rest of my brain tried to convince me that killing Jeff Cotton would somehow fix things.

That's how depression works. It lies.

Part of me even realized what was happening, that I was not being rational.

But goddamn it, I wanted to go finish the job on Jeff Cotton.

I finished dressing, clipped my gun to my belt, and walked out of the locker room. Sheriff Daltry was waiting for me in the hall. "You OK, Ed?"

"Just scratched up, is all. Did a lot of running through briars and brush."

"How about on a mental level? Emotions, I guess? You OK? It ain't easy, being shot at." His words evidenced concern, but his expression seemed somewhat suspicious.

"I am on an even keel, Sheriff." I looked him straight in the eye. "Do you have some specific concern?"

He licked his lips. "I am wondering how Jeff Cotton is still alive, considering the two best goddamn shooters in Mifflin County shot him. Now Ty was up in the air and says it was windy, so hell, he did great. But you were what, ten feet away, maybe twenty? And you shot him in the fucking knee?"

"Sheriff . . ."

"The knee. That boy had some goddamned serious weapon on him, didn't he? If he hadn't dropped it, hell, he could've shot you full of holes. Could've shot the SWAT guys full of holes, too."

"It was a judgment call."

"Yeah," he growled. "It was a bad judgment call. Jesus."

"Sheriff . . ."

"I'm glad he ain't dead," Daltry said. "Jesus, I'm glad he ain't dead. That would make things way worse. But if he is not the killer, Ed, we've got a fucking disaster on our hands here."

"Killer or not, he ran and he shot at us."

"Yeah." Daltry glared at the ceiling. "Look, Ed, you know the policy. Officer involved in a shooting goes on desk duty until such time as we review the whole case. So you are on administrative leave, paid, as of right now. No cases. Dooman will just have to pick up the slack. Bax can help him. He's smarter than I thought—found that fucking tractor that you fucking ignored. But you are not doing any road patrol, fieldwork, nothing like that, until I say so. I have no doubt it was a justified shooting, honest, I don't, and considering how much noise that boy's daddy is gonna make in the press and all, it is for the best that you didn't kill him. But . . . other officers are gonna have a lot of questions, Ed."

"I know."

"You have a lot of PTO coming to you," Daltry said. "Maybe don't even do desk duty. Write your report on this—hell, always gotta write a goddamned report, right? Give me that report, then maybe go somewhere, up to Erie, down to the Smokies, hell, anywhere, and just get your head straight. Take that pretty little teacher woman with you. Relax. You ain't been relaxed lately."

"Maybe. OK."

"Give me your gun. You ain't carrying again until the review is done."

"OK."

"It's policy, Ed."

"I know."

I gave him the gun and left him there.

I saw Shelly near the conference room. She had a bandage wrapped around the wounded thigh and had borrowed a Mifflin County Sheriff's Office shirt to replace her own torn blouse. She used a crutch to keep weight off the wounded leg.

"You OK?"

She nodded. "Yeah. I am. Never been shot before, but . . . I'm OK. You?"

"Yeah," I said. "I'm good."

We stood there together, silent, until it grew too awkward. I could tell she was trying to decide whether or not to say something. I had a guess as to what it might be. Eventually, though, she took it easy on me.

"My captain wants me to take some time off," Shelly said. "I told him I would, after I interview Jeff Cotton and see any other suspects arrested. He was cool with that. I have time coming, God knows, so . . . yeah. After this case wraps, I'll take a break. How about you?" She looked as though she hoped I would say yes.

"Same. Finish this up, then take a break."

Then I lied.

"Sheriff wants me to go with you to interview Jeff—thinks I'll be helpful. But that's it for me once we do that. I get to sit out any further arrests, interviews, etcetera after that, pending a review of my officer-involved case. You'll have to work with Bob Dooman, the black Adonis, if you need more assistance from Mifflin County after this."

She smiled. "That man could change a girl's mind." Then she turned serious again. "But you are off the case as far as any other arrests are concerned, right?"

I nodded. "Yes."

"No more cowboy shit?"

"No more cowboy shit."

"Because that was dumbass cowboy shit. You could have gotten killed."

"Yeah. OK. No more cowboy shit."

"OK, let's go talk to Jeff."

I led us to the parking lot, taking a route through the big garage bay that would keep us away from Daltry's eyes. He didn't need to know I was ignoring my orders.

We decided Shelly would interview Jeff Cotton, with me along for the ride. I drove us in her car to Ambletown General Hospital. Brian Cotton was in the lobby, talking to a doctor. Cotton saw us and almost ran at us. "What the fuck did you do to my boy!"

"I told him the boy would be fine," the doctor said loudly. "Tough kid. Very, very lucky."

Cotton looked as though he would throw a punch, but he drew up short when I squared up to defend myself. "Jeff fled, and shot at a police officer," I said. "He shot at me, for God's sake. Things could have turned out much worse."

Things should have turned out much worse for Jeff, I reminded myself. *I should have shot to kill.*

"You had no business with him!" Cotton said it through clenched teeth, but he unclenched his fists.

"Yes, we did," Shelly said. "We have evidence linking him to a homicide. We want to talk to him. He'll have a chance to convince us he is innocent." I admired the steel in her voice.

Brian started to say something, but his phone beeped and he answered it. "What?" He listened for a moment. "What? What?"

He thrust the phone back into his jeans pocket. "You Nazis are searching my farm?"

"Yes," I said. "We already have evidence possibly linking Jeff to a homicide. We have a team there looking for more evidence." *And we have SWAT all over the place just in case your buddies make that difficult, you miserable fuck.*

Brian Cotton swore and ran out the door. We told the doctor we wanted to see Jeff Cotton, and he told us that was not going to happen because the boy had been through a lot of trauma and needed his rest. The physician, a fairly young head-shaven guy whose badge said he was Joseph Trout, MD, and was assigned to the ER, didn't look as though he trusted cops any more than Brian Cotton did. We told him we were working a homicide case.

"The girl in the creek?" His eyes went wide.

"Yes," Shelly said.

"Oh," the doctor said. "Horrible. Still, I need to act in my patient's best interest." He pulled a phone from the pocket of his surgical garb. "One moment."

We listened as he asked someone, presumably a nurse, how Jeff Cotton was doing and explained that two officers of the law wanted to talk to him.

"OK, thanks." He ended the call. "I guess the patient actually wants to talk to you."

Shelly and I exchanged glances, both somewhat surprised. Dr. Trout told us where Jeff was, and we went straight there.

Gretchen Pearson, the public defender who had rushed to defend Van Heusen the skinny guitar man, met us at the door. "I'm his PD," she said. "I advised him against this. I want you to know he has been administered pain medication, and I want you to wait a while before you talk to him."

"It's a murder case, Gretchen. And we think there are more suspects." I started to move past her.

"All the more reason to talk to him when he is better and not medicated," she said, hand on my arm.

"Let them in," Jeff called. "I want to talk."

We went in.

I figured he would be in a bed, but he was in a wheelchair, his bandaged leg stretched out before him. He stared at his foot, fuming. My bullets had torn meat and bone, and his leg was tightly wrapped. The shoulder wound was really more of an arm wound and was mostly superficial. Bandages hid it from view.

"I might not be able to ever play again," the linebacker said.

It had been less than six hours since I had shot the son of a bitch, and I was surprised, frankly, that he was willing to talk to us at all, let alone so soon. But he was a tough kid.

Gretchen took a seat beside him at the small table-thing attached to the bed. She started writing on a legal pad, probably taking notes about how horrible cops are.

Shelly and I sat in the two small armchairs nearby, and after a few formalities. Shelly started the recorder and spoke aloud all the time, date, place, subject preliminaries.

After that, Shelly didn't fuck around. "Why did you kill the girl, Jeff?"

"Whoa!"

"Don't answer that, Jeff," Pearson growled.

"This is why I wanted to talk now," he said. "Jesus! I didn't kill her!" He was obviously groggy, and slurring words a bit.

"We have physical evidence connecting you to the girl," I said. His attorney looked up, but I did not elucidate. No need to mention the Gadsden flag cloth we'd found with the body. Jeff and his lawyer could stew for a while, wondering what we had. And I was betting once our team finished searching the barn and surrounding property, we'd have plenty more.

Jeff's head whipped back and forth, and his lips were tight together, like a fucking Ziploc.

"What evidence do you have, Detective?" Pearson looked at me expectantly.

"If we file charges, we'll tell you."

Meanwhile, Jeff Cotton broke. "It was Josh!"

"Who?" Shelly looked at me.

"Do you mean Josh Webb?" I asked. "Your quarterback?"

"Yes," Jeff said, grabbing his hair with both hands. "I tried to stop him, but . . ."

"He went to the party with you?" Shelly's voice was gentler this time. Pearson did not jump in with an objection.

"Yeah."

"You told us before you went alone."

"I lied, lady, OK? I was . . . I was . . ."

Pearson leaned toward him and touched his arm. "Jeff, maybe we should—"

"No! Jesus, these cops think I killed a girl! Jesus! Let me tell the truth!"

Shelly looked at me, then at Jeff. "So you lied when you said you went to the party alone."

"Yes, I lied."

"Why?"

"I don't know. To protect my friends, I guess."

"Friends," I said. "Who else went with you?"

"Lee Boggs, Eric Corker."

"More teammates," I added.

"Anyone else?" Gentler still. Shelly was far more calm than I felt. I tried to burn a hole through Jeff Cotton's head with my eyes, but he would not look up at me.

"No one else," Jeff muttered. Tears rolled down his face.

"You met Megan Beemer at the party," Shelly said.

"She said her name was Megan. Never told us her last name. I didn't ask."

"This girl," Shelly said, slipping a photo from the folder.

Jeff didn't even look. He just nodded.

"Answer aloud, please, for the recording," Shelly said. Jeff glanced at his attorney, who nodded.

He looked at the photo. "Yeah, that is the girl we met. Megan."

"For the record, the subject identified a photograph of Megan Beemer," Shelly said to the recorder. "How did you meet her?"

"She was dancing with Josh, and we all flirted around with her, you know. She was cute. Flirty. Fun."

"How did you end up taking her with you when you left the party?"

Jeff snorted. "She had a button. On her shirt. A rainbow thing, said LGBTQ on it or some shit like that. Goddamned alphabet people. I asked her if she was gay. She said she was, kinda, sometimes. I said what does that even mean and she said it meant she preferred girls, but a guy now and then was OK. She was smiling and all, and I thought, yeah, she's into this, you know? So we went out to my truck."

"Just you and her?"

"Yeah."

"Where were your friends?"

"I don't know," he said. "Crashing and burning with other girls, I guess."

"OK, so the two of you went to your truck."

"Yeah, just me and her, at first. We had some beer, and some whiskey, and then . . . you know."

"You had sexual intercourse."

"Yeah."

"Did you force her?"

"Don't answer that," the lawyer said. "Look, I think—"

"I want to talk," Jeff said. "I did not force her. She was into it. Really."

"OK."

"After, I said to her let's go back in, I know the guys in one of the bands, they're on later. She said OK. But then the tailgate opened up and Josh and Lee climbed in. I saw her first, Josh says. Then they close up the gate and I hear Corker start up the truck."

I jumped in. "It's your truck—how did he have keys?"

"Designated driver, dude. The rest of us were shit-faced."

Shelly continued. "So you are all in the back of this truck, the girl and you three boys, and one boy was driving. This truck, with a cover on the bed?" She showed him another photo, this one of his own pickup, taken near Black Powder Creek earlier in the day.

"Yes."

"For the record, the subject identified a photo of his own truck, found at the arrest scene," Shelly said to the recorder. "What happened next, Jeff?"

"Corker drove, we got drunker, and Josh got kinda pissed. Mad, I mean, not just drunk. Pissed off."

"Why was he angry?"

"Because I fucked her and he didn't," Jeff said. "I think, anyway. And we were all talking, about gay marriage and shit. She was all for it, you know? Her and her LGBTQ button. And we were trying to tell her that God didn't want it that way, and what the Bible said and all that. That was it, really. It got kinda tense—she was really pushing the whole gay thing. We argued about that."

"All of you?" Shelly's eyes widened.

"Yeah, all of us against her, man. Just arguing the whole gay thing. But Josh, I think it was . . . was . . . more personal for him. I saw her first, he kept saying, looking at me. I really think he was pissed because she fucked me, and not him."

The room went silent. Finally, Shelly prodded Jeff. "What then?"

"Lee says hey, she's open-minded, she likes girls and boys, and who knows, maybe lots of boys."

"And?"

"And she says no, I want to go back to the party, and Josh says c'mon, honey, I saw you first, and he starts kissing her."

"Did she tell him to stop?"

"Yeah, but laughing, you know, trying to be all calm and all like she was trying to calm him down. I think she was trying to do that, you know. Calm him down. She said let's all sober up, OK? And Josh says OK, bitch."

"He stopped?" Shelly glanced at me.

"Yeah."

"He did not rape her?"

"No, ma'am. I swear."

"What happened next, then?" I leaned closer to the guy. I wanted him to feel helpless.

He looked at me. "So we argued, about gays and gender and all that liberal shit, and Josh tells her she ain't even gay so why should she even care, and she says 'cuz she's human or something like that, and he says you fucked Jeff, maybe you should fuck me, and she says no way and then . . ."

Shelly took a deep breath. "And then?"

"Josh whacked her."

"He whacked her?" I said it between clenched teeth, and wished they were clenched on Jeff's throat.

The boy nodded. "Grabbed a wrench and whacked her. Jesus! He didn't mean to kill her, you know? He was just pissed! It was an accident!"

"A wrench?" Shelly remained Buddha calm.

"Yeah. A monkey wrench."

"Where did he get a monkey wrench?" Shelly's professionalism astounded me. I wanted to choke Jeff and track down his god-damned buddies so I could choke them, too.

"It was a truck, right?" Jeff spoke through tears. "Tools laying around. He got pissed, he found a wrench, I think he just wanted to scare her, you know? He held it up, stared at her, said 'shut up bitch' . . . and . . ."

"And what?"

"And she said 'fuck you asshole'. That set him off."

"And then?"

"And he whacked her. Hard. I did not think he would. I didn't! But she was just in his face, right? Triggered little snowflake bitch! And she pissed him off and he was drunk and . . . and . . ."

"Where did he strike her?" We already knew the girl had been hit in the head multiple times, of course, but Shelly's question was aimed at tying everything together, and determining Jeff's veracity. She was great, professional, thorough.

I was not. I was glaring at the little fucker, hoping he would lunge, or spit, or do anything provocative. In my mind, my fist had already broken his teeth, reached down his throat, grabbed a handful of lung, pulled it back out, twisted it. I regretted not killing him when I had the chance.

The boy, sobbing, touched the back of his own head. "Here. He hit her here. She saw it coming, tried to duck. Got hit in the back of the head."

I stood. Shelly stared at me. "I need coffee," I said.

I left the hospital room, walked down the hall, found a vending alcove, and punched a big-ass dent into a candy bar machine. I could hear Linda in my head, and my therapist, too, telling me to calm down, regain control, behave rationally. I could also hear myself telling them to go fuck themselves, that nothing mattered, that teenagers killing each other over the equivalent of a goddamned Facebook argument was proof that there was no God, no sense, no point. Fuck no, Nancy, I do not want to go to church.

I kept seeing that moment, the precise point in time when Jeff Cotton turned toward me with a gun that could instantly fire dozens of high-powered bullets that could smash my organs, shower the woods with my blood, cut me in half. The moment when I could have killed him, could have erased him from the universe without any questions.

I had wanted to. According to the rules, I could have.

But I didn't.

Jesus. I shook my head. *Jesus. Jesus. Jesus.*

"Hey, Ed, you OK?"

It was the reporter, Farkas.

"Good God, man," I said. "Can't you wait for my report? How did you even find me?"

"I followed you from the S.O. to the hospital," he said. "It wasn't that hard. I already have a story online, by the way, about the arrest and the search on Breakneck Hill and all that. Damn, what a thing. The arrest was a big loud thing, Ed, not really a state secret. Readers have questions, and it is my job to try and answer them. But first, are you OK? Is the officer from Columbus OK?"

"Yeah, we're both OK. She got grazed in the leg. I didn't get hit at all." I slid a couple of quarters into the coffee machine. "And I know you have a job to do."

"Is this all connected to the body found in Black Powder Creek? No one so far will confirm that."

I thought about saying no comment. I don't really like being quoted in the paper. But I pictured Jenna at the market in Jodyville, and my landlords in their farmhouse, and I tried to imagine how scared shitless they and everyone else around there must be. I am sure they heard the gunfire in town and saw the chopper and all the cop vehicles.

"Well," I said. "It is potentially related to the body discovered in Black Powder Creek. Potentially. You can print this, too. The incident is over, and there is no reason for the public to be alarmed."

"No other suspects at this time?"

I thought about that for a moment. "We do not anticipate any other dangerous activities."

"OK, great." Farkas tapped furiously at his phone. "OK, news is tweeted. Can you tell me—"

"No," I said. "Further details will not be released until we have finished talking to witnesses, blah blah blah."

"C'mon, Ed."

"Sorry."

He shrugged. "Any idea when you will have a report?"

"Not sure," I said. "A lot of balls in the air here, you know?"

"Yeah. Just . . . look." He peered at me, eyebrows up, in an imploring manner. "Radio Joe is still chasing this. I have already beaten the competition, thanks to you just now, in connecting some dots, and I want to keep beating the competition. I also want to let a lot of worried people know whether they need to be worried or scared. So, any chance you can let me know about your report before you send it to all media?"

He was grinning like an idiot, and I could not recollect owing him a goddamned thing. But I disliked Radio Joe Wills more than I disliked Farkas, because Radio Joe had misquoted me way more times than Farkas had.

"OK," I said. "I will give you a ten-minute heads-up before I send the press release, but I have to send it to all at once. I have to be fair."

"I understand that, but if I know when it is coming, I can be ready to pounce."

"OK."

Farkas smiled. "Thanks, Ed. I owe you a beer."

"Two beers."

"Deal."

Farkas left, tapping on his phone.

I thought about walking back into the interrogation and choking Jeff Cotton. It would be a public service. To hell with courts. But

Linda stayed in my head, reminded me to breathe, guided me through the quick meditation. Just breathe. Just breathe. Just breathe.

I picked up my coffee from the machine. I took a sip. I closed my eyes, did the slow breath thing again.

Moments later, I walked back into the hospital room. I just sat down and tried to pretend I was a normal person.

"For the record, Detective Runyon has rejoined the session," Shelly said. "OK, so you realized the blow from Josh did not kill her."

"Yeah."

"What then?"

Jeff was talking very softly now, in a monotone. "She screamed a lot, fought us, kicked us. I tried to calm everything down, you know. Josh wanted to kill her. Said we had to, said she'd talk to cops and we'd all be done. No more football, no playing in the Shoe, no shot at the NFL."

Shelly drew a deep breath and closed her eyes a moment. I think she might have shaken her head a little, but the motion was almost undetectable. When the eyes opened again, she was all business. "What then?"

"Josh grabbed her phone. Said fuck they can track this shit, and he threw it out the back of the truck."

"Where was this?"

"I have no goddamned idea."

"In Columbus?"

"Somewhere north of Columbus, on the way back home."

That fit with where the mower had found it.

Shelly continued. "What then?"

"We went to my dad's barn."

"The one on Breakneck Hill."

"Yeah, trying to decide what to do. We dragged her in there. And she is yelling at us. I'm like, look, calm down, it was an accident, OK! He just got mad; he didn't want to kill you. It was the booze, you know? No need to . . . no need to . . . ruin everything."

"And then?"

"She spat at me. And I am like, we have dreams, you know? Football. Ohio State, they came to see me play. Me! And I told her, you have dreams, too, right? She had said some shit about law school—she wanted to be a lawyer so she could defend gay people or some such rainbow shit. She would not back down. She was not willing to listen to reason at all."

My fist hit the wall, without any conscious guidance from me. It left a hole.

I turned away so I wouldn't have to see this degenerate asshole anymore. Shelly glared at me, but said nothing.

"Let's all calm down," Jeff said. "That's what I told her, told the guys. Let's think this through. Don't fuck up the future."

He paused. He was breathing hard, like he'd just run wind sprints.

I gazed at the ceiling, counted to ten in my mind, then turned back toward him. I could feel Shelly's eyes on me. I leaned toward Jeff, keeping my hands back, fighting the impulse to claw his throat. "What happened next, Jeff?"

"Josh laughed."

"He laughed."

"Yeah. And he threw her down, started ripping her clothes off, said we should burn that shit. Evidence, he said. And she kicked."

"She what?"

"She kicked Josh, in the mouth. Hard. Really hard."

I remembered the quarterback's busted lip at practice. He hadn't earned that on the field.

Jeff continued. "He smacked her again, in the face. She said 'fuck you, I am not keeping quiet, goddamn you fucking sons of bitches you are going to jail.'"

He was almost inaudible now.

Shelly whispered. "And then?"

"So Lee gagged her."

"How did he gag her?"

"One of my dad's rags. Barn is like a workshop, tools and oil and rags and shit."

"What kind of rag?"

"Um, old." Jeff looked confused. "From one on my dad's old flags, I think. What difference does it make?"

It made a lot of difference. His dad's flags matched the fibers in Megan's mouth.

"What next?"

"She's fighting and shit, and I'm trying to calm shit down, but she's fighting, and Josh is yelling she's gonna get us in prison and shit, so we tied her up. Lots of rope and cords in there. But she's fighting the whole time, and I am like no, let's just tie her up, guys, and quit fighting and all calm down, we can talk this out, it wasn't supposed to be like all this." He was crying hard now.

"What next?"

"We took her to the tunnels."

Shelly's eyebrows raised. "The what?"

"The tunnels. Dad and his friends, they are ready for anything. There's tunnels under the barn, run all the way to the creek south and Dry Run to the north."

"Jesus," I said.

"Fortified good, bunkers, food, all kinds of shit. When the libtards start the war, Dad is ready."

"Jesus," I said, glad we had not stormed the place.

"So we took her down there, left her tied up, but we fed her and gave her water. We took care of her, really. And tried to make her see reason."

"Reason?" Shelly was close to losing her cool, but somehow didn't.

"Yeah. Reason. Like, no reason to ruin our careers over a party that got a little out of hand, right?"

Shelly sighed. "Did she get away at some point? Break free?" Shelly was thinking of Ally Phelps.

"No. No way."

"How long was she your captive?"

"A few days."

"When did you kill her?" I think I hit him with spittle when I growled that.

"I didn't. Josh did."

Shelly leaned toward him. "When did he kill her?"

"Wednesday night," Jeff said. "We were feeding her. Talking to her. She got a hand free and slapped Josh."

"And?"

"And he said damn it, and he grabbed a lawn mower blade off a bench."

"A lawn mower blade?"

"Yeah," Jeff said. "It was dull. Dad was gonna grind it, put an edge on it, turn it into a weapon. Tunnels are full of shit like that, weapons, food, water, medicine."

I could see it all in my head. "What did Josh do with the lawn mower blade?"

"He clubbed her."

"He killed her." That was Shelly, calm and professional.

"Yeah. That time, no doubt. We thought he killed her before, but . . . that time, yeah. He killed her."

Sob.

"He killed her."

Sob.

"He killed her."

"He murdered her, while she was partially bound." I have no idea how Shelly maintained that Zen-like calm. I had no idea why I wasn't strangling this puke.

"Yes! Yes!"

"And then?"

"And we burned her clothes, and we took off the ropes and gag and we drove her over to the creek."

She showed him another photo, of the spot where we'd found the body. "Here, Black Powder Creek."

He shook his head. "Not there, up by the bridge. We drove her to the bridge."

Shelly showed him another photo. "This bridge?"

"Yes."

"For the record, the subject has identified a bridge just upstream from where the body of Megan Beemer was found."

Jeff Cotton was staring at the wall, seeing a future that really did not include him doing much of anything but staring at walls. I did not feel one goddamned bit sorry for him.

"I would like more time with my client," Pearson said, very quietly.

"Of course," Shelly said. She rattled off the end-of-interview mantra, then shut off the recorder.

Outside, I stared at Shelly. "This might be the most goddamned senseless crime I have ever worked on. How the hell could you be so calm and steady in there? Jesus."

"You should give it a try," she said pointedly. "Do you think you overplayed the good cop, bad cop thing just a little too goddamned much? The way you glared at him, I thought you were going to choke him to death."

I stared at her. "Sorry. He's a puke."

"I know he's a puke," she said. "But you have to maintain, right? Be a pro. It helps me put the bad guys away, Ed. I will drink, a lot, later, and I will feel all the anger, later. I advise you to do the same. Shove the anger aside. Feel it later. For now, do the work. Do the job. Calm down. Do you really want this guy to walk because we fucked up?"

I pointed to her wounded leg.

"That thing really OK?"

"Yes. Paramedics did fine. It is really just a scratch. Hurts when I move, and I kinda loved those jeans, you know? But I am OK. Really. Don't change the subject. You need to calm down."

We stared at each other a while. Every cop knows bullets happen. No cop likes to think of it, and no cop knows how he or she will react until that day comes.

"OK, good," I said.

"You alright, Ed?"

"Yeah."

"Let's get back to the S.O.," she said. "I'm going to get some warrants and calmly round up the rest of these bastards. You go listen to whatsizname, Kristofferson. The poet."

Back at the sheriff's office, we parted ways. She went to put together arrest teams with the sheriff. I waved down Irwin Trumpower in the parking lot. "My truck is impounded as evidence," I told him. "Can you give me a lift?"

"Sure, I am finally going off duty. Home or Tuck's?"

"Neither. Take me to Josh Webb's place, out past Hollis High."

"What for?"

"I have to go on leave, because of the shooting. So I figure I'll stop by and catch up on the football. Big Green won. Josh had a hell of a game, I hear."

"Defense is fucked without Jeff."

"Yeah. Give me a ride out there?"

"OK."

To hell with warrants and red tape and spinning wheels.

CHAPTER THIRTY-FOUR

Saturday, 10:12 p.m.

THE WEBB PLACE was a boring ranch out on Pickle Run, within sight of the high school. It would take us ten or fifteen minutes to get there from the hospital. I'd hoped to beat the arresting officers there, but that was not going to happen.

We were only two miles away when dispatch radioed Irwin to tell him to rendezvous with Shelly near Hollis High. He was not going to be off, after all. He was going to be on the arrest team, because we had three guys to pick up and not near enough bodies on duty. In the course of the conversation, Irwin learned how Josh Webb was involved in Jeff Cotton's arrest.

He glanced at me. "Detective Runyon is with me," he said.

"Detective Runyon is on leave, per policy," the dispatcher said.

Irwin acknowledged, put away the mic, and looked at me. "You weren't going over there to have the star quarterback sign an autograph, were you?"

"I just want to see this case through, Irwin."

"You are supposed to be on leave, Ed."

I stared at him a while. He mostly watched the road, but shot me a glance now and then. "You have been off-kilter lately," he said after a while.

"I just need to see this kid go to jail. No shenanigans. I promise."

"No," he said. "You didn't tell me Webb was in on what happened to that girl. Damn tragedy. Hate to see that happen to anyone. I understand your anger. I feel it, too. But—"

"But hell, Irwin. I've been working this case. Let me see it done. At least let me watch the arrest. I need that."

"No," he answered, pulling the squad car over near the store in Jodyville. He slapped it into park. "Go eat a fry pie, Ed. Play your guitar. Relax. But you are supposed to be on the sidelines, and I need this job too goddamned much to help you go cause trouble."

I looked at him for a long while, but he never flinched.

I got out of the squad car. Deputy Irwin Trumpower went to arrest Megan Beemer's killer.

I couldn't buy a fry pie, because the market was closed. I couldn't go pick my guitar, because I'd busted it up in a goddamned moment of rage. But I could clear up a loose end. I punched at my phone screen.

A woman answered. "Hello?"

"Mrs. Phelps?"

"Yes."

"I am Detective Ed Runyon, Mifflin County Sheriff's Office. I know it is late, but I need to talk with Ally."

"This is about that dead girl?"

"Yes. Ally is not in trouble, but I need to talk to her."

"I am putting this on speaker," she said. "Ally? Detective Runyon wants to talk to you again."

"Hello?" She sounded far away.

"Ally, I am right outside. Can you come talk?"

She paused. "Mom says no."

"OK. Ally," I said. "Buzz did not kill that girl."

I heard her gasp. "He didn't?"

"No. We caught the guys who did. You can see it in the paper tomorrow, or maybe even online now. But Buzz was not involved."

"Oh my God."

"Yeah," I said. "Why did you tell us you saw Megan running near the trailer park one morning?"

"I . . . don't know."

"Ally."

"I thought I did."

"Ally. When you lie to cops, you are interfering in an investigation. You did not see her, did you?"

There was a long pause, so I repeated myself. "Did you?"

"No."

"Why did you lie?"

"I wanted to find out about her, to see more about her." Ally was crying.

"Why?"

"I thought Buzz and her were . . . you know."

"You were jealous."

"Yeah."

"And you thought you'd talk to us, learn more about her, maybe get Buzz in some trouble."

"Yeah."

"He didn't do it. He may not be Mister Awesome, but he did not kill that girl."

More silence, more sobs. Then: "Thank you."

"OK."

"I am sorry I lied."

"Don't do it again."

"OK."

"I could charge you. I am not going to charge you," I said.

"OK."

"Just don't do it again."

"I won't."

I ended the call.

I started walking home. If Ally Phelps had been a better liar, if I had believed her, would I have assaulted Buzz? Would I have gone out of my head and beat him, maybe killed him?

Jesus.

CHAPTER THIRTY-FIVE

Sunday, 8:36 a.m.

I SAT ON the oak stump, staring across the pond, squinting in the reflected late morning sun.

A streak of lightning had torn a wound in an oak on the other side of the water, years ago, long before I came here. I stared at that old scar, shaped like lightning itself, and tried to imagine the flash, and the sizzle, and the burnt smell. Zap. Rip. Done.

Things happen fast in this world. Too fast, sometimes.

I'd had less time than that lightning strike to decide whether to kill Jeff Cotton or not. I still was not sure whether I had made the right call.

I heard a car door slam, but I didn't bother to turn around to see who it was. I knew who it was.

I watched the red-tailed hawk circle, and listened to the sound of footsteps through the tall, dry grass.

There was no convenient stump next to mine, so Linda plopped onto my lap.

She placed her forehead against mine. "You OK?"

I brushed her hair away from my eyes. It took me a while to answer.

"Yeah."

"Yeah?"

"Yeah. Aren't you supposed to be working at the art fair?"

"I took a mental health day," she answered. "By the way, I picked up the guitar parts. Thought I might make something artsy out of them. If that is OK."

I kissed her nose. "That is OK."

We sat that way for a little while, her wrapped in my arms, not talking. A dog barked somewhere, and crows squawked, and the water lapped against the bank.

Eventually, she broke the silence. "I read the *Gazette* this morning. Jesus, that was scary shit."

"Farkas spell my name right?"

"Yep. You know, Ed, you could not possibly have saved her."

"Not so sure," I said. "I did not look for her full-time, you know. SWAT calls. Drunk hooker with a gun. Too many distractions."

"None of which were your fault, right? So nothing you could have done, right? Not your fault at all what happened to her."

"I know. I guess."

"So . . . why so down?"

"I quit my job, Linda."

"I know. Debbie called me. She's worried. I am not sure if I am worried or glad. Tell me about it."

"I just walked into Daltry's office, put my badge and ID on his desk and told him I was going to take all of my unused vacation time. I have a lot of that. And I told him I wasn't coming back."

"I meant tell me about why you quit, not the gory details with Daltry, but OK. He didn't say anything? Try to keep you on?"

I laughed, hoarsely. "Hell no, he's glad to see me go. By the way, I think Daltry tipped off Brian Cotton."

"What the actual fuck?"

"They are buddies, Daltry and Brian, and Jeff was on a hair trigger. He was calm and cool when we talked to him before, but as soon as he saw my lights this time he bolted, and he was packing a serious gun. Anyway, I think Daltry said something to Brian, maybe on purpose, maybe accidental, that tipped the Cottons off that we were coming for Jeff. Or maybe Jeff overheard something and got spooked."

"Jesus."

"Can't prove it, but I mentioned it to Bowman. He'll poke into it, I suspect."

"Jesus," she muttered. "Will Cotton's friends be an issue?"

"No, I don't think so," I said. "His property is a crime scene, and it is crawling with cops. Those guys can't get to all their deadly stuff. They might have stuff at their own homes, probably do. But Brian is talking about lawsuits, not insurrection. We'll keep an eye on them, but I think we're OK. Besides, Jeff confessed to everything, and so did his buddies. Brian and his gang are nuts, but I suspect this all has them stunned. They are probably as confused as anyone."

I took a deep breath. "Anyway. So I don't trust Daltry, and he does not trust me. Other guys are wondering about me, too, no doubt, probably not eager to work with me."

"Why?"

"I should have killed Jeff Cotton."

"No, it is good that he is alive, Ed. He's a kid. He can redeem himself, maybe."

"You don't understand."

"OK. Make me understand."

We sat a while longer. My legs were falling asleep, but I needed Linda in my arms more than I needed to feel my toes, so I just endured it. A splash in the water caught her attention, and she twisted around to see. "What was that?"

"Probably a frog jumped in. We have some fat frogs out here. They make a lot of noise jumping in."

She turned back to look at me. "I am proud of you, Ed. You could have . . . Jesus, you could have killed that boy. And I know you wanted to, and the guys say you are a damned good shot, but you didn't. And I just, I just . . . I am proud of you."

I lifted her off my lap and stood. "Don't be. You don't really understand, Linda. No way you could."

She stood and squinted. "What? I understand that boy is not dead. What is wrong with that?"

"I fucked up," I said. "I broke training."

"Please explain how letting a boy live was the wrong call."

"We had probable cause and evidence to think Jeff Cotton had been involved in a murder," I said, quietly. "We went to arrest him. Jeff ran, carrying a semiautomatic rifle with God knows how many bullets in the magazine and a fucking bump stock attached."

"Bump stock?"

"Lets him shoot way more rounds way faster," I said. "Anyway. I chased him into the woods, alone, which I should not have done. Jesus. I endangered my partner. Suppose he had circled around and shot her while I was running around playing Rambo in the woods looking for him, huh? What if that had happened? He could have cut her to pieces while I was off looking for him. No. I should have waited for backup, we had a chopper, we had SWAT, we had all the pieces in place. We'd have gotten him. But I chased him, and he turned that weapon on me . . . and goddamnit!"

"Ed . . ." She brushed hair away from my eyes. I was staring at the ground, fists clenched, jaw clenched, everything clenched.

"I should have blown him away! God help me, Linda, I should have blown him away."

"Ed . . ."

"No! No! Hear me out!"

"OK."

We stared at each other. A hawk's shadow crossed her face.

"I took the wrong shot," I finally said. "When a perp turns a gun on you, you aim for the chest and you keep shooting until he can't hurt you or your fellow officers or anyone else. That's what you do. That's what I should have done. But I didn't do that."

"You did the human thing, Ed."

"I did the stupid thing! My head was all full of rage, and full of you, and everything else, and . . . and . . ."

"Full of me?" She sounded surprised.

"Yeah," I said. "You. And things you said. About justice and all that. I should have been dispassionately killing the guy with the big bad gun who was trying to kill me. Instead, my brain was AWOL, listening to a hippie angel."

She took my hand. "What next?"

"I aimed for his leg. I took a bunch of risky, stupid, godawful low-percentage shots at his knee. It didn't kill him. If he had not dropped the gun, he could have killed me. Easily, even after I shot him."

"Ed—"

"And, fuck, he could have killed any of the SWAT guys coming out of the trees. With that much firepower, he could've blasted the fucking helicopter out of the sky. You get that? He could have killed guys on my team! And he could have run off through the woods, into town, and hell, if he'd gone off his nut, he could have killed the fuck out of a lot of people . . ."

She wrapped me in her arms. "None of that happened."

"It could have."

"It didn't."

"It could have. And it would have been my goddamned fault."

We stood that way, holding each other, a long time. I was shaking, for a while, until she broke the silence. "Is that why you quit, Ed? Because you think you fucked up?"

"I don't think it. I know it. I may be all off in the weeds on . . . on Megan, and Bree. But this, I fucked up. Ask anyone else in the department, or on SWAT. They know it, too. I fucked up."

She stepped back. "OK. So, you fucked up. Human beings do that every goddamned day. And, for the record, I personally am glad you fucked up on the side of not shooting a boy dead. Bad as he is, as ugly as his crimes are, as bad as his friends are, he is young and he has time for redemption. So do they. Right? You see that, right?"

"Jesus, no theology, OK?"

She smiled. "You know I love me some do-good Jesus, Ed, but OK, I won't preach at you. I am just saying that kid will pay for his crimes, the others will, too, but he has a chance to get past all this, and so do his friends, thanks to you."

"Megan Beemer doesn't have a chance. And you weren't in the interrogation room with him. I did not do the universe any favors letting him live."

Linda sighed. "Fine. We can discuss redemption and change and human spiritual growth and all that shit later."

"All theology is amateur theology," I said. I had said that to Linda many, many, many times.

"OK." She waved her hands in the air, as if to ward off mosquitoes. "So, OK, you quit a job that I think was maybe not good for you anyway. What are you going to do?"

I spat. "I have time to think about it. You would not believe how much unused vacation time I am taking."

"OK."

"I am serious. Want to go to Cancún?"

"Sure. Let's take a trip. Somewhere sunny and bright with drinks that have umbrellas in them. But that is a short-term plan. What are you going to do after that?"

"Well, before that, I am going to church."

Her eyes bugged out. "What?"

"Nancy keeps inviting me. I was shitty to her the other day. So I am going to a party at her church, after all the amateur theology, and apologize to her. I'll take her a couple of fry pies, too. And Bax might be there—I think he goes to her church. I owe him an apology, too. Want to go?"

"You at a church picnic? Won't miss that. OK. So church lunch, Cancún, then what?"

"I thought I might get my PI license."

"PI?"

"Private investigator. Like Philip Marlowe."

"Who?"

"You never read the books I recommend."

"Oh." She sighed. "Yeah, I remember. Guns and shit, not my thing. But really, a private detective?" She did not seem to be on board with the idea.

"As a PI, I could take the cases I want to take, and not have to worry about someone's fucking stolen tractor or getting called aside to handle a goddamned OD or domestic incident. No SWAT shit coming at me out of nowhere. I could focus one hundred percent on whatever case I take on. And if I screw up, it's on me, not on the rest of the team. I won't get anyone else killed."

"OK, I see some logic in that. Maybe? What kind of cases? Cheating husbands? Cheating wives?"

"Might have to do some of that, to pay the bills. But . . . I thought, maybe, I could specialize."

"In what?"

"Missing kids."

She had me in her arms again before I finished saying those words.

"You do that, Ed. You do that."